When

Love

Grows

Deborah Ann Dykeman

© 2017 Deborah Ann Dykeman

Cover design © Deborah Ann Dykeman
Photographs by chriscarroll071158 and jenniecoyote
CC0 1.0 Universal (CC0 1.0)
"The person who associated a work with this deed has dedicated the work to the public domain by waiving all of his or her rights to the work worldwide under copyright law, including all related and neighboring rights, to the extent allowed by law. You can copy, modify, distribute and perform the work, even for commercial purposes, all without asking permission."

All rights reserved.
No portion of this book may be reproduced in any form whatsoever.
All Scripture quotations are taken from the New American Standard Bible, unless otherwise noted.
Scripture taken from the NEW AMERICAN STANDARD BIBLE®, Copyright © 1960, 1962, 1963, 1968, 1971, 1972, 1973, 1975, 1977, 1995 by The Lockman Foundation. Used by permission.
All emphasis in Scripture was added by the author.

This book is a work of fiction. Characters, names, places, and incidents are based on the author's imagination or used fictitiously. Any resemblance to real life is entirely coincidental.

ISBN: 1978088914
ISBN-13: 978-1978088917

Books by

Deborah Ann Dykeman

To Thee I'm Wed

Rubyville Series
A Place to Call Home
A Place of Refuge
A Place to Heal
A Place in My Heart

When Hope Blooms

Dedication

The words *I love you* are easily stated. The actions behind those words are a process that is carried out over time, encouraging our love to grow. This book is for all those that have loved me at my most unlovable. We are all a work in progress.

Acknowledgments

When you have written multiple books, it seems cliché to name the same people each time. But when you are self-published, you tend to work with the same group every time a new book is written. It is because of them that my writing is possible. I would be remiss not to include their names here.

Britta Ann Meadows of Peas in a Pod Editing and Design, my editor and oldest daughter, thank you so much for your hard work where my writing is concerned. Because you do have the most difficult job of all. I get to do the fun parts.

Cindy, thank you for taking a microscope to my books, and finding that missing period or letter. I don't know how you do it, but you always do!

Thank you, Julane Hiebert, for taking time out of your very busy writing schedule to read my books, and offer so much encouragement. We authors need much of it, as you know!

Thank you to those people that wait anxiously for my next book and are excited when it arrives. You don't know how much that means to me! It keeps me writing.

To all my readers, a tremendous feeling of appreciation. I've had so many of you let me know that you've read my books, and really enjoyed them. That makes this author very happy!

My family, there are not words for me to express how thankful I am to all of you and your support. The days, weeks, and months of writing another book are long. You all hang in there.

And to the One that is continuing to grow love in me…without You, I am nothing. To God be the Glory!

Prologue

SYBIL BRUSHED AT HER EYES, glaring at the gravel road ahead as she gripped the steering wheel. *Yes, a cow is a very apt description of you, Elvira Sample. With your frizzy brown hair stuck out from your round, ugly, cow face, right down to your cow legs. I would assume you have cow legs, but who would know? All you ever wear are jeans or really ugly denim skirts.* She gave a loud sniff, the effort shaking her shoulders. *And now you're saved, so you can really walk on water. The last little item my father needed to sweep you off your feet.*

She crammed her foot on the brake and skidded to the side of the road. The black Mercedes bumped along the uneven surface, coming to rest along the deep ditch. Shifting into 'park', she laid her head on the steering wheel, deep sobs racking her body. *I miss you so much, Mom. You know Dad and I never did see eye-to-eye, and it's only worse now that you're not here. I understand that God has a plan for each of us, but it really stinks that He took you out of my life. We needed you here. You were always able to keep Dad in line, make him behave. Now he's just a loose cannon. I never know what stupid thing he's going to do next. Do you know he quit practicing law to be a writer? A writer, Mom! What a stupid waste of his talents and time! He just sits up in that loft, staring at that computer for hours on end. Well, he used to. Now he only does that when he's not chasing after the cow. I think I truly hate her, Mom. And I know I'm not supposed to hate anyone. You always said to just let the little people have their quaint fun because that's all they had in their lives. You told me not to rub elbows too much with them because I didn't want any of that on me. But now your husband is going to go off and do something really stupid, like marry that woman! She's just like what you always warned me to stay away from.*

A knock on her window caused her to turn and she screamed, scrambling back from the glass. A large expanse of brown horse underbelly stretched before her window. One jean-clad leg ending in pointed-toe boots in a stirrup swung dangerously close to her Mercedes. Her eyes traveled up the dusty leg to find slate blue eyes, shadowed under a cowboy hat, staring back at her.

"Are you all right, ma'am?" The tanned face leaned closer as the horse stomped one foot, gravel popping against the side of the car.

Sybil took a deep breath and lowered the window a couple of inches. "Your horse is putting dents in my car. Kindly back away."

The cowboy spun the horse in a large circle, its head bobbing up and down, shaking its long mane. "Slow down there, girl. We'll get going in a minute." He turned back to Sybil as his leather-gloved hands held the reins steady. "I just wanted to make sure that you didn't need help. Sandy and I have been out riding pasture," he nodded behind him, "and you've been sitting here for a while now."

Sybil's eyes traveled up and down the vacant expanse of graveled road. "I can't see that it's any concern of yours if I sit on a public road."

The tanned cheeks split into a grin, dimples deepening. He tipped his hat. "No concern at all, ma'am, just being neighborly. I'll let you get back to crying." He nudged the horse with his booted heel, loosening the reins.

"Wait!" Sybil lowered the window further, calling after the horse and rider as they walked away from the back of the car. "I grew up in Wheatacre and my father lives down the road from here. I don't remember seeing you around."

The cowboy turned Sandy once more and meandered back to the side of the Mercedes. He reined the horse in, holding the reins in his left hand, his right hand resting against his thigh. "I'm not from around here. I grew up on a ranch in Colorado. My uncle died a couple months ago. He owned the land west of the road." He shrugged one denim arm. "I suppose it's mine now, being as he willed it all to me."

"So you're Black Byron's nephew?" Sybil watched as the cowboy nodded. "We had heard that he passed away. We wondered what was going to happen to his place since he never married or had any children."

"Well, you're looking at it, ma'am." He grinned again. "I was just giving Sandy here some much needed exercise. She's a bit excited after not being ridden for a while."

Sybil observed as the topic of their conversation began pawing the ground while nodding her head up and down. "I can see that. I mean, I don't know anything about horses, but she seems a bit jumpy to me."

He nodded. "She's a good little mare. She just needs to run for a bit, work off some of that anxiety. We all need that every once in a while."

Sybil snorted. "Thanks, but I'll stick to the treadmill at my gym. I can't imagine going around smelling like a horse all day." She gave a shiver.

"I'd far rather smell like a horse than some other things I've taken a whiff of." He patted Sandy's neck, smoothing his hand down her withers. "Ma'am, it's been nice—"

"Please don't call me ma'am. My name is Sybil Grafton." Her dark eyes scanned his face. "I'm fairly certain I'm not old enough to be a *ma'am* to you, and who uses that phrase anymore?"

"I'm sorry, ma'am, but I was taught to address a lady with respect until you know her name. Then you call her by her title of Miss or Missus until you are told differently."

"Then I guess it would be *Ms.* Grafton." Sybil swept the bangs from her forehead.

He smiled, a row of straight, white teeth against the tan of his face. "So you're confused."

"Confused about what?" Sybil wrinkled her brow, glaring back.

"I guess you haven't figured out if you're a miss or a missus yet." He lifted his hat and nodded toward her. "My name's Chandler Byron. Good to meet you, Sybil Grafton, but I need to get Sandy running before she dumps me on the ground." He replaced his hat, walking Sandy across the road before giving her full rein. They galloped over the pasture.

Sybil waved the dust away as she closed her window. "I'm not confused! And of course your name is Chandler. You're a gorgeous blond, blue-eyed, tanned cowboy. Everything I want to stay away from because I don't want to ride off into the sunset with anyone. I won't live in a romance novel." She sighed. *You would look great in a three-piece suit and a tie to match those beautiful eyes, Chandler Byron.*

She put the car in gear and pulled onto the road as she followed the silhouette of horse and rider with her eyes. *Who would have known that old Black Byron would have had such a good-looking, friendly nephew? That old man was made of cast iron, and just as cold. I'm sure my father thinks that's just what I deserve in this life: to be married to someone like that old grouch.*

Chapter One

Eighteen months later

SYBIL PRESSED THE PALMS OF her hands against the frigid glass, her red nails seeming to bleed against the pale fingers. Her green eyes traveled over the Kansas City lights, twinkling far below in the setting sun, the snowy landscape blushing peach between the large mansions along the boulevard. Her black lashes swept closed as she placed her cheek on the wall of glass, relishing the cold on her hot skin.

I trusted you, Scott. I released my very soul to you over the past year. One tear slipped from beneath the dark lashes. *I even shared my body with you, with no promise of a ring or marriage, and this is the kind of man you are. Why didn't I see it? My father will be more disappointed in me now than he ever has been. He warned me about you. He and that cow he married.*

There was a quick knock upon the wood door, the click as it opened, and a gasp as it swooshed shut.

"What are you doing, Sybil? Come away from there!" The petite blonde grabbed Sybil's thin arm and pulled her away from the glass.

Sybil shrugged her arm away, scowling down at her friend. "Tarah Clayton, you need to leave me alone right now. I'm not in the best of moods."

Tarah propped a wool-skirted hip upon the desk and crossed her arms. "I can see that. He's not worth it, you know. Believe me; I have first-hand experience."

Gripping the back of her white leather chair, Sybil spun it to face the darkening sky and plopped into it, crossing one long leg over the other. Her leather-booted foot swung back and forth. She braced her elbows on the arms of the chair, clasping her long fingers in front of her waist. "It seems that you and most of the female gender in this law firm have firsthand experience with Scott Weinberg." She shook her head, the straight hair skimming her jaw line. "I can't believe I fell for him and his lies."

Tarah snorted delicately. "Scott embezzled almost one million dollars from this firm over his years here. He falsified expense reports and who knows what else. You aren't the only one he lied to."

She leaned her head back against the white leather. "But I'm the only one I care about right now, Tarah." Sybil twisted the chair to look at her friend. "I let that man sleep with me."

The blonde gave another snort. "I don't think that's all you were doing."

Sybil flattened her lips. "That isn't funny, and it's nothing to joke about."

Tarah leaned forward and patted the long arm incased in black. "I know it's not, honey. But he won't be the first guy for you."

Sybil pressed her red lips together, tears slipping down her cheeks. "But he *was* the first guy. I thought Scott was serious about me, that maybe he would ask me to marry him someday. I was afraid of losing him, so I was intimate with him…" she sniffed, pressing her nose with the back of her hand, "when I knew it was the wrong thing to do."

"Don't be so hard on yourself. People live together all the time now. We aren't in the dark ages anymore." Tarah brushed at a piece of lint along her hemline.

Sybil seethed. "Scott and I did *not* live together. He had his place and I had my apartment." She shook her head. "My father would have a heart attack for sure if he thought I was living with someone."

Tarah nodded. "Yes, the honorable Loren Grafton. How is your father these days? Is marriage suiting him?"

"He's just fine and you know it. You ask about him every time I return from Wheatacre."

The blonde sighed through pursed lips. "I keep hoping he will come to his senses and realized what he missed in me. I may be older than your father's wife, but I can still have some fun."

Sybil brushed her hand at her friend. "Give it up, Tarah. You'll need to find someone else. He's never going to leave that cow. They're just as happy as two pigs in muck."

Tarah laughed. "I think you mean *two pigs in mud*, my dear."

"Whatever! I don't want to talk about them tonight. My life is in too big of a mess to worry about something I probably can't change." Sybil stared up at her friend, her green eyes wide and unblinking. "What am I going to do now?"

"What do you mean?" Tarah lifted the hair at the back of her neck. "Scott was fired. Be thankful you don't have to see him every day anymore." She raised one brow. "You didn't fall in love with the guy, did you?"

Sybil scoffed. "Of course not! He was handsome and had a killer body, but he was too full of himself to love."

Tarah gaped. "I thought you just said you wanted to marry him." She shook her head and chuckled. "You're as bad as I am."

"I did. We had a lot in common. We are...*were*...both partners in a successful law firm. We enjoyed going to the gym, vacationing in the same locations...we would have been good together." Sybil lifted one thin shoulder. "Maybe after a few years we would have grown to love one another, but that's just emotional stuff anyway. We were good in all the ways it really counted."

Tarah sighed and looked off into the distance. "I don't know if all that really matters too much in the long run. There's something to be said for real love and being with someone that cares about you for a lifetime."

Sybil snapped her long fingers at her friend. "Step back into reality. You were the one that just said we weren't living in the dark ages anymore."

"I said that in reference to sex. No one waits until they're married to be intimate, and most people live together before they marry. I think it's an excellent way to see if you're compatible for marriage…kind of a test drive, you might say." Tarah gestured at Sybil. "You wouldn't buy a $600 pair of shoes without trying them on first. But you'll get married for a lifetime without seeing if you enjoy having an intimate relationship with that person?" Tarah shook her head. "I think that's crazy." She crossed her arms once more. "Besides, now you've been broken in a bit. When you get married, your wedding night won't be such a surprise."

Sybil swiveled her chair back to the dark wall, lights twinkling on the street corners far below, cars sweeping past. "That's just the problem. I actually *wanted* my wedding night to be a surprise, for the both of us. It just felt right somehow. And now I feel as though I've gone and ruined it." She looked back at her friend.

Tarah stood with a smoothing of her waistband. "Well, cheer up; your future husband probably won't be as naïve in the bedroom as you're thinking. So you won't have to worry about it." She rubbed Sybil's shoulder and gave it a pat. "I'm going home. It's been a long day and I'm sure we'll have more surprises tomorrow, courtesy of Scott." She rolled her eyes at Sybil before leaving the room.

The soft click of the door left the large room in stillness. Sybil touched the tips of her fingers together, resting her pointed chin on the index fingers. *I have let you down, Daddy. You preached to me my entire life about waiting until I was married to share my body. And now I've gone and done it with someone that I really didn't even care about. It was just a way to try to manipulate the situation in my favor. And it didn't even work! And now, after what Scott's done...well, he's shown what kind of a person he is. He would have made a terrible husband.*

Sybil closed her eyes and sighed. *It'll take some time, but everyone will forget about Scott and me and move on to other people to talk about. His name has been linked with practically every woman in the firm at some point. I'm not any different.*

THE MANAGING PARTNER STRAIGHTENED HIS red tie flecked with gold and repeated his question. "Ms. Grafton, were you aware of Mr. Weinberg's actions involving this firm?"

Sybil blinked, meeting each pair of eyes seated around the large table. "I was not aware of anything illegal, sir." She cleared her throat, looking at her clasped hands upon the glossy table. "Outside of this office, we did not discuss business matters."

The managing partner leaned back in his leather chair. "Mr. Weinberg stated," the older man tilted forward again, pushing his glasses up his nose as he read from the paper before him, "that you, Ms. Grafton, not only knew about his falsifying of expense records, but you contributed as well."

Sybil lifted the heavy glass before her and took a long drink of the clear liquid. She set the glass on the table and met the gaze of the managing partner. "I feel as though I am on trial here for a crime I did not commit."

The glasses were swept from the narrow nose. "Not at all, Ms. Grafton. We merely want the truth from you. That is all."

"I have stated the truth. I had no knowledge of Mr. Weinberg's actions toward this firm other than what he represented in this office. I find it offensive that because of our *personal* relationship outside of this office, I have been accused of something that I did not do." Sybil's eyes met the two other women seated at the table. "Have all the women in this office been interrogated in such a manner?"

The managing partner cleared his throat. "I am sure you are aware that personal relationships outside of this office are discouraged. Unfortunately, they do occur, and unfortunately for you, this situation occurred while you were involved with Mr. Weinberg for several months."

Sybil's eyes traveled over those seated at the table. "None of you here today are more aware than I am of the folly of my relationship with Mr. Weinberg. But as I have stated, I had no knowledge of what he was doing." She took a deep breath. "I would hope that my years of service here would speak for themselves. I have been a non-equity partner for three years now."

"Yes, you have been, but the business you have brought to this firm has been consistently under our expectations."

Sybil widened her eyes, nodding her head. "I see. If this meeting had taken place last week, before all of the…problems with Mr. Weinberg—"

"Mr. Weinberg embezzled money from this firm, Ms. Grafton…a very large sum of money." His hand smoothed his tie.

"I understand that." Sybil lifted her chin. "Under the circumstances, I think it is best that I resign. I will have my letter of resignation to you by the end of the day." Sybil pushed away from the table, adjusting the red belt at her waist. Squaring her shoulders, she took a deep breath as she raised her chin and strode from the room, closing the double doors behind her.

She walked the long corridor, a smile pasted on her face for those she passed. The door to her office opened smoothly, and shut the same, clicking into place. She lifted shaking hands to her cheeks as she walked to her large, mahogany desk and sat down. Drooping against the white leather chair, she pressed her hands to her tummy, kneading away the tight ball within. *My career as an attorney is over. All those years of work are just…gone. And it's because I let some stupid fool of a man into my life. I knew better…I've always known better.*

THE NOISE OF EARLY MORNING in the city woke her. The trash truck rattled behind the large apartment complex, metal grating as the lift set the dumpster on the pavement. Far-off sirens joined the low hum of traffic beginning its daily commute. Sybil opened one eye, glancing at the blue digits upon her night table. *One more hour before I need to be up to begin my last week at work. Monday mornings are always a pain, but this one is especially so.*

She rolled to her back, her emerald-green satin pajamas slipping on her black satin sheets. She pulled the cashmere blanket against her chin, wrapping it around her hands. *This week can't be any worse than last week. The stares and whispers behind hands as I passed by. I think Tarah has been the only one to treat me as she always did.* She gritted her pearly-white teeth. *What I would give to say what I think about you, Scott Weinberg!* She smiled, remembering the two suits and several shirts she had thrown in the dumpster. The silk ties had added just the right touch of color to the pile of clothing resting on the foul-smelling black bags.

What am I going to do? The words rushed around inside her brain, just as they had for the past week. *No one is going to hire me now. Not with accusations of embezzlement hanging over my head. You couldn't just crash all by yourself, could you, Scott? You had to take me down with you…ruin my career and my life. I'll be flipping burgers at the local greasy spoon, walking around in those really ugly white shoes and wearing a name tag. It will be like high school all over again when my father made me get a job at the café. That was the worst summer of my life. I never even made any tips. And it wasn't because I was cranky, like my grandfather said. I just didn't care to have a conversation with everyone that came in.*

Sybil tossed back the covers and sat up, swinging her feet to the wood floor. She brushed the hair from her face. *I might as well get this day started. I can do an extra hour on the treadmill this morning and make a nice smoothie. Everything will be almost like normal.*

A spasm across her middle drew her feet to the bed rail, red-painted toes curled around the edge. She gripped her knees with her hands, burying her face against her legs. *What am I going to do? Why are You making me so miserable, God? I've never done anything against You. I go to church when I'm in Wheatacre, I give a good sum of money each time I visit, and I don't talk badly about You to other people. Why are You doing this to me?* The sobs shook her thin frame.

TARAH FOLLOWED SYBIL INTO HER office, shutting the door. She watched as Sybil took a seat behind her desk. "So, are you trying red eyeliner this morning? Because if you are, I'd like to be the first to tell you it looks horrendous on you."

Sybil leveled her gaze at her friend. "You just walked the gauntlet with me and you make a wisecrack like that?" She picked up a manila folder and opened it, staring at the pages. Sweeping it closed, she shoved it aside. "I don't even care to wrap anything up. I'm having a really bad few days and I have a terrible feeling in the pit of my stomach that it's only going to get worse."

"You've complained about your stomach hurting a lot lately. It could be an ulcer. Maybe you should go to a doctor." Tarah glided over to the large desk and laid her palms on the glossy edge. She smiled. "Come on, Sybil. Chin up. It's not like you to curl up and die. You usually come out fighting when you're struck with adversity."

Sybil slumped against the plush chair. "There's no fight left in me." She brushed aside her long, black bangs, looking up into Tarah's blue eyes. The layers of eye shadow concealing the slight wrinkles at the corners shimmered in the morning sunlight. "Do you know that I stopped and got a donut on the way to work?"

"A coffee too?" Tarah placed a small hand on her chest. "You really must be giving up the fight. No wonder your stomach's hurting. It's all those trans-fats and refined sugars lying like a lump in there."

Sybil shook her head. "I don't know why I've called you my friend all these years. It's obvious that you aren't."

Tarah straightened, setting her hands upon her narrow hips. "Come on, honey. It's not that bad. Another firm will hire you. You just have a few weeks of misery to get through and then you'll be whizzing past all the donut shops on the way to work, just as you always have."

A loud knock on the door interrupted the conversation.

Sybil sighed. "Come in!"

A young woman stuck her head around the door. "You're wanted down in the conference room, pronto." She walked away, leaving the door open.

Tarah turned back to her friend. "The associates are getting a bit uppity around here, I'd say."

Sybil stood, adjusting the cobalt-blue silk at her waist. "She has wanted this office for some time now. That's the way it goes, I guess."

"What do you think is happening?" Tarah followed Sybil to the door, pulling it open.

Sybil shrugged. "I guess I'm about to find out. Maybe they want me to leave today, rather than wait around the rest of the week. That would suit me just fine."

SYBIL SAT FORWARD IN THE black leather chair, clasping her hands at the edge of the large conference table. Her eyes traveled over the empty chairs to the three men seated at the head of the table. "You're telling me that Sco…Mr. Weinberg, took his own life and left a note clearing me of any involvement?"

The managing partner nodded, giving a small cough as he adjusted the striped tie at his throat. "It seems as though he was feeling badly about what he did to the firm and he wanted to set things right." The older man made eye contact with the two other men seated at the table. "Mr. Weinberg said that you were not involved in any way."

Sybil nodded. "Yes, I seem to recall stating the same last week."

The dark glasses were adjusted on the thin nose. "Well, under the circumstances, we would like to offer our sincere apologies. And of course, we ask that you stay on at this firm. You have been hardworking and loyal over the years that you have been here." The two other men nodded their agreement.

Sybil gave a slow smile as she met the three pairs of eyes

avoiding hers. "What about your *low expectations* of the business that I have brought to this firm?"

The managing partner cleared his throat, looking at his colleagues. "I think we would all agree that you are hardworking, and that is an asset to the firm." The two men nodded their heads.

Sybil gestured around the table. "There seems to be a few people missing today. I would appreciate that they be told the truth…that I was not involved in, nor had any knowledge of, what Mr. Weinberg did to this firm." She pushed away from the table and stood, lifting her chin. "My resignation is still in effect for this Friday. Of course, I will be expecting a good reference from this firm for future employment." She nodded. "Good day to you…gentlemen."

Chapter Two

GRABBING THE PILLOW, SYBIL ROLLED to her tummy and smashed the softness over her head, pressing it against her ears. "Go away! How many times do I have to tell you to leave me alone?" The loud knocking continued. Groaning, Sybil threw the pillow to the floor as she sat up, tossing the covers to the side. "I don't want to be bothered! I don't want to be told to get up, get dressed, what to eat, and what to do with my day like I'm five years old."

"Then stop acting like a spoiled child."

Sybil raised her head, staring at the woman framed in the doorway to the bedroom. "It's only you. If you were going to use your key anyway, why didn't you just break in without pounding the door down first?" Sybil scratched the top of her head, barely making a dent in the tumbled, black mess.

Elvira Grafton propped one shoulder against the door frame and crossed her arms. "It's a gorgeous spring day in Wheatacre and you're in bed at one in the afternoon. Your father asked me to *encourage* you to get yourself and this place cleaned up today."

Sybil snorted. "Encourage? Is that the word he used?"

Elvira pressed her lips together and shook her brown head. "No, he told me to drag you out of bed, push you out the door, and toss your suitcases and clothing out behind you." Smiling, she straightened. "I was trying to be a little more compassionate and understanding." Her green eyes traveled around the bedroom of the guesthouse. "But after seeing the mess over here," she bent down, picking up half a cookie off the wood floor, "I think I agree with him." Elvira's eyes roamed over the paper bags with fast food restaurant logos, fries and portions of hamburgers spilling from them. "You're living like a pig, Sybil."

"Yep, it's a regular barnyard around here." The dark eyes slid over her father's wife. "If my father had something to say to me, why didn't he come over and tell me? Why did he send you?" Sybil snorted. "Like I would listen to you anyway."

Elvira tossed the cookie at her step daughter. "Your father *has* been here, twice a week for the past month since you ran away from Kansas City. You haven't listened to him either."

Sybil snarled, baring white teeth. "I didn't *run* away. I left a bad situation. You and Dad know how difficult it was for me to stay there after everything that happened. My name was connected with Scott everywhere I went, even though I didn't do anything." She crawled back into the bed, burying under the covers. "My boyfriend killed himself. How would I expect you to be understanding of that? Did you even have a boyfriend in your life…*ever?*"

Elvira strode over to the bed and snatched the blankets, throwing them to the floor. "Those need to be fumigated along with the rest of the room."

Sybil jumped from the bed, poking Elvira in the shoulder. "You get out of my house…you…you…"

"Cow?" Elvira narrowed her eyes at the younger woman. "I know what you call me, Sybil. You have a hateful heart. I've tried to be nice to you; I've tried to get along for your father's benefit. But you've crossed the line with this mess." Her arm swept the room. "Your father is at the office today. He is at the end of his rope with you. He wants you to get out of bed, clean up this pigsty and get a job, or...leave."

Sybil crossed her arms, raising an eyebrow. "And if I don't?"

"If he arrives home in," Elvira looked at her watch, "five hours and you haven't made any progress, he is calling the police."

"The police?" Sybil chortled. "You've got to be kidding me. He won't call the police to kick out his own daughter. He told me I could stay here while I got my life in order." She thumped her flat chest. "That's what *he* told me."

"Yes, he did, over a month ago. But you have abused that, Sybil. Your time is up. Clean up or get out." Elvira clasped her hands, meeting Sybil's eyes.

"You strut around like you're the queen since you married my father." Sybil tilted her head. "Well, you aren't. You came from nothing and you are nothing. You have no right to tell me anything. If my father wants me to leave, he'll have to tell me himself." She pointed to the door. "Now get out. I don't like you, I never have, and I really can't stand being in the same room with you."

Elvira remained where she stood. "You know the law better than I do, Sybil. Your father and I are married, this is *our* home, and I have every right to ask you to leave. I'm not too fond of you either, but I *am* willing to work on that for your father's sake. Personally, I believe you wouldn't be such a pain if you'd just grow up and quit acting like a spoiled-rotten brat." She turned, walking slowly to the door, before pausing and looking over her shoulder. "I almost forgot. Chandler Byron will be by at three. Your father gave him the sofa and chair in the front room."

Sybil squeaked, her mind racing back to her encounter with the blond cowboy almost two years before. "He's coming *here*?"

Elvira faced Sybil. "Yes, at three." Her green eyes slid up and down the thin form. "If I were you, I'd want to shower and change before then. You look awful, and..." she brushed her nose, "the smell in here isn't too pleasant either."

"What am I going to sit on? Dad can't just sell the furniture out from under me."

Elvira smiled. "Actually, he can." She shrugged. "Besides, your father gave it to him as a pre-wedding gift, so he didn't *sell* anything."

Sybil's mouth gaped. "He's getting married?"

One brown brow arched. "Do you know him?"

Sybil looked away. "We met once, a couple of years ago. He's Black Byron's nephew, inherited the ranch, I guess."

"Yes, that's what your father said. He's been out there a few times giving Chandler a hand on the house. It was in rough shape...not someplace you would want to take a new bride, from what your father said. It's more of a bachelor's shack, not a lot of comforts."

"Yeah, well, it doesn't sound as though I'm going to have very many of those around here either."

Elvira laughed. "Well, if you don't get it cleaned up over the next few hours, you won't have to worry about that. Your father said there is plenty of furniture in the stone barn for you to use *if* you clean this up first."

Shaking her head, Sybil sighed. "I don't know why I thought coming back to Wheatacre was a viable option. I should have just weathered this all out in Kansas City."

Elvira's eyes slid over Sybil. "You really need to jump off the pity wagon."

Sybil gaped. "I don't feel sorry for myself. I've had a very difficult few months. My boyfriend embezzled from the law firm we were both partners at, and then he took his own life. How would I expect you to understand all that?"

"You're right, I have no clue about adversity in this life. My own life has been a walk in the park." Elvira reached down, taking the blankets from the bed off the floor and balling them up. She tossed them into an armchair. Her eyes met Sybil's. "I'm going to tell you what your father and grandfather told me. You're still here, so God's not finished with you yet. It doesn't matter whether you are here or in Kansas City, but it's certainly easier to hide in a big city. You stick out like a sore thumb around here. Believe me, I know." Elvira gave her stepdaughter a smile. "And you're correct about me being a queen since marrying your father. He treats me like royalty. I guess everyone can see it." She walked from the bedroom.

Sybil seethed. "That's *not* what I meant."

SYBIL NARROWED HER EYES, READING the blue, digital numbers on the stove from her perch on the overstuffed armchair. "Gloria, please answer the door for me. It's probably just Elvira, seeing if I've made any progress over here. The cowboy for the furniture isn't due for half an hour yet." She continued flipping through the glossy magazine.

A gray-haired woman entered the living room of the guesthouse, her arms clad in yellow rubber gloves dripping water from the fingertips. She braced her hands on her wide hips and stared at the younger woman. "I don't work for your parents anymore, Chiquita, and I never was the butler. Answer the door yourself." Gloria's dark eyes glanced at the door when the knocking resumed. "And if that's Elvira, I'll let her know what a mess you've made of this place."

Sybil threw down the magazine, running long fingers through her wet hair. "She's already been here, that's why I called *you*." She gestured around the room. "I don't know what to do to clean this place up. That's your area of expertise." She glowered at the older woman. "And I'll remind you that I'm paying you extremely well for a few hours of work here."

Gloria harrumphed. "And I'll remind *you* that I'm only doing this for your papa. I don't know how such a nice man could be cursed with a child like you." She shook her head, grumbling as she walked back to the bedroom.

"Whatever!" Sybil pushed up from the chair. *Let's see if you're still complaining when you see the check I'm going to give you. It's not like you have anything to do with your life. My parents were the last family you worked for, and that was one cushy job!*

She swung open the door. She watched as the tall man opened the door to the run-down truck, a low trailer hooked to the back of it. "Where are you going? I thought you came for the furniture."

He turned, slamming the door shut as he swept the cowboy hat from his blond head. He gave her a smile. "Good afternoon, ma'am. I didn't think there was anyone home. I was going to come back later."

Sybil crossed her arms. "That would have been better, since it's only 2:30 and you were supposed to be here at 3:00."

The hat was replaced. "I always say it's better to be early and ready, rather than late and wondering."

Sybil rolled her eyes. *Give me patience to deal with this country cowboy. It might be more than I can take.* She pointed at him. "Where's your help to load the furniture?"

He pointed to his bicep with one long, tanned finger. "This is about all the help I need, ma'am."

"Oh brother, here we go again with that *ma'am* stuff. I told you my name was *Ms.* Grafton."

He snapped his fingers. "I thought you looked familiar. But the last time we met you were sitting in your fancy car, crying your eyes out. I didn't quite recognize you. I guess you still haven't figured out if you're single or married."

"You must think you're funny, but I don't. You'll have to keep trying the one-liners on your fiancée and get your laughs from her. I have better things to do with my life."

Shoving his hands into the front pockets of his worn and dirty jeans, he threw her a frown. "I don't have a fiancée."

Sybil tapped her fingers on her upper arms. "Elvira told me not two hours ago that you were coming here to pick up the sofa and chair for your shac—" She pressed her lips together.

He tilted back his head and laughed. "You're not offending me. It *is* a shack." His slate blue eyes roamed over her face.

"Why are you staring at me like that?"

He tilted his head. "I was just wondering why you wore that red lipstick. It seems kind of harsh against your white skin."

"So now you're an expert on makeup." She uncrossed her arms and pointed inside the little house. "Why don't you just get what you came for, *Mr.* Byron, so I can get back to my day."

He strode toward the door. "You may call me Chandler. I think I can get the chair, and if you'll give me a hand with the sofa, we'll have them loaded and I'll be out of here in no time at all."

Sybil gaped, pointing to his upper arm. "I thought that was all you needed. I'm not a furniture mover."

Chandler shrugged. "I didn't say you were. But your father did offer your services if I needed any help. He said you are in great shape from all your hours at the gym and you wouldn't have a problem helping with one end of a little sofa." He laughed. "Besides, I have a hand truck. I'll just strap one end on there, and you can guide it through the door. No lifting required on your part."

She shook her head. *Just wait until I see you, dear father of mine!* "I don't know what a hand truck is, but let's get this over with. I have things to do." Sybil eyed Gloria as the older woman set a bucket on the kitchen counter, draping the yellow gloves over the edge as the couple entered the living room.

"Hello, Mrs. Flores. What a surprise to see you here." Chandler greeted Gloria with a wide grin.

Gloria rounded the counter, giving Chandler a hug, her gray head barely reaching his chest. She patted his arm as she pulled away, smiling up at him. "So good to see you! Are you ready for some more empanadas, maybe some enchiladas?"

He chuckled. "I'll eat whatever you want to make, Mrs. Flores. Your baskets of food have kept me from starvation many a night now."

"A big, strapping boy like you needs lots of food to work. My son, Jorge, was not so tall as you, but he could eat. I remember well!" She smiled, her dark eyes twinkling as she turned to Sybil. The smile left the wrinkled face as she addressed the younger woman. "I am finished here. You have a load of laundry in the washing machine, and your bedding is in the dryer. That will be no problem for you to make."

Sybil's eyes scanned the small space, drifting to the bedroom doorway. "You scrubbed the bathroom, and dusted?" She crossed her arms. "My father won't be happy if this place isn't spic and span."

Gloria chuckled. "I know your papa, Chiquita, and he would say I did more than enough here." She took her purse from the counter and slid the short handle over her arm.

Sybil shook her head. "Well, don't be in such a hurry. I have to get your check."

Gloria raised one work-worn hand and brushed her statement away. "I don't want or need your money, Chiquita. As I said, I did this for your papa. Just return the kindness to someone else." She gave Chandler a wink. "Like maybe help this tall boy with the furniture. He needs a place to sit in the evenings when he's done working, even if he's there all alone."

"Well, I heard that's about to change for him. If he's getting married, he won't be alone. He's probably not alone now." Sybil's dark eyes slid over his tall frame and she scoffed.

Gloria pointed at Sybil, shaking her finger. "He's a good boy. No girl will be there until he be good and married to her. He's not like my Jorge, living like he was married when he's not."

Sybil raised her hands. "Sorry, I was just repeating what I heard, that's all."

Chandler cleared his throat, his eyes sliding from one woman to the other. "I think I can explain this little problem we seem to be having about me and a fiancée."

"I thought there was no fiancée." Sybil crossed her arms once more. "Either way, it doesn't matter to me. I just want to get this furniture out of here. I've been thinking this little place needs some sprucing up anyway. Maybe a décor change."

Gloria patted Chandler's arm. "I bring over more food in a couple days." She turned to Sybil, shaking her finger. "And you…behave!"

Sybil gaped as Gloria left the little house. "She cannot tell me what to do any longer."

Chandler laughed. "Mrs. Flores has a way of keeping the younger folks in line. I think it's nice that she cares. This world needs more people that take an interest in others."

Sybil glared. "You mean old women that have nothing better to do with their lives than to stick their noses in and gossip?"

He shrugged. "I suppose you could look at it like that. I prefer to believe that she cares. She misses her husband, and her son doesn't visit much. At least she doesn't sit at home feeling sorry for herself."

"That is *not* what I'm doing!" Sybil's voice rang in the small room.

Chandler's eyes widened as he backed to the door. "Look, Miss Graf—"

"It's *Ms.* Grafton, but everyone calls me Sybil. You might as well, too, since we're sharing furniture." She rubbed her forehead and sighed. "Look, maybe it would be better if you came back when my father was here to help you load this stuff. I'm getting a migraine and the only thing that helps is to lie down."

"That's fine, Miss…I mean…Sybil. I'm in no rush." Chandler hurried to the door, walking out into the bright sunlight of the April day.

"Your fiancée won't mind, will she?"

Chandler sighed and shook his head, his eyes narrowing at the glare. "The only women that have been out at my place are Mrs. Flores and a childhood friend, Crystal Waters. We are more like brother and sister than a couple." He pulled a pair of aviator sunglasses from his shirt pocket and slid them on his face. "She was visiting with her brother a couple months back, helping with some of the work around the place. My uncle really let it run down. Your father came out one day when they were there…he must have thought something else was going on."

Sybil swallowed deeply, looking away when his face turned back to her. *Who knew a pair of sunglasses could make your heart beat like that? He's better-looking than any man has a right to be, if you ask me. Childhood friend, my foot! And what kind of name is that…Crystal Waters? Did her parents think they were funny?*

"Are you okay, ma'am?" Chandler brushed her arm. "I mean, Sybil. You look a little pale."

Warmth spread over her arm, joining with the rapid beat of her heart. "I'm…I'm fine. Just this migraine to deal with. It'll be gone in the morning. That's usually the way it works."

Chandler walked to his truck and opened the door with a loud screech of metal. "I'll contact Loren about the furniture. If you would rather not part with it, I can find something else. I'm not picky. I hope you get to feeling better. My mother had those kinds of headaches a couple times a year. Not much she could do but wait them out."

"I'll be fine." Sybil walked into the guesthouse, shutting the door. She crept to the front window, edging aside the blind to watch the old truck and trailer rattle down the gravel drive to the stone barn, where he turned the rig around. Music blared as he raced past the guesthouse, a plume of dust hanging in the air.

Country music! I'd know that twang anywhere. I can't even begin to be attracted to a guy like that! He's everything I've spent my entire life trying to escape. She let the blind slide back into place. *But that feeling in the pit of my stomach and the warmth spreading over me isn't a good sign. It must be the headache. I'll sleep it off and that cowboy will be just as abhorrent to me as they always have been.*

CHANDLER TURNED ONTO THE PAVED road, leaving the gravel of the driveway behind. He lowered the volume on the radio, smiling at the words to the song. *No, I'm not the one for you, Ms. Sybil Grafton, and I'm not the one you're looking for. But even as bristly and growly as you are, there is something I want to dig deeper to find. I think there's a loving woman in that hard shell you hide in…I just don't know if I have the patience to wait for it to grow.*

He gave a laugh as he signaled to turn down the long, gravel road that led to his acreage. *But it sure would be fun to poke just a bit at such a cute little porcupine.*

Chapter Three

WHAT IS WITH THE POUNDING on the door today? So much for living in the country where it's supposed to be quiet and peaceful." Sybil tossed the cold, wet washcloth from her forehead, grimacing as it hit the floor with a wet *thunk*. She pushed up from the bed, and stomped to the front door, swinging it open as she set one slim hand on her hip, and sighed. "Did you lose your key?"

The slender, older man crossed his arms and rocked back on his heels. "No, I don't need a key when you're here to answer the door." His green eyes slid over her pajama bottoms and camisole. "I hope you were dressed when Chandler came by for the furniture."

Sybil rolled her eyes and tapped one bare foot on the wood floor. "Of course I had clothes on, Dad. I'm not a complete idiot. I don't walk around half-dressed with strange men."

"Well, that's good to know. It gives me some hope where you're concerned. I thought your mother and I also trained you to treat your elders with more respect, as well. But that's not what Gloria said." Loren raised one brow and continued to rock.

Sybil shook one finger at her father. "I knew she would run and tattle. Gloria was always doing that when she worked for you. She never did know her place in our house."

Loren rocked forward, setting his lean fingers at his waist. His eyes darkened. "Gloria's place in our house was a loved and trusted part of our family. She just happened to help with the cleaning and cooking around the house, two daily tasks you seem to be having a problem with."

"I haven't been feeling well today, Daddy." She flicked her red nails at her forehead. "I just wanted to rest a bit and that woman you married came over here and read me the riot act. Tried to pass it off as something you said. I told her you said I could stay here at the guest house until I had my feet on the ground. You need to let her know of *our* agreement so she stops bothering me."

Loren's eyes narrowed, deepening another shade. "Elvira, my *wife*, came over here at *my* request and gave you *my* message. Clean this place up, or get out. You've had more than enough time to get your act together, Sybil." His eyes looked past her and into the dark interior of the little house. "The message was for *you* to clean up the mess *you* made, not call a dear friend to do it for you."

"See, Gloria tattled, just as I said."

"No, Gloria visited with Elvira before she headed back to town, which was a very welcomed gesture. Gloria didn't say a thing about cleaning up your mess. I'm not an idiot either, dear daughter. I know how you operate." He rubbed the back of his neck. "And for future reference, nothing I say or do is a secret from Elvira. It was *her* idea to let you stay here, not mine. I knew the trouble you would cause. So, put that in your pretty little red purse and snap it shut." One corner of his lips lifted. "Now close your mouth. Gaping isn't one of your better facial expressions. Put on some clothes so you can help me load the furniture for Chandler."

Her lips widened further. "I told Chandler you would help him some other time. I have a migraine—"

"You've never had a migraine in your life and you know it." Loren shook his head.

"Well, I have a headache, and that's unusual for me."

"I don't doubt that you have a headache. You've been holed up in here for a month, eating all sorts of junk that you never eat. Your body is probably going through agony wondering how to process it all. Not to mention, you haven't seen the light of day in all that time."

Sybil squinted at the sun. "If you had a swimming pool, I would have been outside every day enjoying it. But I'm not going to just sit out in this Kansas sun getting old and wrinkly for no reason at all."

Loren gestured one thumb over his shoulder. "I can think of several reasons for you to be outside. The yard needs mowing, and it's a rather enjoyable job on the riding lawn mower. Elvira could always use some help with the garden. She has it planted now, but it needs weeding. The early morning is the best time to be out there."

Sybil crossed her arms and scowled at her father. "I am *not* a yard man! I didn't even mow the yard when I lived at home. Why would I do it now?"

"Your mother was the one that didn't want you mowing the yard. I thought it would be a fantastic way for you to spend a few hours each week." Loren sighed. "But that was a long time ago. I was hoping that you had grown up a bit and saw the need to be a help rather than a pain in the—" He raised his hands in the air. "I'm finished talking. I want Chandler to have the furniture that I promised him before the sun goes down tonight. Since you didn't see the need to help him when he drove over here to get it, you can help me now." One finger motioned up and down her frame. "Put on some clothes to work in, if you have any. Some sturdy shoes would be good too. None of those strappy, sandal things you usually wear in the summer. It's a bit rough at Chandler's place."

Sybil stomped one bare foot. "I'm not a child anymore. You can't tell me what to do."

Loren laughed as he stared at her feet, red toenails against the pale skin. His eyes traveled to her face as he continued to smile. "Then don't act like one. As long as I'm paying your way here, in the form of utilities and not charging rent, you can help out. If you don't like that arrangement, you can get in your cute little black Mercedes and head down the road…tonight."

Sybil's lip puckered. "You don't love me at all, do you? You have no compassion for me and what I've been through these past several months."

"Don't open the floodgates, Sybil. People have been through much worse that what you've been through. You quit a good job because of pride."

Sybil pressed her lips together. "*I* quit because of the accusations. They just lumped me in with Scott and what he did, not even listening to me. It was too late for them, they threw away a great employee."

Loren shook his head. "Their firm is alive and well in Kansas City, and I guarantee they found someone to replace you just like that." He snapped his long fingers. "You should have swallowed your pride and stuck it out for a few more months, and then resigned when you had made arrangements with another firm. You leaving like you did made you look guilty." He pointed at her. "But that wasn't the worst of it, or the most stupid thing you ever did. That was living with a man you didn't love, and someone from your place of work. That was just dumb."

"Here we go. I knew you wouldn't be able to keep silent on that one. I'm shocked it's taken you this long to bring it up." She raised her nose. "People do live together, you know. It's done every day."

"Yes, it is. But just because people do something doesn't make it right. I can stand out in the middle of a pasture with a metal pole in my hand during a lightning storm—"

Sybil sneered and laughed. "You really are in a stitch. The writer scenarios are just bubbling over."

"Actually, that doesn't have a thing to do with my writing. I was thinking about a case I was reading about a few months ago. Some guy was carrying a metal pole and was struck by lightning. His family wanted to sue the company that made the pole, stating that was what caused his death." Loren shook his head. "People never cease to amaze me."

"Well, I don't see how some guy getting electrocuted during a storm has a thing to do with me living with Scott." Sybil sighed. "We really didn't even live together. We always went back to our own apartments. It was just easier than trying to share a space for a few hours every evening."

"And that's where the problem lies, my dear." He gave her a sad smile. "When you really love someone, you *want* to be with that person every moment of your life. They are the other half of you, and you really don't even function that well without them. That is God's design. Man can't top that." Loren reached out and brushed her chin. "I pray that you have that kind of love someday. The kind of love that is worth waiting for, worth saving your body for." Loren turned and walked back to his truck, calling over his shoulder, "I need to get the hand truck. I'll be waiting for you to get dressed, so hurry."

Sybil closed the door, wrapping her arms about her thin waist. "I guess I'm going to find out what a hand truck is today, whether I want to or not." One tear slipped from her dark lashes. *You have it all wrong, Dad. There are no men in this world that are willing to wait for that kind of love. If you don't share something with them, they will leave. And when you're getting as old as I am, you don't have that many options left in the marriage department. Men want to do their thing, and women as well. No one wants to be a part of a whole anymore. You're just old-fashioned and living in a world that doesn't exist.*

THEY TOPPED THE LONG HILL, the old truck rattling over the gravel, and Sybil gasped. Her eyes traveled over the valley below them, a narrow river weaving through the cottonwoods. More grass-topped hills rolled in the distance, seeming to go on forever. The green line ended at the blue sky. "I would have never dreamed this was here. It's almost as though we aren't even in Kansas."

Loren smiled as he steered the truck over to a small building, a dilapidated porch framing the peeling front door and sagging screen door. "We have hills here in the eastern part of Kansas. You've known that your entire life."

"I haven't seen anything like this view before. It's almost as though you are at the top of the world." She sighed. "This place is probably a great tornado catcher." Sybil turned her head, looking at the small building. "That shack looks as though the tornado has already been through here. What a dump!"

Loren chuckled as he parked the truck and shut off the engine. "Remember that things aren't always what they seem." He threw her a sideways glance. "Chandler said he is leaving the house for last. He wanted the barn and fencing in place for the animals. It's taken him a while, but he's a hard worker. He's just about finished with that part."

"Well, he'd better tear down the house before it falls down. If it looks that bad on the outside, I can't even imagine the inside. It's probably overrun with rats and cockroaches." She gave a shiver. "I'm going to wait right here while you guys unload the furniture. My furniture-moving days are over." She examined one nail. "I'll need to get into Wheatacre for a manicure as soon as possible. I chipped several nails."

Shaking his head, Loren opened the door and slammed it shut, talking through the open window. "If you clipped those claws, you could actually function as a human being. You must be a danger to yourself getting dressed."

Sybil narrowed her eyes, rubbing at one nail. "That was where one nail went…zipping up these stiff jeans." She brushed at her knee. "They are about the most uncomfortable things I've ever worn, and of course much, much too big for me. Even though your wife has lost weight since you married her, she's still larger than I am."

"You should be thankful Elvira was willing to loan you a pair to wear since all you have is silk, satin, and linen. A good pair of jeans will take you through a hard day's work and then some." He turned his head with the slamming of the screen door on the little house.

"What brings you all out here? I'd offer some supper, but I just finished it all up." Chandler grinned as he strode to the edge of the porch.

Thank goodness! I'll never be hungry enough to eat with you! Sybil slid down on the vinyl bench seat, watching the duo out of the corner of her eye.

Loren backed away from the truck and walked to the trailer. "We brought your furniture. I said you could get it today, and I meant it."

Chandler stepped off the porch, his easy gait eating up the distance to the truck. "I told your daughter that I wasn't in any hurry. You didn't have to do this tonight, Loren. You should be home with your wife, enjoying this beautiful spring evening."

Loren smiled. "And that's what I'll be doing in just a bit. Elvira is making some shortbread to go with strawberries. I'd love to stay and chat, but I'm kind of in a hurry. Nothing like strawberry shortcake on a warm day."

"Well, let's get this stuff unloaded then!" Chandler clapped Loren on the back before climbing onto the trailer.

Sybil rolled her eyes. *It's the good old boys club! Dad seems to regress into a different kind of man when he's around hicks. Mother would have been disgusted to see how he acts at times.*

Chandler took the straps from the chair and lifted the tarp covering it. He gave a whistle. "I can't wait to try this out. It will sure beat that old recliner my uncle had since the dark ages. Now I can have company over and offer them a place to sit."

Sybil stretched her neck and looked out the back window of the truck. Her gaze met Chandler's and he gave her a slow smile. "Well good evening, *Ms.* Grafton. I didn't even see you there, being so quiet and all."

Loren chuckled. "Yep, that's my daughter, just like a church mouse."

Sybil scowled and straightened her shoulders, snatching her head to the front as she crossed her arms. *Just go ahead and talk about me as if I'm not even here.*

Chandler chuckled, lowering his voice. "I think that's one church mouse that needs to spend more time in the church service, if you ask me."

"I think you're right about that one." Loren laughed with his low reply.

"I can still hear you." Sybil called back.

CHANDLER STOPPED IN FRONT OF the large window and shoved his hands into the back pockets of his jeans. He gave a low whistle as he read *Highlights* written in a gold flourish across the tinted glass. "You've sunk to a new low. But you've got to do what you've got to do." He strode to the glass door and entered the hair salon, narrowing his eyes in the dim interior.

"Welcome, cowboy! What can I do for you today? Or any other day, for that matter." The tall blonde behind the counter tilted her head, her eyes traveling over Chandler as she presented a huge smile. Her pink tongue caressed her too-white upper teeth.

Chandler swept the Stetson from his head and approached the counter. *That door you just came in will take you right back out. You can wait for the barber to get out of the hospital.* "Well, I was needing a haircut, but I heard the barbershop was closed. I thought maybe I could get it done here."

"Well of course, cowboy!" The blonde wrinkled her brow. "I know, such a sad thing to happen to Mr. Carver. I was just in shock when I heard he had passed away this morning." She shook her head. "Carver the Barber, that's what we always called him in school. He had to be about a hundred years old. He's been Wheatacre's barber for years."

An older stylist with burgundy-colored hair paused over her client's shampoo. "Cissy, you know he wasn't that old."

Cissy shrugged, turning her smile on once again for Chandler. "Seemed like it to me. He was the barber when my grandfather moved to Wheatacre back in the '60's, and he'd been here for ages by then."

The stylist returned to rinsing her client's hair. "Mr. Carver came here after the war and opened his barbershop. He was a really nice man, and you kids shouldn't have called him what you did. His wife told me years ago that it really hurt his feelings."

Chandler pulled his eyes away from the burgundy strands. "Well, I'm sorry to hear that he died. I was told he was in the hospital."

Cissy smoothed back her hair with her long fuchsia-pink nails. "He *was* in the hospital. He had a stroke last week and then I heard he got pneumonia. That's what killed him."

The stylist squeezed the water from her client's head and wrapped a towel around the wet mop. "He will be missed, that's for sure. Go ahead and take a seat over there, Sybil, and I'll be right with you."

"It's about time you finished, Thelma. I was getting a terrible pain in my neck from that position." Sybil stood, one hand upon her towel-wrapped head, the other fluffing the cape around her slim form.

"Well fancy meeting you here, *Ms.* Grafton. I didn't know it was you with your head in the sink." Chandler tossed Sybil a smile.

Sybil glared back. "I thought I recognized your voice amongst all the senseless chatter." She sat down in the chair at Thelma's station. "This is a strange place for you to be. I didn't think cowboys had their hair cut. I thought maybe they just kind of chopped at it themselves or shaved it all off."

Chandler chuckled. "No, I have to get my hair cut every few weeks, as a matter of fact. And I eat with a fork as well."

Sybil shrugged her shoulders with a huff and looked away.

Cissy brushed her hand at Sybil. "Don't mind her. She thinks she's better than the rest of us because she moved to the big city."

Sybil threw Cissy a sneer. "There *is* life outside of Wheatacre. But I guess you wouldn't know that, would you?"

Thelma walked from the back room. "Now girls, you aren't in high school anymore, so let's act like grown-up women."

Cissy leaned across the counter and whispered, "She's always been a snoot. I never understood it because her father and grandfather are just the nicest people. That new wife of Mr. Grafton's is really friendly too."

"Cissy..." Thelma glanced over her shoulder as she pumped

the chair up. "Why don't you help the young man. We're going to be getting busy and you don't want to keep him waiting."

Chandler raised his hands. "If you're too busy, that's okay." He nodded toward Sybil. "I can just go home and shave my head."

Cissy rounded the counter and took Chandler's hand. "Now don't be talking like that. You have gorgeous hair for a guy. It would be a shame to cut it all off. I'll have you spruced up in no time." Cissy guided Chandler to the station at the end of the room. "You can set your hat on that chair," she gestured to the empty station, "and you can sit right here. I'm going to do such a great job that you'll be back, and you won't even miss Mr. Carver." She flipped a cape over his shoulders. "I mean, we're all going to miss him—"

Chandler smiled at her in the mirror. "I know what you meant."

Cissy patted his shoulders and smiled back. "You're Black Byron's nephew, aren't you? You're living out at his old place."

"Yes, I am, to both questions." He grinned. "My name's Chandler. I've lived here awhile now, but I don't visit the hair salons much."

Cissy giggled. "It's so nice to finally meet you. I heard that you were a handsome thing, but it's really great to see you with my own two eyes. We need more men like you around here. Bring some new blood to this old town."

Sybil's snort traveled down the room.

Chandler raised a brow, glancing at Cissy's ring finger. "I'm going to be presumptuous and assume that you're not married?"

Cissy held her hand up, wiggling her fingers. "No, I'm not, with no prospects in sight. I'm 'footloose and fancy-free', as they say."

"I have a bit of a problem you might help me with." Chandler's eyes swept down the room. "There seems to be a rumor going around that I have a fiancée, which is not true. You might be able to help me squash that bit of talk with a bite of lunch later. I hate to just let bad rumors go unheeded."

Cissy giggled. "I'd love to have lunch with you, Chandler. I get a break around one. We always have women that come in during their lunch, so I don't eat until later. The café is just around the corner, and it's really good."

"Yes, I've eaten there a few times now, and it *is* good. I'll be there just before one." He winked at her. "Now maybe you should cut my hair."

"Well of course, Chandler." Cissy giggled as she met his eyes in the mirror.

"Thelma, you just about cut my ear off. Why don't you pay attention!" Sybil's shrill voice carried down the room.

Thelma responded, the honeyed tones gliding over the harsh words. "Now you know I told you to keep your head down. You can't just jerk it around like that when I have scissors an inch from your head."

"I didn't *jerk* my head." The loud sigh floated through the room. "Haven't you heard that the customer is always right?"

Chandler tilted his head, watching as Sybil leaned forward, fluffing the black hair over her ear. "What am I going to do now? I have a hunk taken out of the side of my hair the size of Texas."

Thelma shook her head. "We can always go a bit shorter. The weather will be getting hot, you might enjoy it off your neck."

"I know it's going to be hot. I've lived in Kansas my entire life." Sybil sighed once again, sitting back, her shoulders high and stiff. "Go ahead, do what you have to do to fix it." Her eyes met Chandler's smile. "What are you staring at?"

Chandler chuckled. "Absolutely nothing, *Ms.* Grafton."

Chapter Four

*T*HE LATE-JUNE SUN PEAKED OVER the horizon, spreading its yellow, orange, and pink glow across the dark fields. Sybil swiped at the sweat dripping down her face. *You're almost there, less than a mile to go. Then you can cool off with a nice, long shower and a glass of iced tea. And you won't have to worry about running again until tomorrow morning. Ugh!*

Two beady, shining eyes in the middle of the gravel road skidded her to a stop. She put one hand to her heaving chest and gripped the sweat-drenched t-shirt she wore. The eyes stared back at her, not moving.

Oh no! I've dreaded this moment for the past month. Hoping I wouldn't run into a snake or some wild animal, and now I have! I can't even see what it is. Just eyes. It could be a raccoon, or a skunk. And of course it's between me and home, not moving, maybe carrying rabies. If it's a skunk, it could spray, and I'll smell for days. What if it is *carrying rabies, and it attacks me? No one will be down this road for hours. I could be lying in a ditch all that time. I've been an idiot running out here in the middle of nowhere. If only Wheatacre had a gym, or a decent track. But no, there's nothing here! No one cares to stay in shape. They just want to eat junk food and visit with their neighbors. No one has any goals beyond this small little world. Why did I ever leave Kansas City?*

"Sybil? Why are you standing in the middle of the road? Someone is going to come along and run you over."

She took her eyes off the two staring at her and glanced toward the field. Chandler's lean form strode swiftly toward her. She raised one shaking arm and pointed to the empty road. "There...there was an animal in the road just a moment ago. It just stood there, staring back at me. I didn't know what it was."

Chandler stopped beside her, his eyes sweeping over her before looking in the direction she pointed. He chuckled. "You mean that little guy making his way through the grass?"

"He's still here?" Sybil screeched and moved closer to Chandler.

Shoving his hands into his pockets, he glanced down at her. "He has better things to do than bother you. He's headed to a nice place to sleep the day away before he heads out again tonight."

"What is it? All I could see was beady little eyes and something the size of a cat." She gave a shiver, crossing her arms at her waist.

"It was an opossum, very common around here. Sometimes you can see them carrying their babies on their backs. It's kind of cute."

"Well there was nothing cute about those eyes. I didn't know what to do." Sybil licked her lips and looked up at the man beside her. "I guess I'm happy to see you. Heaven only knows what you're doing out here this time of the morning. Don't cowboys eat big breakfasts and lots of coffee before the sun comes up?"

He smiled. "Already taken care of." His eyes brushed over her once again. "The question is, what are *you* doing out here? I thought women like you stayed in bed until noon and waited for the maid to arrive."

Sybil shook her head. "You *would* think that. How did I keep a job for so many years, if that was my routine?"

"I'm sorry." He shrugged. "I don't know you. I shouldn't be saying anything about the type of person you are, especially if it's a jab at you. You seem to bring out the sarcastic side in me."

Sybil rubbed her forehead. "Don't be sorry. I do seem to bring that out in people. There are times when I just get sick of the mental sparring and the verbal attacks."

"Then why do it?"

The words hung in the damp air before evaporating in the gentle breeze.

Sybil sighed. "I don't know. It's just who I am. The older I get, the more it seems as though this is just the way I'm always going to be. I know people don't like me, and that they think I'm uppity. It seemed to work in Kansas City, rather like armor that I wore. But here…well it's just not the same."

"I read somewhere once that it's much easier to be happy and smile, than it is to be angry and frown. Maybe you should give it a try." Chandler tilted his head.

"You're staring at me again."

"How can you see that? It's still dark along the road here." Chandler's hand gestured back and forth.

"I can feel it. You are judging me and my actions, and the words I say."

He laughed. "Actually, I was wishing the sun would rise more quickly so I could see your new haircut."

Sybil put both hands to her head, fluffing the wet mass. "Don't even look at my hair right now. It's a mess. I don't like the cut at all. Thelma layered it all over after she took out that huge hunk over my ear. Now it's just fluffy and unmanageable. I can't wait until it grows out so I can go back to my old style. I've had it for years and it suits me."

"You're wrong, you know."

The sun's rays lightened the space around them, and Sybil looked into Chandler's blue eyes. "I'm wrong about what?"

"That hairstyle you had was harsh, and it made you seem the

same." His eyes caressed her face. "The tousled, wavy look makes you more approachable, more vulnerable, somehow. I like it."

"Well, you aren't wearing it, so it shouldn't matter to you." Sybil frowned. "See, there I go again. I'll just be happy when it grows out, so I can cut it back to one length."

"Yes, you said that already. You want your armor in place as soon as possible so you can go back to attacking at will."

Sybil set her hands upon her hips and glared at Chandler. "So how was your date with the town floozy?"

He wrinkled his brow. "I haven't gone out with anyone..." He nodded his head. "You mean Cissy, from the salon?"

"Of course that's who I mean. Have you been dating so much around Wheatacre that you can't keep the women straight?"

"No, I just said I haven't gone out. I had lunch with Cissy that day, back in April, and we've talked a few times around town, but she's not really my type." He adjusted the Stetson. "You shouldn't be so hard on her. I think she's had a difficult life."

Sybil rolled her eyes. "I've known her my entire life. She was the school flirt, nothing more."

Chandler narrowed his eyes at the distant fields. "She talked a bit her family. It seems she had a rough childhood."

"That's impossible. Cissy's parents were at church every time the doors were open. Her father was a deacon for many years. I think Cissy was just trying to get you to feel sorry for her."

Chandler kicked at a rock with the pointed toe of his boot. "I don't think so." He glanced at the rising sun spreading warmth over the fields. "I've got to get back to Sandy."

Sybil's eyes traveled over the road and fields. "Isn't that the horse you were riding the first day we met?"

"Yep. I have her ground-tied just over there." He nodded to a slight hill. "I was checking fences when I saw you standing in the road. I thought I'd better see what you were up to." His eyes moved over her. "You look like you could use a shower and a cold drink." He smiled. "You know, if you're wanting exercise, I could give you more of a workout than running down a dusty road will ever do."

Sybil gasped.

Chandler's tanned face colored red. "That didn't come out right at all. I only meant that there is plenty of hard work to do around my place. It burns a lot of calories and builds muscles. No need to waste time running down a dark road." He cleared his throat and looked away.

"It's not completely dark out, as you can see, and I run when it's early to beat the heat and humidity." Sybil rubbed the back of her neck. "My father told me the same thing. He wants me to work like a common laborer and keep up his yard. But I think jogging is a bit different then, then…" she waved her hand in the air. "Then whatever you do all day."

"You're welcome to stop by any time and see what I do all day. I would love the company. It can get rather lonely up there on the hill sometimes."

"Cissy would be more than happy to keep you company, I'm sure." Sybil leaned over, bracing her hands on her knees.

"Yes, she would be, but I've already told her that it wouldn't work between us."

Sybil glanced up, narrowing her eyes. "That didn't take long. I almost feel sorry for the girl not getting a better chance. Maybe you made your decision too quickly about her."

"I don't think so. There are other roads I need to travel down. When you feel the push to go, you should. God will direct your path." He lifted his hat in farewell. "Have a great day, *Ms.*

Grafton, and steer clear of those opossums. They can be a bit snarly if given the chance."

Sybil straightened and watched as he strode away. She heard him chirp as he topped the slight hill, Sandy bobbing her head in the distance. Kicking a rock, she began the walk home, the desire to jog completely gone. *I've told you over and over to call me Sybil. Just Sybil, not Ms. Grafton. I hate the way you say it. And you know it!*

"*I DIDN'T MOVE BACK TO* Wheatacre to be free labor for you and my father all summer long." Sybil stood, brushing at her mud-encrusted knees. "I agreed to mow the yard this morning. I'm still shaking from riding on that poor excuse for a mower."

Elvira laughed, shading her eyes as she looked up at Sybil. "You know, it will go slower. You don't have to race around the yard like a crazy woman."

"I didn't want to be out there all day. I have a life, you know." Sybil crossed her arms, raising her fingers and gasping. "So much for that manicure."

"Thelma will be glad to have you back. You're just about keeping her shop open at this point in time." Elvira went back to thinning the radishes. "You *can* wear gloves, you know."

"You aren't."

"No, I don't wear them. I like to feel the dirt." Elvira glanced at the younger woman. "But I also don't spend hard-earned money on manicures and pedicures. A stiff brush works just fine for me."

Sybil rolled her eyes, muttering, "I bet you use it on your hair, too."

Elvira chuckled. "I heard that. I've pretty much given up on the idea of you and me ever being close. But it would be nice if you could be civil." She gestured at Sybil's feet. "Your flip-flops are sinking."

Sybil pulled up on her foot, one red flip-flop sticking in the mud. She lost her balance, her narrow foot coming down on the row of radishes.

"Now look what you've done." Elvira shook her head, reaching out to the abused sprouts.

"You're throwing most of them away anyway."

"It's actually called *thinning*. I'm making room so that they will grow bigger."

Sybil pulled the flip-flop out of the sticky mud. She slid her foot into it, wiggling her toes. "It looks like a pedicure will be in order as well. This yard work is going to get expensive."

Elvira's eyes slid over Sybil's bare legs, across the denim cut-offs she wore to the red tank top. "You aren't exactly dressed for yard work."

Sybil shrugged, making long strides out of the garden space, her flip-flops making sucking noises with each step. "I dressed this morning to mow the yard. It's boiling hot out, and I wanted a bit of sun. I didn't plan on crawling around in this muck." She gestured at the garden. "We've had too much rain for you to be rolling around out here. Why don't you wait for it to dry out?"

Elvira laughed. "When it has just rained is the absolute best time to weed. Everything pulls out easily. Much better to weed in the early morning or after rain."

"Well, you have fun with that. I'm done for the day. A cool shower and iced tea are calling."

"I would love some iced tea!" Elvira pushed to her feet, wiping the sweat off her brow with the back of her hand. "I made some lemon cookies this morning that would be perfect with it."

Sybil set one hand on her hip. "You know, Dad is getting a little chubby around the waist. Maybe you shouldn't be baking all the time. My mother was very careful with her weight. She rarely baked cookies or cakes."

Elvira gave Sybil a smile. "I know, your father told me your mother didn't like to bake. But, I love it and your father enjoys eating it." She stepped past Sybil. "And I think your father is just perfect the way he is."

Sybil snorted.

"Are you coming in? I made sun tea earlier. It should be nice and cold in the fridge by now." Elvira opened the screen door off the stone terrace, turning back and raising one brow.

Sybil shook her head. "No, I need a shower." *And so do you.* "I might make a salad for lunch."

"There are some cucumbers ready to pick. They would be delicious in a salad."

"Thanks, but I'm not walking back into that mess. I don't know why you spend so much time on that garden. You can just go to the organic section in the store, and you don't even have to get your hands dirty. So much easier." Sybil gave a shiver.

"I enjoy gardening, and it gives me pleasure to know that I've accomplished planting, watering, and weeding." Elvira smiled. "Plus, it tastes so much better than anything in the store…including the organic stuff. Have you seen the prices on it? I guess the more natural way you do things, the more it costs. That doesn't make sense to me."

"You pay for what you get." Sybil frowned, brushing at her arm.

"You certainly do." Elvira's eyes scanned the tidy garden space. "Thanks for mowing today. It will save your father from having to do it when he gets home. I know he will appreciate that."

Sybil shrugged. "I'm not making a commitment to do it every time, but it worked for me today."

"And that's what is *so* important." Elvira lifted her hand and stepped into the house, the screen door shutting quietly behind her.

Sybil frowned. "I guess I said something I shouldn't have." She shrugged, crossing the driveway to the guest house, her flip-flops smacking against her heels.

CHANDLER TOOK A STEP BACK and surveyed his work as he shoved the hammer into the loop on the leather tool belt he wore at his waist. *A few more boards and I'll be ready for the railing. I might be sitting on this deck enjoying the view by autumn, after all.* He grinned, pleased with the progress he had made. Stepping down the couple of stairs to the dirt he called a yard, he whistled as he rounded the corner of the house. He paused, narrowing his eyes at the black Mercedes creeping up his long driveway. *Now, I wonder what she's doing here. Can't be good.*

He walked over as the car stopped, puffs of dust lingering in the humid air. The tinted driver's window slid down, revealing Sybil's dark sunglasses and red lips. Chandler smiled. *She'd be a great-looking woman if she dropped that haughty attitude she wraps herself in.*

"I'm sorry to bother you like this. Elvira baked lemon cookies this morning and said they were your favorite. She insisted that I take some to you on my way into town." The red lips resumed their straight line as she pushed a plate of cookies through the open window.

Chandler took the cookies. "Good afternoon. It's so nice to see you—"

"Don't say it!" Sybil lifted one finger into the air as she stared over the steering wheel.

Chandler straightened, grinning as he lifted his wide shoulders. "I was just going to say *today*."

Sybil shook her head. "No you weren't. You were going to say *Ms.* Grafton in that irritating way of yours." She turned to him, the black orbs of the sunglasses covering her eyes.

"I assure you, the thought didn't cross my mind...this time. But I can accommodate you if you wish."

"No, I hate it when you say it like that. I regret that we ever had that conversation. You'll never stop now."

Chandler chuckled. "If you agree to take off those sunglasses so I can see your eyes, I'll try to remember to call you by your given name. Because it really irritates me to have a conversation with someone wearing sunglasses."

Sybil smirked. "Really? Then I'll be sure to have a pair on hand just for you." She placed her right hand on the leather gearshift knob. "I'm in a bit of a hurry. I wanted to see if Thelma could fit me in."

"You're getting your hair cut already?" He narrowed his eyes.

Sybil removed the sunglasses and blinked up at him. "What do you know about women getting their hair cut?"

He shrugged. "Not much I guess. My mother always wore her hair in a long braid, and Crystal does the same."

Sybil nodded. "The illustrious, not-your-fiancée. Well, I'm sure that women in the wilds of Colorado just let their hair grow natural. I on the other hand have always had my hair trimmed every eight weeks, and I'm a week overdue."

"There is nothing wrong with natural. I happen to think that God did a pretty good job on the feminine form. Most women don't need a lot to make them beautiful."

Sybil snorted. "You need to get out more. I've seen some women that would raise the hair on your head if you saw them first thing in the morning. There's nothing wrong with helping out when needed."

"No, there isn't. But I know I don't like to snuggle up to someone that has a ton of goop on, either."

Sybil raised her black brow. "Sounds like you have lots of experience in that area."

Chandler shook his head. "No, not really. Just kind of common sense, in my mind."

"Well, your mind goes a lot of places that others never see." Sybil sighed. "I'm going to stop this senseless chatter and get on with my life. Some of us are busy, you know."

Chandler grinned, pulling a buttery-yellow cookie from beneath the plastic wrap. "I can see that. Haircuts, manicures, and shopping must keep you exhausted."

Sybil shoved the sunglasses back into place. "You are always making light of my life and what I do. It's become boring."

Chandler took a big bite of the cookie, talking out of the side of his mouth. "Elvira is correct. These lemon cookies are my favorite *summer* cookie. Peanut butter and oatmeal are delicious in the fall." He tilted his head toward the side of the house. "Speaking of which, why don't you turn off that expensive car of yours and save the gas. I'd like to show you what I've been working on, even if it does bore you."

Sybil shook her head. "I'm not really a farm girl. I don't know a thing about barns, fences or animals...and I don't really care to learn more. You'd better save the tour for when your Crystal is here."

Chandler reached out and pulled on the black door latch. "Will you unlock the door so I can be a gentleman and open it for you?"

"I didn't know that I had agreed to your tour." Sybil smirked.

Chandler's eyes softened, the blue blurring at the edges. "I would really like to show you around. It gets lonely out here at times. It's just nice to share some of my achievements with someone."

"Even if it's someone like me?"

He grinned. "Even you, Sybil."

She sighed and turned off the car.

Chandler opened the door, gesturing grandly.

"Don't be ridiculous. It doesn't become you." Sybil swung her legs from the dark interior, and placed her sandaled feet upon the dirt.

Chandler's eyes followed the long line of her bare legs from her brown, strappy sandals to the hem of the denim sundress at her knees. *If she wasn't so crotchety, you'd be very attracted to this woman.* He shook his head. *Who are you kidding? You're attracted to her anyway!*

Sybil stared up at him. "Are you going to move so I can get out of the car, or just stand there?"

Chandler cleared his throat, tearing his eyes away from the view before him. "I'm moving." He pointed to the plate of cookies. "I'm going to put these in the kitchen. You're welcome to come inside and look around."

Sybil stood, smoothing the front of the A-line skirt of the dress. "I might as well. The excitement of seeing the inside of this mansion is almost more than I can stand." She slammed the door shut and turned to follow Chandler across the yard and up the front porch steps.

Chapter Five

*S*YBIL STEPPED INTO THE COOL interior of the little house and gasped as she swept the dark glasses from her nose. "This is beautiful!" She turned around, taking in the four walls of the spacious room. "The sofa and chair fit right in. You have really good taste." Sybil gaped at Chandler. "I never would have thought this looked like…like *this* inside."

Chandler chuckled, setting the plate of cookies on a long sofa table as he took the hat from his head. He smoothed his tousled hair. "It didn't look like this when I moved in. This room was the entire house. My uncle had a metal bed over there in the corner," one long finger pointed to the wall opposite the front door, "and a sort of kitchen in that corner. Just an old porcelain sink and a cupboard, a tiny cook stove, and a beat-up refrigerator from when they were first invented." He gestured to the front door. "He had an old recliner and a table there."

"He didn't have any bathroom facilities?" Her eyes widened.

"He had an old outhouse out back and a metal tub hanging on it. His needs were simple, I guess."

Sybil shook her head. "I'm in shock. I didn't think people still lived like that these days. I'm surprised someone didn't come out here and light a fire to the place."

Chandler nodded. "I wondered the same. But if you ever met my uncle, you probably know it was best to just leave him alone. He wasn't hurting anyone out here."

"Probably not, but I can't imagine living like that...and for years." Sybil ran her hand over the woodwork. "Did you refinish this?"

"No, there wasn't any woodwork in here. This place was literally a shack someone threw up years ago."

"So why does it look so bad on the outside?" Sybil walked to a front window. "The porch is rotten and practically falling off the house. The same with the screen door."

Chandler laughed, joining her at the window. "I rather like it that way. It reminds me of the way things were. The life my uncle lived here all alone." His eyes swept over her. "I'll fix it someday, just as I did this room when I first moved in. But I have lots to work on." He grabbed her hand.

Sybil looked down and tugged.

His grip tightened. "Just relax. I didn't ask you to marry me." He pulled her to the door leading into another room and dropped her hand. "I built this last year. It doubled the size of the house."

"You did this by yourself?" Sybil walked around the large dining room and kitchen. "You wouldn't even think this was back here when you come up the driveway." She strode to the French doors. "And look at that deck. It's huge!"

Chandler grinned. "That's what I wanted to show you. It's my current project. I hope to have it finished in time for cooler weather and sitting out with a cup of coffee in the mornings."

Sybil's eyes swept over his tall form. "I don't see how you have time for coffee. I'm really amazed...and that doesn't happen often."

"You are?" He raised one golden eyebrow, smiling down at her.

She returned the smile. "I am. You're very talented for a cowboy." She looked away and walked slowly over to the long island separating the kitchen and dining room.

"I'm thinking cowboys aren't high on your list of people to

respect." Chandler joined her at the island, pulling out a wrought-iron bar stool and sitting down.

"They aren't. Or at least they weren't." She smoothed pale fingers over the glossy wood surface of the island. "They always seemed a bit full of themselves to me. The way they swagger into a room—"

"That's from sitting in a saddle all day." Chandler laughed.

"Or never take their hat off when they enter a building or eat at a restaurant. I think that's just rude."

"I agree. I always take my hat off when I enter a building. My mother would have taken it off for me if I hadn't." He gave her a sideways grin. "Times have changed for everyone, including cowboys. I don't think many of the new ones spend that much time in a saddle. Not like my uncle did. Those four-wheelers are used a lot these days."

Sybil frowned. "I haven't seen you on one of those."

He shrugged. "I don't have one. I much prefer to ride a horse. My uncle didn't have a huge spread like some. Horses worked just fine for him. It's a little different for my father. He owns a lot of land, and he has several people that work for him to keep the place running smoothly."

"And you didn't want to stay there and be a part of that?"

Chandler shook his head. "I love my family, but I'm the youngest of three boys. My father has lots of help." He pointed to the French doors. "All of this is mine. Something I can pass down to my own children. It's more than worth the work I've put into it so far."

Sybil's gaze swept around the room. "I love that your kitchen is so homey, but updated as well. This would be a great space for family dinners. You could kind of flow out onto the deck in cooler weather."

"My plans exactly." Chandler gave her a warm smile.

Sybil took a deep breath and cleared her throat. "I haven't seen any bathroom facilities for you, either. Don't tell me you still have an outhouse."

He shook his head. "I couldn't even keep that for nostalgic reasons. It was about the first thing to come down." He laughed. "The black snake living beneath it wasn't too happy either. I think he and his family had called it home for many years."

Sybil shivered. "I hate snakes! I know they say black snakes eat mice and they are good to have around, but no thank you!"

"I agree. My heart always stops for a second whenever I see one." Chandler pushed away from the island and stood. "I didn't even offer you something to drink." He held up one finger and rushed from the kitchen, returning with the plate of cookies. "Or a cookie or two with your drink."

Sybil laughed, her green eyes sparkling. "Well, it's not like I came here expecting you to feed me."

"I can do that too." He flashed her a smile and went to the large refrigerator. He opened the doors, shuffling around on the shelves. "I can grill a couple of steaks, and I have a bag salad we could share. I even have some leftover baked potatoes I could warm up." He turned to her. "What do say? Are you hungry? I'm a great cook…really." He let the doors shut.

Sybil laughed, leaning over the island and linking her hands together. "I would assume you could cook to some extent or you would have starved by now." She pressed her red lips together. "Suddenly, I'm really hungry. I will forgo the bag salad…and you should too. It's really not good for you, even though it's easy. I would love a grilled steak, and I would even eat a baked potato, but no sour cream of course."

Chandler frowned, shaking his head. "Of course…no sour

cream. What was I thinking? What do you dribble across your baked potato? A little water perhaps?"

Sybil rolled her eyes. "I would usually put a tablespoon of olive oil on it, but if not, I can use a smidgeon of butter."

Chandler nodded vigorously. "Butter I have… *lots* of butter. You can't live without butter…it's like nectar."

Sybil laughed, her smile wide and contagious. "You are really being a dork."

He gave her a wink. "Maybe, but it made you laugh, and it's a beautiful sound."

Sybil brushed his comment away. "People laugh all the time. There's nothing special about it."

"Smiles and laughter are always special. They are a window into a happy soul."

Sybil groaned. "You're a poetic cowboy as well. Wonders never cease around you."

Chandler leaned across the island, gazing into her eyes. "I hope not. Life is full of them if you only look."

Sybil straightened, smoothing her hands down the sides of her dress. "About those bathroom facilities…"

Chandler tapped the counter. "We did get sidetracked, didn't we? But I warn you, that section of the house is still in progress." He pointed to a doorway at the end of the long counter opposite the island. "Just go through there and you'll see where you need to be."

Sybil raised a brow. "It sounds a bit ominous."

"Just not ready for company, but it's all right. Your father said he would give me a hand with the tub when I was ready." He pulled open a drawer and took grilling tools from it. "I'm going to get started on those steaks."

Sybil walked through the doorway and into a small utility room before seeing another doorway leading into a large bedroom. A twin-sized bed stood to one side, a crate serving as a nightstand table next to it. French doors were framed in the insulated walls. Sybil walked to them, her eyes sweeping over the gorgeous view of the river lined with cottonwoods. The pile of treated lumber just outside the set of doors spoke of another deck to come. *This will be lovely when it's finished.*

She walked to the rough opening in the opposite wall, and pulled back the curtain. She stepped onto the plywood floor, gasping at the large tub leaning against the wall. *Now that's a bathtub! I could do some serious soaking in that.* She admired the tiled shower and the double sinks set in a rustic cabinet. Not one she would have chosen, but it fit beautifully with the décor of the house. *You can't tell me you figured this all out on your own, Chandler Byron. This place definitely has a woman's touch to it. Now the question is, what woman?*

"*ARE YOU SURE I CAN'T* put a little burst of a firework or a star on one of your nails, Sybil? It would be fun for the Fourth of July celebration." Cissy glided the last stroke of red polish over the nail and set the brush in the bottle.

Sybil tilted her head back and held her fingers before her face. "You missed a tiny spot, Cissy. You always do."

Cissy stood up, looking down at the red-tipped fingers. "Where? I think you carry a magnifying glass around with you, Sybil Grafton, just so you can find people's mistakes."

"Believe me, it doesn't take much to find the mistakes. Nobody pays attention to detail." Sybil tilted her head back and forth. "I guess it will have to do. I don't have time for you to start over."

Cissy rolled her eyes. "Well, stop waving your fingers around and let's get those nails dry before you mess them up."

Sybil narrowed her eyes, looking at her former classmate. "So, have you and that Chandler Byron been seeing one another?"

Cissy shook her head. "No, we just had lunch that one time. He told me he wasn't really looking for anyone to date." She leaned across the table and lowered her voice. "I think he really *is* interested in that woman. I think it's more serious than what he lets on, just between you and me."

Sybil wrinkled her brow. "What woman are you talking about?"

Cissy sat back in her chair, taking the bottle of red polish from the counter. She rolled over to the cabinet and placed it on the shelf. "You know, the one he said wasn't his fiancée. I think she really is, or if she isn't, she will be soon. That's what I think."

"Is that what he told you?"

Cissy shook her blonde head, the highlighted strands glowing in the sunlight coming through the window. "Sometimes you just know these things."

"And sometimes, most of the time, people are wrong." Sybil pulled her fingers from under the dryer and stood. "I don't have time today for that haircut after all."

Cissy lifted her brows. "Suit yourself. It's your hair. But it's getting kind of long. I haven't seen it like that since we were kids."

"Yes, I know, Cissy. I look in the mirror every morning. I know what my hair looks like." Sybil fluffed the uneven layers. "I'm thinking of doing something different with it. I'm rather tired of the same old cut."

"Well it's about time!" Thelma entered the salon with a stack of folded black towels. She gave them to Cissy. "Would you be a dear and put those away for me? I had to get out of that back room. It's as hot as the Sahara." She crossed her arms and tilted her head, her eyes examining Sybil's hair. "It's about time you had a different hairstyle. When you were a lawyer—"

"I am *still* a lawyer."

Thelma waved her comment away. "You know what I mean. When you were in an office situation every day and you were dressing that part, I think your blunt cut worked well. But now you need something softer, more feminine."

"Because I'll be working where?" Sybil placed the strap of her purse on her shoulder. "Maybe I need a softer more feminine style for waiting tables at the café, or when I'm mowing my father's yard." Sybil clicked her fingers. "Yes, that's it."

Thelma sighed. "I'm just trying to give you my professional opinion, Sybil. You don't have to take it, and knowing you, you won't. I just think it's time for a change."

"Well, I guess I will just keep letting it grow longer while I decide what I want to do."

Thelma reached out and examined a black strand. "Well, I don't see any split ends. It seems to be really healthy."

"That's probably because I don't ever blow it dry, and I only wash it a couple times a week now. It just seems senseless to wash it every day when I don't have anywhere to go."

Thelma smiled, patting Sybil's shoulder. "Chin up, my girl. Good times are just around the corner. I can feel it."

"I hope so."

"Are you going to the celebration on the Fourth?" Thelma grabbed a broom and began sweeping the floor at one of the stations.

Sybil let out a long breath. "Probably. I'm sure Dad and Elvira will drag me out kicking and screaming if I don't go voluntarily. Grandpa will join right in, of course."

Thelma laughed. "Honey, you know they just want what's best for you. It's not good for you to be sitting at home alone feeling sorry for yourself, and you know it. You have a good family and they love you. Let them help you get through this rough time."

"I don't even know if it's that rough. I just feel out of sorts...like I don't know what to do, or where I belong. All my life I always knew what the next step was. Now I just feel uncertain and scared to make *any* decision. I don't like that." Sybil rubbed her forehead.

"Well, I know I've been missing you at church." Thelma raised her hand. "Now don't go get all huffy on me."

Sybil rolled her eyes. "I know what you're going to say. I hear the lecture at least once a week from someone in my family."

"I don't want to lecture you. You're a grown woman. But you know it's hard to listen to God when you don't give Him a hearing. You don't know what He wants if you won't give Him the time of day. I'm just saying it would be nice to see you once in a while on a Sunday morning. I know you never did come regular-like, but you came every now and then." Thelma went back to sweeping. "You know, that Chandler Byron has been an asset at the church. He's handy with a set of tools. He can say a pretty good prayer, as well."

Sybil wrinkled her brow. "Chandler's been at church?"

Thelma nodded. "He started coming once in a while when he first took over his uncle's place a couple of years ago. Now he's there every Sunday, for Sunday school too. I'm surprised your daddy or grandpa didn't say something about it."

Sybil chewed on her bottom lip. "Yes, I'm surprised too. A house-building, church-going cowboy. Who would believe it?"

"What was that?" Thelma paused in her sweeping.

"Nothing. I need to get going. I told Elvira I would help with some baking for the picnic."

"The picnic you're not going to?" Thelma gave Sybil a wink. "See you there."

Sybil waved, leaving the salon. She stepped onto the sidewalk and slid on her sunglasses as she walked to her car. Opening the door, she tossed her purse onto the passenger seat and started the car before sitting down. She waved her hand in front of her face, trying to move the heavy, humid air. Laughter across the street drew her attention and she turned, watching as Chandler helped a tall, thin woman with very long blonde hair from his truck. The woman was pretty in an athletic, carefree way, her bare arms tanned golden. She looped her fingers through the back of Chandler's belt, her slim hip bumping against his, the hair swaying at her waist as they walked into the hardware store.

"A house-building, church-going, *womanizing* cowboy!" Sybil slid into the front seat and slammed the door shut, her chest heaving. *Why do I care what he does? I had dinner at his house one time, and it wasn't even something he had planned. It just happened because he didn't want to eat alone. I'm so gullible! I could just slap myself. The way that woman was hanging on him, they have to be together. No fiancée, my foot!*

Chapter Six

THE MERCEDES RACED UP THE driveway and came to a stop with large plumes of dust surrounding it. Sybil got out of the car and slammed the door, stomping over to the terrace. She frowned, staring at the couple seated there. Loren's arm wrapped around Elvira, her head resting against his shoulder.

"Well, aren't you two cozy. Isn't it a bit hot to be out here cuddling? I need to talk to you both and I don't want to do it out here. It's positively miserable." Sybil crossed her arms, and stared at the couple. "Did you both hear me?"

Loren kissed the top of Elvira's head. "Of course we heard you, Sybil. If we had neighbors, they would have heard you, and they would be choking on the dust you stirred up tearing down the road like you did." He glanced up at her as he stroked Elvira's arm. "What's the problem now? Did you smudge a nail on the wild trip home?"

Elvira patted Loren's knee. "Don't be cruel, Loren. She said she needed to talk to us."

Sybil gestured at Elvira. "At least your wife cares about me. I don't think you do."

Loren cleared his throat and took a deep breath. "What's happened to make you so upset? I care, Sybil, but all the drama gets very old after a while."

"Why didn't you tell me that Chandler Byron has been going to *our* church? And that he has been for a long time...ever since he moved here?"

Loren shrugged. "I didn't think you would care one way or another. You've made it perfectly clear that you don't want us asking you to attend the services with us."

Sybil bit her lower lip. "Well, not *every* Sunday, but every now and then it would be nice to be thought of. Especially when someone I know is there."

Loren pulled his arm away from Elvira and leaned forward on the bench they shared. "So, that's it. Because a handsome, young, *available* man is going, you're interested. You and the rest of the unmarried women in town."

"Loren..." Elvira's voice glided in.

Loren shook his head. "Well, it's true. We've never had so many young women attending the services at our church. They've come over from the other churches in town just to be near Chandler. If I was the poor guy, I'd be hightailing it back to Colorado. Who needs that?"

Sybil crossed her arms, tapping her fingers at her elbows. "I don't care if Chandler is going to our church. That's his business. But I think you could have at least let me know. I *am* a part of this family after all."

"So now you want to be a part of it?" Loren looked up at his daughter. "That's news to me."

Elvira nudged her husband once more. "Loren..."

Sybil raised one hand at Elvira. "It's all right, really. I don't need you sticking up for me. I've handled my father for years and I'll just keep right on doing it without your help."

Elvira pushed to her feet. "On that note, I think I'll get us all some iced tea. It's nice out here on the terrace with the breeze."

Loren leaned back against the bench and crossed his arms. "I agree. I was enjoying it immensely just a few moments ago." His eyes slid over his wife's form as she walked to the back door.

Sybil pulled a chair from the wrought iron table and sat down, crossing her legs with a flourish. Her leg swung back and forth, keeping time with her nails upon the table. "Really, Dad, can't you keep the looks to a minimum when I'm around? It makes me uncomfortable."

Loren tilted his head back and laughed. "It makes you uncomfortable if I look at my wife…in my own yard. You had better turn your eyes in the opposite direction, my girl, because I'm going to look at my beautiful wife any time I get a chance. *Especially* in my own yard."

Sybil rolled her eyes. "I don't recall you looking at Mother that way."

"I don't remember if I did or not." Loren shrugged. "It doesn't matter anyway. Your mother has been in Heaven for several years now. She is a very happy woman. I love Elvira, she delights me, and I will express that whenever I have a chance. I'm a lucky man, and I can't help but show it, I guess."

Sybil tilted her head, pursing her lips as she stared at her father. "Can we get back to what we were talking about, please?"

Loren gestured at Sybil. "Please do, I'm all ears."

Sybil stared up at the heavens as she released a sigh. "You are so difficult to talk to at times."

"I don't mean to be…really. But I don't understand why you would be upset about a young man you barely know going to our church. The church you haven't attended one service at since Elvira and I were married there."

Sybil quickened the pace of her swinging leg. "Can't you understand why I might be uncomfortable being there? That church was where we went as a family. You, Mom, and I went there for special holidays. It was the church I was baptized in. It always meant a lot to me."

Loren harrumphed. "You're going to have to come up with something better than that, Sybil."

Sybil scowled. "Okay, I just get plain tired of the old people, the happy families, and the hypocrisy that goes on there. Everyone is all smiley and spiritual on a Sunday, but come Monday morning, it flies out the window. Besides, I like to sleep in on a Sunday. After I moved away from home, it was the one day each week that I could do that."

Loren nodded. "Yes, you and most of the people in the world today think that. It's been forgotten as the day set aside to worship our Lord, and gather with other believers. I know, I lived the same way for many years."

"So, if you understand, why are you pressuring me to attend church with you?" Sybil squared her shoulders, staring at her father.

"*I'm* pressuring you to go to church?" Loren laughed. "You sure turned the direction of this conversation around. You tore out here madder than a catfish in the desert wanting to know why we hadn't invited you to church lately. All because our neighbor has been going. Our single, available neighbor, I might add."

"Well, that's not true either!" Sybil's eyes flashed as they turned to Elvira exiting the house.

Loren raised a brow. "Now I'm thoroughly confused."

The back door swung shut with a nudge from Elvira. "Here's some iced tea, lemonade, and some cucumber sandwiches I made. I thought you both might be ready for a bite to eat." Elvira carried the large tray to the table and set it down.

Loren stood, rubbing his hands together, a wide grin on his face. "Is that the bread you made today?"

Elvira smiled, touching Loren's arm as she glided by on her way to the house. "It is. I just remembered that there are some of those kettle chips you like in the pantry. I'll be right back."

"Hurry, please!" Loren returned her touch. "I'm suddenly starving."

Elvira's laughter disappeared into the house.

"You're always starving, Dad. I don't know why you don't weigh the same as a small car." Sybil reached out, taking a tall glass and pouring tea over the ice. "Do you still like a dash of lemonade on top?"

"I do." Loren pulled out a chair and sat down. "So…did Chandler get married over the past few days? When I was helping him with the bathtub on Saturday he was still single."

"He keeps telling everyone he's single, but when I came out of Highlights today, he was arm-in-arm with a tall blonde, sauntering into the hardware store. She had hair practically dragging on the cement. It looked ridiculous." Sybil poured another glass of iced tea and took a long sip. "They looked pretty cozy to me."

Elvira set the bag of chips on the table. "That sounds like that friend of his…Crystal." She glanced at her husband as she sat down. "Didn't you say Chandler had some friends coming for Independence Day?"

Loren placed a thick sandwich on his plate, and reached for the bag of chips. "I guess I did. Friends from Colorado, a brother and sister he's known most of his life. I thought he was serious about the girl, but I guess not." He shrugged. "I didn't think much of it. They've visited several times over the past couple of years."

"They sure looked like more than friends to me." Sybil took a plate and a sandwich, and, laying the bread to one side, she picked a slice of cucumber off the bread and popped it into her mouth, chewing rapidly. "The mayonnaise is just sliding off that bread, Elvira. Maybe next time you shouldn't put so much on."

Loren reached over, taking the cucumber slices off the bread on Sybil's plate, and dropping them to the side.

Sybil frowned. "What are you doing?"

"Saving a perfectly good slice of delicious bread from someone that doesn't appreciate it." He pointed to the garden plot just beyond the terrace. "If you just want a cucumber, I'm sure there's more in the garden." He took a huge bite of the bread and chewed slowly, closing his eyes. "It's like biting into a cloud."

Sybil sighed, shaking her head. "It's a wonder that I grew up with any manners at all. I must have learned them from my mother."

Elvira nodded. "I've heard that mothers usually teach the manners. May I get you anything else to eat?"

"She is just fine, Elvira. She can nibble on some lettuce leaves when she gets home." He tilted his head to the guest house across the driveway. "Which is right there."

"Are you asking me to leave?" Sybil raised a brow.

"No, he's not. He loves having dinner with his daughter every now and then...don't you, Loren?" Elvira smiled at her husband, pouring herself a glass of lemonade. She topped it off with tea.

"You know, Elvira, if you had more tea than lemonade it would be much better for you. Less sugar." Sybil's eyes moved over Elvira's figure. "You don't want to slow down your weight loss with useless calories."

Elvira smiled at Sybil, blinking her eyes. "You're correct, of course. I'd much rather save the calories for the several scoops of ice cream I'm going to have later while watching a movie. It's my favorite thing to do on a hot summer evening."

Loren chuckled, coughing into his hand.

Sybil pushed to her feet, dabbing at her lips with her napkin. She dropped it on the table. "You two are made for one another. I can't even talk to you most of the time, and I don't know why I bother."

Loren leaned back, looking up at his daughter. "I'd like to be the first to invite you to church on Sunday. We're going to have a special service after our worship time, a couple of songs, the Pledge of Allegiance, and then a potluck dinner to celebrate the Independence Day weekend." He grinned. "You could bring a salad. We don't have a lot of those, usually."

Sybil growled and stomped from the terrace. *I can't believe the amount of disrespect I put up with in this small-minded town! And from my own father!*

Loren's words reached her ears as she crossed the driveway. "I'm sure Chandler will be there with his friends."

Just the reason I should stay far, far away!

"Loren, you know that wasn't nice." Elvira's soft voice carried over, her father's reply lost as she reached the door to her little house. *Quit defending me! I'll take care of myself!*

"LOREN, YOU REALLY SHOULDN'T PROVOKE your own daughter in such a way." Elvira took a bite of her sandwich.

"I know, but she is so dramatic, and she won't be truthful with her own emotions. How am I supposed to talk to her when she's like that? What can I say?" Loren rubbed his temple.

Nibbling on a bite of chip, Elvira narrowed her eyes. "I really think she's attracted to Chandler, even though everything in her is saying he's wrong for her. That's why she came out here tonight in such a flurry. She saw Chandler and Crystal in town, and that made her jealous. That was piled on top of the comments circulating around Highlights about him attending church." Elvira laid a hand on Loren's arm. "Your daughter feels stupid to care for someone like Chandler, and now she thinks she's missed an opportunity to get to know him better at the church."

Loren shook his head. "You women don't make a bit of sense to me. *Like* Chandler? He's a hardworking, very nice young man that happens to wear jeans and a cowboy hat. He also attends my church on a regular basis." Loren nodded, popping another chip into his mouth. "Yep, he's a real bum."

Elvira took Loren's hand in hers and gave it a squeeze. "Your daughter is struggling with who she is. She doesn't like the person she has been most of her life, but she doesn't know how to change. And she certainly doesn't want someone like me to help her with it."

Loren scratched his head. "There you go again. *Like* you? You've treated Sybil better than she has ever deserved, *especially* in light of the way she's been with you."

Nodding, Elvira gripped Loren's hand tighter. "Just as God has treated me with love and understanding, never leaving my side when I've messed up. How could I not extend love and understanding to others…even in my very limited way?"

"Limited way?" Loren frowned. "You have grown so much in your Christian walk over the past couple of years."

Elvira nodded. "But I'm still learning about the Bible, and the paths I should take as a Christian. Sybil won't want to hear anything from me."

Loren sat forward in his chair, supporting his elbows on the armrests. "Sybil accepted Christ as her Savior when she was a child. There is no excuse for her to be acting the way she does most of the time. She is disrespectful of you, and our relationship. My patience has worn very thin where she is concerned."

Elvira pulled her hand from Loren's and rubbed his arm. "I know it has. But she needs to understand that God is there for her, and always has been. Not just on the special holidays, but every day. He is waiting to guide her, and as her father, you need to be praying for her, and what God has planned. Not your own agenda, Loren."

He snorted. "Believe me, I stopped trying to guide Sybil long ago. When she has a plan, or a certain way of doing something, nothing and no one is going to change her course of action."

Reaching into the chip bag, Elvira smiled. "God knows that about her better than we do. He has a way of getting our attention, and He'll get Sybil's. It's just a matter of time." She looked down at the chips cupped in her hand and sighed. "I guess Sybil's departure means I'm alone for the baking she told me she'd help with."

Loren snuggled up to his wife. "You're not alone, my dear. I know a little bit about baking. I can help you."

Elvira raised a brow, looking down at Loren's head on her shoulder. "I volunteered for six dozen cookies, two apple pies, one cherry pie, and an angel food cake."

Loren straightened, lifting one shoulder. "So, the picnic is scheduled for tomorrow at five. We can do it. I don't know a thing about pie-making or the cake, but I can do cookies without too much trouble."

Elvira closed the chip bag and stacked the dirty plates on the tray. "The baked goods need to be at the town hall by ten tomorrow morning. The ladies wanted to be able to take inventory and get things set up."

"Ten…in the morning?" Loren groaned. "Well, there goes sleeping in, or taking a walk, or even fishing."

"Fishing?" Elvira laughed. "Since when do you go fishing? Do you even have a pole?"

"No, but I could get one." He took a deep breath. "My point was that I was pretty excited about doing nothing, and spending the day with my favorite person…you."

Elvira gave him a pout. "Aw, that's sweet. And you can spend it with me, we'll just be a little busy until ten in the morning."

"Exactly! Why did you volunteer for so much stuff? Are we feeding all of Wheatacre? Isn't anyone else bringing anything?" Loren brushed the crumbs from the table to the terrace.

Elvira placed the glasses on the tray. "Of course they are. I was just excited about all the festivities going on, and…and I may have overdone it in my exuberance." Elvira winced. "I also have a couple dishes to make for the potluck on Sunday."

Loren stood, stretching his back. "Let's get through tonight first. It's going to be an all-nighter. I haven't pulled one of those in a *long* time."

Elvira slid her arms around Loren's waist and placed her chin on his chest, looking up at him. "At least we'll be together. We'll have fun."

Loren kissed the top of her head. "We will, we always do. But what about that ice cream and a movie? I was kind of looking forward to that."

"We can sneak in the ice cream. We'll have to taste test the cookies anyway." She stood on her tiptoes and kissed the tip of his nose. "I love you immensely, you know. There's no one I'd rather bake with."

Loren cupped her hips, pulling her closer. "We can make a real early night of it, then get up before the sun and get cracking."

Elvira set her hands on his chest and pushed away. "No, that is a terrible plan and you know it. We'll still be snoozing at eight in the morning, and I'll ruin my reputation by having to go to the store to purchase six dozen cookies and three pies."

"You forgot the angel food cake, my dear."

She frowned. "Do they even sell it at the store?"

Loren nodded. "They do, but it's similar to munching on a mattress. I wouldn't recommend it."

Laughing, Elvira took the tray from the table. "How many mattresses have you eaten lately?"

Chapter Seven

*S*YBIL STEERED THE MERCEDES OVER the rough gravel topping the driveway. She pulled up in front of Chandler's house, shifting into park. *It's only a matter of time before I get a flat tire out here. I wonder if he's heard of blacktop?*

She took a deep breath, one hand over the V-neck of the red t-shirt she wore. *There you go, a bad attitude with caustic remarks. You told God you were going to try and do better. Today is a great day to start. After all, you came out here. If asking a guy out to a picnic isn't out of your comfort zone, I don't know what is.*

Taking a quick glance at her lips in the rearview mirror, she opened the car door and slid from the black leather seat. Smoothing her hands over the navy-blue capris, she walked to the dilapidated porch, noting the American flag snapping in the ever-present Kansas wind. She knocked on the door and was greeted by the tall blonde she'd seen hanging on Chandler the day before.

The attractive woman gave her a big smile, perfect white teeth lined up neatly. "Hello! What can I do for you?"

Sybil's eyes swept over the willowy form with the curves in all the right places. Golden arms and legs peaked from the jean cut-offs and white men's t-shirt, bare toes just as golden, and pure in their absence of nail polish. Out of the corner of her eye, she caught the pop of her own red nails and she curled her toes against the suede sole of her sandals.

"Ma'am, can I help you with something? Maybe directions? I

haven't seen a nice car like that around these parts."

Sybil squared her jaw and pulled in her tummy. "I'm here to see Chandler. Is he available?"

The woman smiled. "Yes, he's just around the side of the house, working on the deck. May I give him a name?"

Sybil gave an eye roll. "He'll know who I am. The name is Sybil, Sybil Grafton."

"Well, of course! Your dad is the one that has helped Chandler around here so much. Why didn't you just say so?" The woman gave a welcoming laugh, gesturing her into the house.

Sybil pointed to where the woman had said Chandler was. "Thank you, but I left my car running. I just had a quick question for Chandler. I'll talk to him over there."

"Of course. It will give me a chance to finish making lunch. You know how hungry working men get." She gave Sybil a wink and stuck out her long-fingered hand, the bare nails trimmed close and buffed. "I'm Crystal Waters, very nice to meet you."

Sybil glanced at the hand. "Yes, of course you are." She turned and walked to the edge of the porch, the wind catching her loose hair and plastering it against her lipstick. Yanking it away, she took a deep breath and glanced at her car. *I can just leave now, before I really make an idiot of myself. No, you've come this far, you're not turning back. Even if Miss Golden America is waiting for you to land on your face!*

She walked around the side of the house, male laughter and deep voices beckoning her. At the sight of a pair of tanned, bare chests glistening in the sunlight, she paused. "Hello?"

Chandler turned, shading his eyes. "Sybil, what are you doing out here?" He laid the drill on the deck and reached for his t-shirt draped over the deck railing. He shrugged into it as he strode over, and then wiped his hands on the back of his jeans. He gave her a smile. "Did Elvira bake some more lemon cookies?"

Sybil's eyes drifted to the tall man with the dark blond hair at the other end of the deck, pulling his own t-shirt over his head. "She *has* been baking today. I'm on my way into town with her pies."

Chandler beckoned to the man. "Hey, come here and meet my neighbor."

Long strides carried him over and he stopped beside Chandler, placing his hands at his waist. "You didn't tell me you had such a *pretty* neighbor." He grinned, sticking out his hand. "Howdy, my name's Blu, Blu Waters. It's nice to meet you, ma'am."

Chandler shook his head, rubbing one tanned finger beneath his nose. "She doesn't like that, Blu."

Blu glanced over before focusing his attention on Sybil once more. "What doesn't the pretty lady like?" His blue eyes traveled over her, his grin contagious. "They sure don't make them like this in Colorado."

Sybil smiled, feeling the heat in her face. *I can't believe I'm actually blushing!* She took the warm hand in hers. "Kansas, born and raised right here in Wheatacre." She slid her eyes to Chandler. "I don't mind *ma'am*, when it's said in the right way. But I prefer Sybil."

Blu squeezed her hand, rubbing his thumb over the back of her knuckles. "It's a pleasure, Sybil. I don't think I've ever seen hair as black as the night like yours." He continued caressing the back of her hand. "I bet it smells pretty too."

Chandler reached out and grabbed Blu's wrist, breaking the clasped hands. "Blu, what's got into you? You don't even know the woman. Her grandfather's the town judge, so you'd better simmer down."

Sybil smiled, throwing a look at Chandler. "Yes, he is, but he likes polite, hardworking, young men in Wheatacre. I don't think he'd have a problem with you."

Chandler scowled. "Blu is the same age as I am, and we're not young by any stretch of the imagination. He's always been a flirt, but he's really putting on a show today."

Sybil stuck out her bottom lip. "And here I thought it might be about me."

Blu chuckled. "Believe me, it's *all* about you."

Crystal opened the French door leading to the dining room and stepped out onto the deck. "Lunch is ready, guys. You'd better get started if you want to make it in time for the picnic tonight." She nodded to the deck. "I'm assuming you want to finish this, and you both have to get cleaned up." She smiled at Sybil. "Would you want to be seen in town with two guys as filthy and rugged-looking as this?"

Sybil tilted her head back and forth, smiling up at Blu through her lashes. "It's not that bad."

Blu poked Chandler in the ribs with his elbow. "Hear that? I'm not too bad." He turned his eyes on Sybil. "What are you doing tonight, pretty lady? I was going to play third wheel for these two, but I'd much rather have you on my arm."

Sybil gaped and stuttered. "Well, I was going to ask Chan…" Her eyes darted from Chandler to Crystal and back to Blu. She flashed him a brilliant smile. "I would love to tag along."

Blu slapped his hands together. "It's a date, then." He turned to Crystal. "Sis, why don't you bring the food out here? We're too dirty to eat inside." He smiled at Sybil. "Maybe our new friend will join us?"

Sybil backed away from the deck, holding up her hands. "No, I just ate before I came over and I really need to get those pies delivered. I can meet you at the town hall around the time the picnic starts, if that works for all of you?" Her eyes smiled for Blu, drifted over Crystal, and escaped Chandler's dark gaze.

"I'll see you then, pretty lady." Blu jumped off the side of the deck where the railing was being installed. "I'm going to wash up a bit with the hose," he called back.

Crystal shook her head. "That brother of mine. He keeps everyone on their toes. But he's a sweetheart." She looked at Sybil. "Is this a dress-up occasion in Wheatacre?"

Sybil gestured to her own clothing. "This is what I'm wearing. Everyone is casual. You might want some bug spray later on for the fireworks. People bring blankets and sit on the grass. The chiggers can be rather pesky."

Crystal winced. "I'm finding that out. I have bites in the strangest places."

Chandler walked to the edge of the deck and stepped down next to Sybil. "I'm going to walk Sybil to her car. I'll be right back."

"Okay, see you later, Sybil." Crystal waved and walked back into the house.

Sybil took off at a fast pace, Chandler keeping up with her.

"What's the hurry? A few minutes ago, you acted like you had the rest of the afternoon to sit and flirt with my best friend." Chandler stopped beside the black car, his chest heaving.

Sybil stared up at him. "So, if he's your best friend, I'm not allowed to go out on a date with him?"

"That's not what I said." Chandler ran a hand over his hair, rubbing the back of his neck. "Blu is a great guy. He'd give you the shirt off his back, and his shoes too, but he also does things without thinking. He goes with what his heart and emotions are telling him at the time, and he'll deal with the reality later."

"You're warning me away from him?" Sybil raised her brow. "I'm a grown woman, and I can take care of myself. I know what I'm doing."

"I just don't want to see either one of you get hurt. Blu falls fast and hard. I don't know if he could stand being used…" Chandler looked away, biting his lower lip.

"You think I'm using him?" Sybil raised her voice. "What would I be using him *for*? He's just a nice guy that I met, and he thinks I'm pretty. I haven't heard that a lot from *any* man, and it was rather nice to have someone think I'm pretty *and* worth flirting with. But you wouldn't understand that, would you? You have your gorgeous Crystal all bundled up and tied with a lovely ribbon, just waiting for you."

Chandler wrinkled his brow. "What are you talking about, Sybil? My relationship with Crystal isn't that way. I've told you that over and over."

Sybil shoved a finger at his chest. "And you're a liar, Chandler Byron. I saw you two yesterday, walking into the hardware store. No woman hangs on a man like that unless she's encouraged to do so."

Chandler grabbed her finger. "I've known the Waters family since I could barely walk. Crystal and Blu are like brother and sister to me…maybe even better. I *like* them most of the time. We weren't doing anything out of the ordinary for us."

Sybil jerked her hand away. "Well, maybe you should rethink *your* ordinary."

Chandler took her elbows in his hands, capturing her eyes with his own. "Why did you really come out here today, Sybil?"

Looking away, she took a deep breath. "It doesn't matter."

"It matters to me."

"Well then, it wasn't important, and it doesn't make any difference now." She moved her arms, trying to free them from his grasp.

He loosened his hold, reaching up to rub her cheek with his finger.

Sybil jumped back, her hand going to her face, her eyes accusing. "Why would you touch me like that?"

"You had a red streak across your cheek. I was hoping it wasn't blood."

She smoothed her fingers over the area that burned like fire where his hand had been. "It's probably just my lipstick. This never-ending wind up here keeps making my hair stick in it, and then it smears all over my face."

"You would be just as beautiful without the red lips…maybe even better." He spoke softly, his eyes caressing her face and hair.

Sybil pressed her lips together, narrowing her eyes as she looked out over the undulating hills in the distance. *What am I feeling here? Why is my heart beating as though it will spring from my chest?* "I really need to go. I've probably run all the gas out of my car, and you need to eat lunch."

He reached out and opened the door. "I'll see you tonight."

Sybil slid into the seat and looked up at him. "Yes…tonight." She closed the door and shifted into gear, turning the Mercedes in a large circle before heading down the driveway. Her eyes drifted to the rearview mirror framing the tall cowboy, the dust from her car enveloping him in a sandy cloud.

CHANDLER BRUSHED AT THE DUST, watching the black car disappear over the hill. *Why didn't I have the nerve to ask her to the picnic tonight? I just stood there like a complete idiot while Blu snatched her right from under my nose. I've known of the woman for two years now, and my best friend says more to her in two minutes than I have in the past three months. I don't deserve a chance with her if I can't even open my mouth and ask her out.*

"What are you doing out there standing in the dirt? Aren't you hungry?" Blu's voice traveled over the distance from the house.

Chandler turned and strode back, a sheen of sweat covering his forehead. He brushed at it with his upper arm. "Man, it's hot out here. You sweat just standing around. I'm never going to get use to this heat and humidity." He stopped beside Blu and looked down at him seated on the edge of the deck, his booted feet dangling.

"You could always sell this place and go back to Colorado." Blu took a long swig of his bottled water.

Chandler shook his head. "And work for my father? You know my brothers have that all sewn up. The ranch will be theirs someday. And that's just fine with me. I have this place, and I'm going to make it into a nice home for my family."

Blu shrugged. "Suit yourself. Just trying to help, is all." He closed one eye and squinted up at Chandler. "You weren't trying to steal my girl, were you?"

Chandler snorted. "*Your* girl? You just met her ten minutes ago. Why don't you see what happens tonight before you make proclamations like that one?"

Blu chuckled. "I can tell you what's going to happen tonight. I'm going to eat some great picnic food with the prettiest woman in town, and then I'm going to watch the fireworks with her." He nodded. "Maybe even make a few fireworks of our own."

Chandler leaned one shoulder on the corner of the house and crossed his arms. "Sybil's not like that, you know. She's not going to make out with you like some sixteen-year-old under the bleachers back home."

Blu finished the bottled water and crushed it in his hands. "You sound like you've already tried and got rejected."

"No, I've only talked with Sybil a few times. But I know her father and grandfather and they're men of honor. I think she's been raised right, even if she does have a bit of an attitude most of the time." Chandler scuffed his boot in the dirt. "Sybil's a lawyer."

Blu guffawed. "You're kidding, right? A pretty thing like that?"

Chandler nodded. "She was a partner at a firm in Kansas City."

"So, she's pretty *and* has a head on her shoulders. I wonder what she's doing back here." Blu stuffed the rest of his sandwich in his mouth and chewed. "You'd think she would have stayed there if she was successful."

"I don't think that was the problem. There was some issue with the man she was seeing…" Chandler straightened, staring down at his friend. "My point is, be careful with her. She's softer than she realizes."

Blu pushed to his feet and gripped Chandler's shoulder. "She's not the only one with a soft spot, if I'm hearing things right." He shook his head, dropping his hand. "You should have moved faster…this one's mine." He climbed the steps, walking over to the railing. "Crystal left your sandwich in the kitchen. She's eating in there. She said it was too hot to eat outside. I can finish up."

Chandler climbed the steps, the joy of his friendship sucked out of his soul. "I'm not really hungry anymore. Must be the heat. Let's get this wrapped up so we aren't late for the picnic."

Blu leveled his gaze at his childhood friend. "You can't have them all, Chandler. You've played the blond, blue-eyed cowboy for too many years. I've watched you turn down one good thing after another, and I've taken your scraps. I also know that girl in there has loved you since we were in grade school—"

"Like a brother, Blu."

Blu thumped Chandler on the shoulder. "No, not like a brother. Quit lying to yourself. That girl has her heart set on marrying you. Both our families expect it. You know you care for her, why do you keep stringing her along?"

Chandler stepped back. "Don't start this again, Blu. I care for Crystal, but not like *that*. I think of her like my little sister. And I want God to lead her to a man she can respect and love…have a family with. She deserves that. But it's not me." Chandler shook his head. "It's just not me."

"Well, you'd better be praying awful hard then for someone else to come into her life. She's wasted a lot of years hoping on you." Blu kicked at a piece of treated lumber. "I'm done out here for today. I have to get ready for my date." He walked across the deck, snatching his Stetson from the railing post.

Chandler picked up the tools strewn across the treated boards. *I don't know what I want, Father. I don't know the plans You have for me, but I can't see Crystal being part of my future as a husband and father.* Green eyes framed with black lashes drifted through his thoughts. *And Sybil just seems like a suitcase full of trouble.*

Chapter Eight

*T*HE BRILLIANT ARRAY OF COLORS exploded in the dark sky, illuminating the blankets spread over the grass and the lawn furniture carried in from Wheatacre's yards. Young couples snuggled on the blankets in spite of the warm, humid air, stealing kisses when the sky darkened. Young children dressed for bed sat on their parents' laps, eyes wide, hands covering their ears as they gazed up at the heavens.

The sound like a cannon reverberated around the people gathered on the courthouse lawn.

"Look, Mommy! That's the flag sparkling in the sky." The small boy pointed, his mouth forming an 'o'.

Music began to play as the young mother said, "Yes, it is, and we need to stand while we sing our National Anthem."

"Because we respect what my daddy is doing for our country?" The boy climbed off his mother's lap, taking her left hand as she stood.

The mother placed her right hand over her heart, tears sparkling down her cheeks. "Yes, because we respect and honor what all the military is doing for our country."

"Can I salute the flag like Daddy showed me? Like he does when he's at work?" The small head tilted, gazing up at his mother.

She nodded. "Yes, Daddy would like that. Now no more questions."

Sybil listened to the exchange, tears slipping down her cheeks.

Chandler leaned over and whispered against her ear. "Are you all right?"

Sybil nodded. "That mother was in the salon yesterday. She was telling Thelma and me that her husband will be gone for a year. It's so sad."

"We need to remember them in prayer. Ask that God return him safely home." Chandler continued singing the last lines of the song, his eyes closed.

Sybil watched him, the fading sparkles of the flag lighting his face. *He's praying for a family he doesn't even know.*

As the crowd began to disperse, Sybil watched Chandler approach the woman. "I'd like to thank you for your sacrifice, ma'am." He smiled down at the boy. "And for yours too. It must be very difficult to not have your father at home right now."

The little boy nodded, his brown hair falling into his eyes. He brushed at it. "My daddy's in the United States Army. He's very far away."

"I'm sure he has a very important job to do." Chandler reached out to ruffle the boy's hair. "Thank you both. I will be praying for you all."

The mother smiled up at Chandler, brushing at her cheek. "I appreciate that. I know my husband would too. Happy Fourth of July to you."

"The same to you, ma'am."

Sybil tilted her head, hugging the blanket to her chest as Chandler returned. "That was very nice. I know they appreciated your kind words."

Crystal came up and brushed Chandler's arm. "He's always been like that. Always offering a word of encouragement, helping others in need."

Blu nudged his sister's arm. "Yeah, he makes the rest of us look like ungrateful slobs."

Chandler shrugged. "I can't help that. You'll just have to put yourself out there more, Blu."

Blu patted his lean abdomen. "I don't know about you all, but it's been a long time since that picnic. Do you want to get something to eat?" His gaze swept the almost vacant court house lawn. "Is there anything open this time of night in this little burg?"

Sybil shook her head. "Not usually, unless the café is having special hours because of the holiday. The town shuts down around nine every night."

Chandler crossed his arms. "I don't see anything wrong with that. It suits me just fine. I like to go to bed early and get up with the sun." His gaze shifted to Sybil's face. "Just like some others I know."

Sybil cleared her throat and smiled at Blu. "It's been difficult to get used to Wheatacre again after living in Kansas City for so many years. I'm remembering all the little things that annoyed me so much."

Crystal moved closer to Chandler. "I think Wheatacre is a lovely little town. The people are friendly, and I don't need anything after nine." She brushed Chandler's arm. "I couldn't agree more with the going to bed early idea."

Sybil rolled her eyes, then watched as Chandler's gaze darted over the grass. He bent down and picked up a candy bar wrapper, shaking it at the group. "If everyone takes away their own trash, there's no clean-up needed."

Blu laughed, kicking an empty pop can over to Chandler. "There's some more for you. I want to do everything I can to help your Boy Scout reputation."

Chandler picked up the can and tossed it at Blu. "Maybe *you* should work on being a better citizen."

Blu dodged it, giving a chuckle. He gave Sybil a wink, his teeth illuminated in the street lamps lining the courthouse lawn. "I'm such an upstanding citizen that I'm going to escort this young lady back to her car." His smile included the group. "Unless you all want to find something to eat."

Chandler shook his head. "I'm still as full as a tick, and about bushed." He swept his hat from his head, and smoothed back the short layers of hair, using the hat to gesture at Blu. "You should be thinking about getting some sleep too. You agreed to help me finish that deck tomorrow." He set the hat on his head, tipping it back from his forehead.

Blu nodded. "It'll get done, Gramps. We don't head out until Monday morning."

Crystal crossed her arms and gave a shiver. "I should have brought my jacket."

Blu tilted his head at his sibling. "See, Crystal is ready for a ride back to your place." He grinned at Sybil. "I'm sure this little lady wouldn't mind dropping me off. You don't even have to go up the driveway. Just slow down so I can land softly."

Sybil laughed. "Don't be ridiculous. I don't mind taking you back to Chandler's place. And it's not that far up the driveway."

Blu draped one arm around Sybil's shoulders. "So it's settled then. You both can head back, and I'll be along a little later. There's got to be a convenience store or someplace I can grab a bag of chips and a Coke." He flashed another smile at Sybil. "That'll give us a chance to get to know one another a little better."

Chandler cleared his throat. "Maybe Sybil has plans for the rest of her evening. You're assuming a lot of someone you just met."

Crystal took Chandler by the arm. "I'm not hearing Sybil complaining. She's a woman of the world. I'm sure she can speak for herself very well."

Sybil leveled her gaze at the blonde. "Of course I can. If I had a problem, I'd let you all know." Her eyes slid to Blu's face smiling down at her, only inches away. "It's a Friday night, and it's been a long time since I enjoyed one *with* someone. The gas station in town has a little store. I'm sure you can get something there. They're open until midnight."

Blu dropped his arm from around her shoulders and took her hand. "Well, let's go, little lady! The night's still young, the way I figure it." He headed to the sidewalk, Sybil stepping quickly to keep pace. He waved his free hand in the air. "Don't stay up too late, you two. I'll see you bright and early to finish that deck."

CHANDLER SCOWLED, HIS EYES FOLLOWING the laughing couple, their hands entwined and swinging as they walked to Sybil's car.

Crystal laid her forehead against Chandler's arm. "Don't worry. He'll be back in time to get that deck finished. You know he's good for it."

Chandler pulled away, stuffing his hands into the pockets of his jeans. "Yeah, he'll be there to work. That's not what I'm worried about, and he knows it." He took to the sidewalk, his long strides going in the opposite direction of the happy couple.

"Hey, wait up!" Crystal jogged over. "He's just having some fun, Chandler. You know Blu likes the pretty ones, and Sybil *is* attractive, in her own way." Crystal laughed, tossing the long, blonde strands at her waist. "Kind of like a baby skunk. So cute, but you don't want to get too close."

Chandler shook his head. "And it doesn't bother you that your brother is interested in someone like that?"

"Oh, come on! They're just spending a couple of hours together. They barely know one another."

"Exactly!" Chandler reached his truck and swung open the passenger door, gesturing for Crystal to get in.

Crystal placed one slim hand on the rim of the truck bed. "What's got into you? You've never minded Blu and his antics before."

"I've minded, I've just kept it from you over the years. He works too fast and jumps in too quickly where women are concerned. I know this one and she's out of his league."

Crystal narrowed her eyes. "Well, if Sybil Grafton is out of Blu's reach, she's out of yours as well." She climbed into the truck, staring straight ahead as she crossed her arms.

Chandler took off his hat and slapped his leg with it. "Why are you upset now? Why can't you, Blu, and I just be friends like we always have been? We've had some good times together over the years."

Crystal turned her eyes on Chandler, tears collecting on the lashes. "You just don't get it, do you? We aren't little kids anymore." She shrugged. "We aren't even young adults. I'm going to be thirty in a couple more years."

He lifted his shoulders. "What's that got to do with anything?"

"Did you ever think that maybe I'd like to settle down sometime, get married and have a couple kids?"

He shrugged again. "I always thought you *would* get married...kind of surprised that some handsome cowboy hasn't snatched you up by now."

The tears spilled over. "I've been waiting for *you*, Chandler! You're about as dense as an old piece of oak. Everyone expects us to get married. My mother has had our wedding planned for years. We're supposed to be together!" She brushed at her cheek and then pointed one long finger at him. "And then you stand there talking about that *shrew* like you care about her!" Swiping at her cheek, she yanked her door closed.

Chandler lurched as his support slammed loudly in the night air. He struck his hat against his leg once more. "This is going to be one fun ride home." He rounded the back of the truck and paused. *This isn't just some girl, this is Crystal. You've known her since she was in diapers, and you've seen her upset before. You can handle this.* He reached his door and opened it slowly, sighing when he heard the sobs from the opposite side of the bench seat.

"I want to go home." The words were muffled against her hands.

Chandler slid in, closing his door. He started the truck. "We'll be at my place in just a few minutes. We can talk this out on the way there. It's just a misunderstanding."

Crystal turned her red face to him. "This is *not* a misunderstanding!" She thinned her lips. "I don't want to go to your house, I want to go home, to Colorado."

Chandler shook his head. "Don't be ridiculous, Crystal. You and Blu are leaving on Monday morning. We'll have this all worked out by then." He buckled his seat belt. "Besides, I'm not bothering Blu right now to let him know you're upset." He wrinkled his brow. "What's got into you? You're usually pretty level-headed. That's what I've always liked about you."

Her chest heaved. "You care about that woman! I saw it on your face this afternoon when she was at the house, and I just watched you again. I've never seen you act like that about a woman before."

Chandler put the truck in gear and pulled away from the side of the curb. "Crystal, you're upset, and I don't even know why. I don't have any feelings for Sybil. I know her father, and I like the guy. I just don't want Blu doing something stupid to ruin the relationship I have with him."

Crystal rolled her eyes and stared out her window. "You'll have to come up with something better than that."

"Crystal, I really don't understand why you are so upset. We've never talked about marriage." He snorted. "We haven't even been on a date."

Crystal turned to him and gaped. "We went to your senior prom together."

Chandler chuckled. "Yeah, because I didn't want to go, and I let you and Blu talk me into it. I only went because you agreed to go as my date…not my *date*."

"That's seriously the way you look at it?" Her eyes widened.

Chandler nodded. "Of course! There is no other way to look at it. I think of you and Blu the same as I do family. I've known you all my life. I care about you, and I love you—"

"Like a sister!" Crystal sneered. "I can't believe we are having this conversation."

Chandler lowered his head, looking out the front window. "I guess we should have had it a long time ago."

"Haven't you heard the comments people have made about us over the years? People are always asking when we're going to get married. Did you think they were just joking?"

He gave her a quick glance. "Well, yes, of course I did. I would always play along, but I thought everyone knew we were just good friends. I never told anyone…" he shook a finger at her, "including you, that I loved you or we were going to get married someday."

Crystal turned to him. "I think you're scared."

Chandler frowned. "Scared of what?"

Crystal nodded. "I think you *do* care about me, and you're afraid that everything will change for us. That you, Blu, and I won't be the same anymore…like we always have been." She slid over, placing her hand on his shoulder. "I'm perfect for you, Chandler. I've known you my whole life. I know the way you like your eggs in the morning, and just how strong you want your coffee. I'm a hard worker, and we'd make a terrific team." She laughed. "We could have that place of yours looking beautiful in just a few years. I know all about caring for a place like yours. Sybil can't fry an egg, much less help with the running of a large ranch."

Chandler raised one hand. "Whoa, there. You're getting way ahead of yourself." He gripped the steering wheel. "First of all, I don't want a ranch like you're talking about…like the ones we grew up on. I love it here, and I'm very content to keep it small…jut some cattle and a couple of horses, maybe a garden and some chickens."

Crystal reared back. "You want to be a farmer?" She chewed on her bottom lip as she nodded. "I'm fine with that too. My point is that Sybil wouldn't have a clue about any of it."

Chandler turned onto his driveway. "I'm not asking for a résumé from *anyone*. I really appreciate the help you and Blu have been on your visits here, but I'm okay on my own."

She braced her arm along the back of the seat. "So you're just going to continue to fight this? You won't admit that we belong together, that everyone expects us to be together?" She shook her head. "Come on, Chandler. You always do what's best for everyone. Can't you see that us getting married is what's supposed to happen?"

Chandler stopped the truck in front of the house and turned off the engine. "You're right. I've always done what's been best for all concerned, putting anything I wanted to the side. But I stopped that when I moved here, Crystal. I'm my own person now. Not the youngest son of a big rancher in Colorado. I'm doing things my way and in my own time. And I like it that way."

Crystal opened her door before turning back. "I never thought I'd say this about you, Chandler Byron, but you're being an idiot. You're turning away from the very best person to spend your life with. I know you like the back of my hand, and…" she sniffed, jumping from the truck. She turned, placing both hands on the vinyl seat as she leaned in. "I love you, you big, stupid, block of wood! I always have. I'll love you more than that simpering, mean Sybil ever could." She swiped at her eyes. "And because I love you so much, and I want the best for you, I'm going to be here for you…waiting as I always have, for when you get your head on straight!" She backed away, slamming the door.

Chandler's eyes followed her as she ran to the little house, her sobs floating back to him. She treated the front door the same as she had the truck, the porch railing shuddering with the impact. *I'm going to have to get that porch taken care of before it falls off the house and takes the front room with it.*

He struck the steering wheel with the palm of his hand. *I've got to hand it to you, Chandler. You've made a royal mess of this day. You're going out with a bang, just like those fireworks.* He shook his head. *Crystal's right. Sybil* is *mean and ornery, and I shouldn't be worried about her and Blu. I should be thankful to have him interested in her. We're nothing alike, and she would never be happy living here. She'd fit better into Blu's plans for his future as the only son of a big rancher.*

Staring out the window, he narrowed his eyes as he laid his cheek on the palm of his hand. His elbow rested on the open window, the night sounds drifting around the old truck. *Nothing makes sense right now. Crystal has ruined our friendship by saying she loves me, and Blu is out with the only woman that has ever interested me. Even if she* is *ornery! And because of that, the relationship I have with Blu will never be the same again. What a mess! And all because of some woman! My life has been just fine without all that hassle.*

Sandy nickered from the pasture fence.

Chandler turned, calling over to the horse. "Hey there, Sandy girl, are you enjoying the cool night air?"

The answer was a pawing of the ground, and a nodding of the butterscotch yellow head, the pale mane fluttering.

"I know, it's been a couple of days since we went for a decent ride. Whenever Crystal and Blu come to visit, you take a backseat, and that's not right."

Sandy nickered, shaking her beautiful head.

"Let me get a few hours of sleep, and we can get some miles in before it gets hot. How does that sound?"

Sandy pawed the ground again and kicked up her feet as she ran down the fence line, stirring dust into the air.

Chandler opened the door. "At least someone likes me right now." He slid from the truck, giving one last glance down the driveway before slamming the door closed.

Chapter Nine

SYBIL LAUGHED, BRACING HERSELF WITH her hands as she leaned back on the blanket spread on the ground. She crossed her slim feet at the ankles, shaking her head at Blu. "You really didn't learn to ride a horse when you were still in diapers. That's just cowboy cliché talking."

"Sure I did!" Blu took a corn chip from the bag and popped it into his mouth. He chewed vigorously, smiling at her from where he reclined, his strong jaw resting in the palm of his hand. He nudged her bare toe with the tip of his boot. "My mother wiggled those little blue jeans over my well-padded behind, pulled on my boots, slapped my hat on my head, and took me to my daddy." His grin widened with Sybil's laughter. "That's the way it's done for little cowboys in training."

"Well, maybe someday I'll get the chance to talk with your mother and see what kind of stories you've been telling me." Sybil shook her head. "I can't imagine any mother sending her toddler out like that."

Blu nudged her toe again. "I would really like for you to meet my parents. I think they'd like your spirit as much as I do."

Sybil raised a brow. "Spirit...I don't know if I've ever had my attitude called that before. But I like it much better than what I've heard in the past." She shrugged, looking out over the meandering stream before them, the moonlight shimmering a silver path to the low bank on the opposite side. "We just met, so we have lots of time to get to know one another."

Blu rolled to his back, clasping his hands beneath his head. "I'm not much of a letter-writer. I'll be leaving on Monday, and usually we only visit once every few months." He turned his head, smiling at her. "So it seems to me, we'd better get acquainted as much as possible in the time we have."

"Isn't that what we've been doing for the past couple of hours?" Sybil sat up, pulling her knees to her chest. She curled her toes against the blanket. "I don't think I've ever spent so much time just talking with someone. My friend Tarah would be shocked."

"Tarah doesn't speak?" Blu reached out and slid his finger down her arm.

Sybil shivered. "Of course she does. I guess we've known one another so long we don't have to really say a lot. We know what the other one thinks."

Blu nodded. "It's like that with Chandler and me. Kind of nice to be with someone and just enjoy the silence. Not always have to say something."

Sybil gripped her knees. "Are Chandler and your sister really getting married, or is it just talk? My father told me he thought Crystal was Chandler's fiancée, but Chandler said she's not. What's up with that?"

Blu curled to a sitting position, draping his arm across his bent knee. "Haven't we talked enough tonight about my sister and Chandler? I'd much rather hear all about you and what makes you such a gorgeous, spirited lady."

"Flattery won't get you very far, Mr. Waters. It's usually insincere, and a way to manipulate someone into thinking or doing something your way." She smiled over her shoulder at him. "Even though it *is* nice to hear."

Blu laughed. "If I thought you were ugly and boring, I wouldn't be here right now."

Sybil's laughter filled the night air. "Touché!"

Blu chuckled. "All right, I'll answer one more question about my sister and Chandler, and then no more talk about them. I want to get to know *you*." Blu swatted at a mosquito. "It's not official, meaning he hasn't given her a ring or set a date, but everyone assumes it's going to happen." He shook his head. "My mother has had the wedding planned for years now. She's just waiting to call the minister and the caterers to give them the date and time."

"So it is pretty serious between them." Sybil pressed her lips together, staring into the distance.

"I'd say so. Chandler tries to deny it, but I think he just has cold feet. I've told him over and over that nothing's going to change between the three of us, that it will only get better." Blu rubbed his nail over the denim material covering his knee. "Crystal's loved him since we were kids. She always said she was going to marry him. I don't think she thought it would take this long, but Chandler's cautious. He doesn't make decisions easily."

"That's probably a good thing in the long run. Believe me, I've seen case after case that wouldn't have had to go to court if someone had just slowed down and thought a little bit first."

Blu reached out and poked her arm. "But that wouldn't have helped you one bit."

Sybil smiled. "Probably not."

Blu adjusted his position, his shoulder rubbing against hers. "So, pretty lady, why aren't you taken? There must be a boyfriend around somewhere."

She cleared her throat. "Not anymore. It wasn't very serious anyway."

Blu ran his finger down her arm. "I probably should say I'm sorry to hear that, but I'm not."

Sybil pulled away. "I really need to get home. It must be very late."

Blu shrugged. "And what if it is? We don't have much time. You might be taken by the time I get back to Wheatacre."

"I really doubt that. I haven't had men lining up at my doorstep."

Blu placed the palm of his hand on the blanket behind her and nudged her shoulder with his chin. "I can't imagine why."

Sybil took a deep breath. "I think my sharp tongue and nasty demeanor keep most of them away. The ones that break through all of that don't stay around very long."

His breath was warm against her neck. "Maybe a little loving would help. Maybe it would soften that cool exterior you're trying to show."

Sybil reared back, putting one hand against Blu's chest. "Do you try to sleep with every woman you go out with?"

Blu chuckled. "I don't usually do much sleeping, but why not? Like I said, the time is short. I think a person should make the most of it, and have a little fun." His lips brushed her hair. "Don't you like to *sleep*?"

Sybil struggled to her feet. "As a matter of fact, I do!" She slid her feet into her sandals. "I also like to do it *alone*. I don't know you well enough to do what you want to do right now, Mr. Waters."

Blu pushed to his feet, his hands before him. "I'm not going where I'm not wanted. I just thought we could have some fun together, nothing too serious. I really like you, Sybil. I think there's another whole person under that turtle shell you're wearing."

Sybil crossed her arms. "So now I'm a turtle? That's definitely not flattering."

Blu grinned. "Well, you know, turtles move kind of slow, and they hide in their shells when they're afraid." He nodded. "I think that describes you pretty well."

Sybil reached down and took a corner of the blanket, giving it a yank. "Would you move your big boots off my blanket, please?"

Blu stepped off. "Of course. Can I help you with that?"

Sybil gave the blanket a shake. "I'm just fine. I know how to fold a blanket." She jerked the corners together, folding it into a large lump.

Blu gestured at the cotton mass held against her chest. "I think you need more practice with that. Maybe we can check out this spot again tomorrow night?"

Sybil stared at him, blinking slowly. "I'm going to pretend you didn't just say that." She turned with a huff and strode to her car. "That way we can save ourselves the embarrassment of what almost happened here." She opened the trunk and tossed the blanket in.

Blu took her hand. "I'm not embarrassed at all. I like you, and I'm attracted to you. I don't see the problem with us having a little bit of fun like two adults."

Sybil jerked her hand away. "I thought for most of the evening that I liked you too. But I think you'd be attracted to a goat, and adults don't just share spit. Adults get to know one another before they do intimate things together." She shut the trunk lid.

Blu tilted his head. "So I don't have to marry you, just get to know you better?"

Sybil wrinkled her brow. "I didn't say that…exactly." She groaned. "It's late, I'm tired, and I like you too much to do something stupid with you."

Blu cupped her cheeks and placed his lips on hers.

Sybil pulled away, brushing the back of her hand across her mouth. "What did I just say?"

Blu shrugged, raising his brow. "I just wanted to see if I was really missing anything. You're right, we should probably get to know one another better before we share spit, as you so beautifully put it." He walked to the passenger door and slid into the car.

Sybil clenched her fists. "How dare he say something like that to me! What a rude man." *Just goes to show that I made the best decision. But it did feel rather nice to have someone hold my hand and touch my arm. Even that short kiss felt good!*

Blu's voice carried to the back of the car. "Are you about ready? I have to be up in a couple of hours to finish a deck."

"I'm coming, just keep your shirt on!" Sybil opened her door and slid behind the wheel.

Blu gave her a wink. "You insisted, so I did. You didn't get a chance to see what you're missing."

Sybil closed her eyes and groaned. *Yes, I saw more than enough this afternoon.*

CHANDLER STABBED AT HIS SCRAMBLED egg, sliding it around his plate. His eyes moved over Crystal standing at the stove, and then Blu seated at the counter with him. "You must have gotten in pretty late."

Blu took a piece of crispy bacon and chewed on it. "Not too bad…around two."

"That seems kind of late to stay out with someone that you barely know." Chandler chewed the bite of egg, watching Crystal's shoulders straighten.

Blu turned on his stool to face Chandler, putting his knuckles against his thigh. "I didn't do anything with her, if that's what you're asking. We talked for a long time, and then when I tried to get friendly, the claws came out. I don't think she's as innocent as she wants to portray, but she wasn't having any of me, that's for sure." Blu turned back to his plate. "Now, can we eat breakfast and get on with the day without you glaring at us?"

Chandler nodded. "I'm sorry, I didn't realize I was making you uncomfortable." His eyes strayed to Crystal's back once more. "Thank you for the breakfast, Crystal. It was delicious, as usual."

The curt, "you're welcome," was followed with a loud sniff.

Blu nudged Chandler's knee with his own. He lowered his voice, his eyes swerving to his sister's back. "What's up with you two?"

"I'll tell you later." Chandler stood, taking his plate and coffee cup to the sink.

"YOU REALLY DO HAVE MARBLES for brains!" Blu shook his head and drilled the long screw into place. He took another screw from the box, pointing it at Chandler. "I told you Crystal loved you. But no, you never listen to old Blu."

"You're her brother. You don't know what she thinks half the time." Chandler laid another piece of treated board on the deck frame.

"I obviously have more sense than you. I figured out that she loved you and wanted to spend the rest of her life taking care of you and having babies." Blu punched Chandler's bicep. "Now you've gone and broke her heart."

Chandler winced, rubbing his arm. "What was that for?"

Blu shook one finger at his best friend. "That was for Crystal. She wouldn't hurt a fly in her pudding, so I know she's not going to say anything to you."

"She had plenty to say last night." Chandler laid down another board. "You need to stop talking and start drilling. You're getting behind."

Blu narrowed his eyes, shaded under the brim of his hat. He stared at Chandler. "I can't wait until our mother gets her hands on you. She's been planning a wedding for the two of you since Crystal graduated high school."

Chandler thumped his chest with his thumb. "*I didn't do anything!* I've never told Crystal that I loved her, and I certainly didn't ask her to marry me. I'm innocent of the accusations you're making."

Blu drilled in another screw. "Yeah, about as innocent as a raccoon in a cornfield after dark."

"Well, I wasn't the one staying out all night with someone I just met." Chandler glared. "In the dark!"

Blu nodded, closing his eyes and taking a deep breath. "And it was so pleasant down by the river, the grass nice and cool—"

Chandler shoved Blu, knocking him from his knees.

"What'd you do that for?" Blu dropped the drill and sprang to his feet, his eyes flashing.

"Don't talk about Sybil like that! You don't know her." Chandler pushed to his feet, meeting Blu eye to eye.

Blu perched his hands on his wide leather belt, sweat trickling down his tanned chest. "You need to back off, Chandler. I already told you at breakfast that nothing happened. I wanted to, believe me, but she was out of there, snatching up her blanket before I knew what was going on."

Chandler rubbed his sweating forehead across his upper arm. He pulled off his leather work gloves and tossed them on the deck. "I'm sorry. I don't know what's got me so worked up." He took the edge of his damp t-shirt and wiped his face. "I feel terrible about—"

"You should!"

Chandler chewed on his bottom lip. "Don't push me, Blu. I'm trying to make things right between us."

"You need to be telling this to Crystal, not me."

Chandler walked to the railing and sat down, his booted feet dangling. "I did. I told her that I loved her like a sister, and not in the way she wanted."

Blu snorted. "How did she take that?"

"She told me I was an idiot and she'd be waiting for me to get my act together."

Blu laughed. "That's my sister. Of course, you deserved that."

Chandler dropped his head, staring at his feet. "If you say so. I'd rather Crystal said rotten things about me and got on with her life, than think that I hurt her. I want her to be happy…" Chandler's eyes focused on Blu. "But it's not with me. Not in that way. I can't feel something that's not there."

Blu sighed, tilting his cowboy hat off his forehead. "Well, I'm sorry to hear it. I was looking forward to having you as a brother for real, and I guess it's not going to happen now."

"Don't say that. I want us to be friends, just like we've always been. I can understand why that won't happen for Crystal and me, but I don't want to lose you too."

Blu hitched up his jeans and set his hands on his hips once again. "Crystal will come around. It may take her awhile, and she may make life a bit uncomfortable until we head out on Monday, but because she cares, she'll be back."

Chandler shook his head. "I hope you're right, Blu. She was crying last night, and I felt really bad. I've never seen her like that before."

Blu knelt down on the deck, taking up the drill. "What can I say? She loves you. She can't help her feelings any more than you can help yours." Blu gestured to Chandler with the drill. "Let's get this wrapped up. I'm hot, and a swim in your pond sounds good. Crystal won't be back until suppertime."

Chandler jumped from the railing. "You can swim in that swamp if you want to. The cows are probably in it since it's so hot."

Blu nodded. "That's true. When you dredged it a couple years ago, it made it really nice this spring. But the cows think so too. Maybe just some fishing down by the creek would be better. You really should think about putting in a swimming pool. You know, one like your dad put in back when we were kids. We had some fun times there."

Chandler smiled. "Yeah, we did, but pools like that cost a lot of money. I'd rather have a house I can live in all year than a pool I can only swim in for a few months."

Blu chuckled, wiping the sweat off the back of his neck. "A few months! As hot as it is here in Kansas, you could swim from April to November, no problem."

"Sounds as though you have it all figured out, Blu. And since you have way more money than I do, why don't you put one in here and you can use it every time you come visit." Chandler clapped his friend on the back.

Blu shook his head. "That's not a good investment for me. Besides, you work me like a dog whenever I'm here. Who has time for a swim?"

Chandler shrugged. "That's what I was thinking!" He pointed to the deck. "You have a screw sticking out. You need to sink it. I don't want to skin my toes when I come out here with my morning coffee to watch the sunrise."

Blu looked up at his friend and shook his head. "Just remember to put on your fuzzy pink slippers and you'll be all set."

Chapter Ten

CRYSTAL STOPPED BESIDE SYBIL'S TABLE and cleared her throat. "Would you mind if I sat with you?"

Sybil's eyes roamed over the café, noting the many vacant tables. "Where are the guys? I thought you all were inseparable."

Crystal dropped her leather fringed purse on the vinyl seat of the booth and sat down next to it. "They're at Chandler's place, finishing up the deck. I came into town to get some supplies from the grocery store. Chandler's bad about not keeping staples in the kitchen."

Sybil raised one eyebrow. "Really? Imagine that. I thought all guys knew how to stock a kitchen." Her eyes traveled the café once more. "I'm about finished, but you are welcome to sit here."

Crystal smiled. "Why thank you for the invitation, Sybil. I hate to eat alone." She pointed at Sybil's large salad, barely a bite taken. "Besides, you just got here. I saw you walk in a few minutes ago."

Sybil dabbed at her mouth with the paper napkin. "I didn't know I was being spied on. I don't know if I should be flattered or scared."

"I wouldn't try to flatter you. I was just being observant." Crystal smiled up at the waitress as she neared the table. "I don't need to see a menu. Just bring me the biggest cheeseburger you have, with all the toppings, onion rings instead of fries, and a large chocolate shake."

The waitress wrote it all down, glancing at Sybil's glass. "Would you like more water?"

"Yes, please, and another slice of lemon, as well. It covers up the taste of Wheatacre's tap water."

The waitress shook her head. "I've told you over and over, Sybil, that our water is filtered."

Sybil shrugged. "It doesn't taste like it to me, Genie. Besides, I know you didn't filter it back in the summer I worked here. It was straight from the tap."

"That was also a hundred years ago." The waitress sighed, giving Crystal a smile. "I'll be right back with your order."

"Thank you, ma'am!" Crystal grinned, watching the Genie walk back to the kitchen. "She is always so friendly. I like to think about living in a place such as this, where you know everyone and talk about your life while you're grocery shopping or getting your hair done."

"Yes, Genie is friendly…very friendly, which is why I would guard your tongue. You will hear the strangest things about yourself if you let too much information slip." Sybil pushed the romaine around her plate.

Crystal leaned over, examining the salad. "Are you eating that without dressing?"

Sybil scowled. "I have balsamic vinegar and a dribble of olive oil on it. Just the way I like it, thank you." Sybil pointed her fork at Crystal. "And you should be more careful. That lunch you ordered is enough to send you right to the hospital with blocked arteries."

Crystal leaned back, patting her lean frame. "I've made it to almost thirty without a problem. Besides," she leaned forward, lowering her voice, "I'm usually so busy on the ranch that those calories are worn off, and then some. I end every day with a huge bowl of ice cream."

Sybil winced. "I'm so very happy for you."

"Chandler has told me over and over that he likes the way I eat. He says that it assures him that he's going to get a great, home-cooked meal." Crystal's eyes flittered to the salad. "And I'm not talking about a pile of leaves, either."

"Really?" Sybil smiled. "The evening I was there, we had a lovely salad and the steaks he grilled were the best I've ever eaten."

Crystal tossed her long braid over her shoulder. "Don't get me wrong, Chandler is a fantastic cook. Of course, he'd have to be, living on his own like he does. But I happen to know that his mother, a very good friend of mine, took the time to teach him the basics of cooking when he was younger. She tried to with his brothers, but it just didn't take like it did with Chandler."

"There you go." Genie set the plate heaped with onion rings and a huge cheeseburger before Crystal. She placed the tall glass of chocolate shake beside it and Sybil's water at her place. "One cheeseburger with all the toppings, onion rings instead of fries. Can I get you ladies anything else?" Genie looked from Crystal to Sybil.

"No, thank you, Genie, but I will need my check." Sybil laid her napkin on the table.

Crystal waved the last comment away and smiled at Genie. "Please put Sybil's salad on my check…my treat."

"*Really*, it's not necessary." Sybil's eyes darkened as she leveled her eyes on Crystal.

"No, I insist. I want to do this for you." Crystal's gaze shifted from Sybil as she smiled up at Genie.

Genie raised her brows. "All righty then, I'll bring your check after you've had a chance to eat. Just let me know if there's anything else I can get you." Genie rushed from the table, walking into the corner of another table.

"I hope she's okay." Crystal frowned. "Did you see that? She jabbed her leg right into that table. She's going to have a bruise."

Sybil crossed her hands in her lap. "Crystal, this is all very pleasant for you, I'm sure, but you need to get to the point of why you're here."

Crystal laughed. "I'm here to visit Chandler, of course. Blu and I have been coming to Wheatacre every few months ever since he moved here. You know that." Crystal took a big bite of her burger and rolled her eyes. "This is *so* good! You really should try it sometime." She shoved the cheeseburger under Sybil's nose. "Have a bite…it's delicious."

Sybil tilted back, looking down her nose. "No, thank you. I don't share food, as a general rule."

Shrugging, Crystal took another bite, mayonnaise and ketchup dripping onto her onion rings. "You don't know what you're missing."

Sybil ran her tongue over her bottom lip. "If you came into the café today to warn me to stay away from your brother, you don't need to be concerned with that. Blu is not my type."

Crystal smiled around her onion ring. "I'm not worried about Blu. He can hold his own. But I do agree that you're not his type. He needs someone fun-loving, someone that could handle the everyday running of a ranch. He's going to inherit it, and he needs someone that has a clue about ranching. I think you would agree that's not you."

Sybil smirked. "I have no desire to become a rancher's wife, no matter how big the spread is. I have an education and a career, and I would like for the man in my life to respect that."

"Well, I guess I got a two-for-one today. I'm relieved to know that my brother is not an option for you." Crystal leaned forward, placing her hamburger on the plate. "But my biggest concern is Chandler. You do realize we are to be married very soon, right?" Crystal took the napkin beside her plate and wiped her hands.

Sybil watched the simple gesture. "Yes, I've heard that several times." She narrowed her eyes, staring deep into Crystal's. "But Chandler seems to disagree with the talk that's going around. Maybe *you* are confused as to how he's feeling."

Crystal pursed her lips and shook her head. "No, I really don't think so. We talked about it last night. He knows that everyone is expecting us to be married." She laughed. "Why, my mother has it all planned. Chandler would never disappoint her…or me." Crystal's blue eyes darkened as she smiled. "Chandler's just like that, always doing what's right. It's one of the many things I love about him."

Sybil pushed her plate to the middle of the table. "Look, I don't know you, or your brother, and I haven't really had a chance to get acquainted with your dear friend Chandler. For some reason that I cannot fathom, you think I care about all of you in some way." She took a deep breath. "So, to set your mind at ease, let me assure you I have no interest in your brother *or* Chandler. I detest cowboys and their swaggering ways, and I always have."

Crystal crossed her arms, a slow smile spreading over her face.

"Since that last statement seems to please you, I'll say that cow*girls* fit into that same category for me." Sybil took her purse from the vinyl seat and stood. "Now you can finish your delicious meal in peace and get back to your cowboys to do whatever the three of you do together."

Crystal's mouth gaped.

Smiling, Sybil tapped Crystal's chin. "Careful, the flies are terrible in here this time of year. Thanks for the salad." She walked away, her low-heeled sandals clicking on the tile floor. She paused in the small entrance way, one hand covering her racing heart. She turned back to glare at Crystal.

Oblivious, Crystal shoved her plate away, looking out the window.

Genie sauntered up to the table. "That woman is a piece of work. She always has been."

Perturbed, Sybil quietly crossed her arms. *Excuse me? You're a bossy old witch.*

Crystal turned to Genie.

Genie shook her head. "I could never figure out how Loren Grafton could have produced offspring like that. He's so nice."

"Yes, I've heard that a time or two around here." Crystal laid her napkin on the table and collected her purse.

Genie pointed with her pencil to Crystal's plate. "You didn't eat much. Was your burger okay?"

"It was the best that I've ever had…really. I can't eat that much at one time. If I could get a take-home box, I'll finish it later." Crystal gave a half-grin. "I've kind of lost my appetite as well."

Genie nodded. "Sybil Grafton will do that to you. I'll be right back with your check and a box."

Crystal smiled. "Thanks!" Her gaze returned to the parking lot.

Sybil huffed, yanking the door open as she stormed out to the parking lot. *This small town and the gossip is more than I can take. You're not so sweet, Crystal Waters. You don't fool me. You can have your brother, and Chandler, for all I care. I don't need any of this.*

SYBIL TOOK A LONG SIP of her iced tea and set it on the wrought iron table beside her lounge chair. She crossed her hands on her flat tummy and closed her eyes, smiling. *Now this is the life! No irritating dad, no pesky stepmother wannabe, no Crystal Waters…just me and the cicadas. All I'm missing is a swimming pool.*

She took a deep breath of the warm, humid air and crossed her bare feet at the ankles. *If I wasn't afraid of all the creepy, crawling things out here, this wouldn't be too bad for a night's sleep.* She laughed at herself. *Wrong! A cool shower, air-conditioning and a nice, soft bed are calling. Why would anyone sleep outside when they had those items available?*

A noise on the gravel driveway jerked her eyes open. Shading them against the lowering sun's rays, her eyes skimmed the length of the driveway leading to the stone barn, and then back along the portion in front of the guest house and the terrace. She shrugged, closing her eyes once more. *Guess I'm imagining things.*

Heavy steps on the driveway caused her to jump to her feet, and she stared at the corner of the house, her hand against her chest. *Now I know I've heard something! Is someone here? But it sounded too heavy for a person...and surely no one would visit this late in the day.* She gathered the skirt of her maxi-dress in her hand, lifting it as she tiptoed across the warm stones of the terrace. As she neared the back door, the shadow of a horse and rider elongated on the driveway. She gasped, grabbing for the door. Relief and terror coursed through her.

"Well there you are!" Blu tipped his hat, giving her a grin. He patted Sandy's neck. "I was about to head back to Chandler's place. I wasn't seeing any life around here."

Sybil sagged against the door, gripping the loose material across her middle. "You just about gave me a heart attack. What on earth are you doing out here...and...and on that?" She pointed at Sandy.

Blu laughed. "I was trying to find you. And this here animal is called a horse. Her name is Sandy."

Sybil rolled her eyes. "Yes, we've met. But she's not yours."

Blu swung from the saddle and dropped the reins to the ground. "I'm just borrowing her for a bit." He rubbed Sandy's nose as he walked around her. "Take a break, old girl, we'll head home in a little while."

Sybil wrinkled her brow. "You're just going to leave her there? Won't she run off?"

Blu shook his head. "No, she'll be fine. You don't know much about horses, do you?"

"No, and I'd like to keep it that way. They look big and scary, and like a lot of work." Sybil shivered, rubbing her bare arms. "I think you took about ten years off my life. I'm going to have bad dreams tonight for sure."

Blu chuckled as he sat down on her vacated lounge chair, leaning back and crossing his arms behind his head. He put one booted ankle over the other and gave her a smile.

Sybil raised her hands at her sides. "Sure, just make yourself at home." She ran her fingers through her hair. "May I ask what you're doing out here this time of night?"

"I told you, I was looking for you. Crystal and I are leaving early in the morning and I wanted to see you again, maybe visit for a while…" he lifted his shoulders, "you know."

Sybil pulled a chair from the table and sat down facing him. She crossed her legs, one slim foot swaying back and forth. "Yes, I think I *know*." She sat back, positioning her arms along the chair. "How did you find me? This house isn't exactly on the road."

"Chandler's mentioned where your father lived a few times, and I've been here with him once or twice." Blu grinned, flashing his white teeth. "You're not too hard to track down."

"I'm so happy to hear that." Sybil leveled her gaze at him, not smiling as her eyes swept over him. "It seems strange that you'd be out riding with the sun about to set. You'd think you would be with your friends. I'm fairly certain your sister would not be happy if she knew you were here."

Blu grunted. "Crystal told me about your encounter at the café. It's none of her concern who I keep company with." He gave her a wink. "And if you want to be certain about something, it would be that I'm keeping you away from Chandler."

"Yes, her precious Chandler. The love of her life, the man she is going to marry, etcetera, etcetera." Sybil covered her fake yawn with her hand. "It's all too boring for words. To think your sister is worried about me hooking up with Chandler." She harrumphed. "It's a ridiculous thought."

"Is it, pretty lady?" Blu's lashes lowered and opened slowly, giving her his full attention.

Adjusting the wide strap of the maxi-dress, Sybil fidgeted, looking away from the intense gaze. "As I told your sister, I have no interest in cowboys. I won't go into all the reasons why."

Blu sat up, scooting to the edge of the lounge chair. He braced his elbows on his knees, inches from Sybil's swaying foot. "That's really too bad. Normally I wouldn't be attracted to a woman like you, either."

"What's that supposed to mean?" She raised her chin in the air.

Blu laughed, shaking a finger at her. "That kind of woman. The kind that looks down her nose at every human being she doesn't deem worthy of her attention. The kind of woman that would take on the career of being a lawyer."

"There are many very successful women lawyers out there, me being one of them."

Blu raised his brow. "You're working?"

Sybil crossed her arms. "Not right now, but I will be again. I think it's pretty arrogant of you to say a woman shouldn't be a lawyer. Next, you're going to be telling me all women should be barefoot and pregnant. I thought men like you had died off a long time ago." She sneered. "You know…like the dinosaurs?"

Blu threw his head back and laughed. "See, that's why I say I normally wouldn't be attracted to someone like you." He scooted forward, placing his hand on her knee. "There's something about you that really gets me going, pretty lady."

Sybil shoved his hand away. "Might I suggest a cold shower, and then find a woman that you agree with."

"You see? Feisty, ready to claim your ground at every turn. I like that." His blue eyes swept over her, stopping at her lips. "I like a lot of things about you."

Sybil placed one hand over her trembling heart. *It would be so easy to go along with you. I've never had anyone flirt so outrageously with me. And it's been a long time since Scott and I, well, since anyone has cared to touch me. Just once won't matter. I'm not a virgin anymore anyway, and Blu certainly isn't. There's too many rules to follow all the time. What's wrong with a little fun now and then?*

"Sybil?"

The singsong calling of her name caused her to meet his gaze. "I think we both know why you came out here tonight, Blu."

"And?" Blu tilted his head, running his tongue over his lips.

Sybil uncrossed her legs and stood, her breaths coming in short gasps as she stared down at him. She closed her eyes and sighed. "I don't know why I'm attracted to you, but I am." Her eyes swept open. "I don't do this, Blu. I don't have one-night stands. I've had one boyfriend, if you could even call him that. I've been raised to live my life differently than others do, to save myself for marriage. Just because I've made mistakes—"

Blu cupped her elbow. "How's that working out for you?"

"It's not...I'm lonely."

"Well, so am I, pretty lady." Blu's hand slid up her arm and back down. "I don't see anything wrong with having a little fun and enjoying one another for a few hours."

Sybil bit her lower lip. *His hand is so warm. He's sending shivers to the tips of my toes.* "You don't understand, my father was greatly disappointed in me when he found out I had been having a *relationship* with Scott."

Blu chuckled. "I thought you were the big career woman. You're letting your father's opinions decide what you should do?" He looked toward the house. "Speaking of which, where *is* your father?"

Sybil pulled away and put the table between them. "He and Elvira left after the potluck at church today. They spend every July out in Vermont. Elvira has a house and extended family there."

He nodded. "That's right. Chandler mentioned that today at church."

"*You* went to church? Is that just an obligation you fulfill when you're here in Wheatacre?" Sybil tapped the table with one finger, lifting one side of her mouth.

"Okay, you got me there." He smiled, taking his hat from his head and laying it on the table. He ran his hand through the longish, brownish-blond waves. "I go to church, and yes, I mostly do it to keep my parents off my back. I go when I'm here to keep Chandler happy. I guess we all do things to please others." He tilted his head. "I noticed that you don't attend services…unless you go someplace else in town."

"No, I don't go anyplace else. That's the church I attended growing up, the one I was baptized in." Sybil ran her nail over the wrought iron scrolls of the tabletop. "I guess I should get back into the routine of it. I know it would please my father."

"Going to church to please others is all right, but being with me to please yourself isn't?"

Sybil gaped. "Well, of course not! You're talking about two different instances here. Going to church is a good thing to do. Being with you tonight, probably not."

Blu grinned. "Oh, it will be good, I can promise you that."

Sybil pointed at her chest. "And you say *I'm* arrogant?"

Blu walked around the table slowly. "Look, I've made it pretty clear why I'm here." His eyes traveled over the terrace. "I thought I'd have to convince you to ride off into the sunset—"

"I'm *not* getting on that thing with you!" Sybil pointed to where Sandy stood.

Blu put one finger to his mouth and calmed her. "But we're here alone…" he raised one brow.

Sybil nodded, her breath catching.

He stood before her. "I want to be with you, and I think you feel the same thing. No commitments, just a few hours of enjoying one another. It's nothing to be ashamed of." He cupped her shoulder. "You're a grown woman, Sybil. You know what you want. Don't let others tell you differently. I don't think they do in any other situation."

Sybil snorted. "You've got that right!" She looked up into the blue eyes and was engulfed.

Blu's hand caressed her shoulder, moving to her neck, his strong fingers sliding over the long, pale column. "You're so soft and smooth, your hair like silk."

"You probably tell all the ladies that."

Blu grinned. "Of course! It's usually true." His left hand moved to her opposite shoulder, his thumb making circles on the soft indentation where her arm and collarbone met.

Sybil placed her hand on his broad chest, spreading her fingers across the warm expanse. "Your heart is beating so fast."

He smiled down at her, moving his hand over hers and squeezing. "It's beating just for you." His lips glided over her forehead and down to her temple.

Sybil sighed, tilting her head so her lips would meet his. *So soft, so warm, so…good!*

Chapter Eleven

CHANDLER SHADED HIS EYES AS the old truck rumbled up to the barn. He leaned the shovel against the stall door, taking off his gloves as the truck door opened. *Sybil?*

The woman in question jumped from the front seat and waved him over. "You have to see this."

Chandler smiled. "Good afternoon to you too. It surprised me to see Loren's truck. I wasn't expecting them back yet."

Waving the comment away, Sybil reached into the truck and pulled a basket over. "They won't be home for another week or so. I hate driving my Mercedes up here on all that gravel." She smiled back at him. "I've been out working in that silly garden of Elvira's every day. She told me to not let the weeds get too bad." She turned, displaying the basket full of green tomatoes. "Aren't they beautiful?"

Chandler rubbed his hand across his forehead. "Well, they are, but you usually eat tomatoes red, not green. Unless that's a certain kind that I've never heard of."

Sybil shook her head, wrinkling her brow. "I know what color tomatoes are supposed to be. But there are so many of these in the garden right now, I thought I'd share them with you."

"So, you want me to put them in a paper bag until they're ripe?"

"No...I want you to show me how to make fried green tomatoes. I had some at the café the other day and they were really good."

He shoved his gloves into his back pocket. "You're serious?"

Sybil nodded.

"You think I know how to make fried green tomatoes?"

"Yes. Crystal informed me that your mother taught you how to cook. You made me an excellent steak that night I was here." Sybil placed the basket on the bench seat. "Oh, never mind. I have better things to do than convince you to help me."

Chandler laughed. "I'm still processing the fact that you actually ate a *fried* green tomato. They are better for you once they ripen."

Sybil jammed her knuckles on her hips. "Here I am, trying to be friendly, and all you want to do is make fun of me. Never mind!" She shoved the basket over and grabbed the steering wheel, putting one leg in.

Chandler took her bare arm. "Now don't get all huffy." His eyes met hers and he swallowed deeply. *She is pretty today, with her hair swept up, her eyes free of all that gunk she puts on them.*

Sybil looked down at her arm and pulled it away. She rubbed her hand over the spot his hand had covered. "Why are you staring at me like that? I know I look horrible. I didn't even stop to change my clothes or fix my face. I was just so excited, and now you're not even interested. I know I'm not Crystal, but I'm trying to be your friend, if that matters at all."

Chandler's gaze traveled over her face. "No, you're not Crystal, and I'm happy that you're not." He grinned. "And I'm really happy that you want to be my friend. That's definitely a step in the right direction."

Sybil rolled her eyes. "So, are you going to help me or not?"

Chandler looked up at the sky. "You mean right now, in the middle of the afternoon?"

"What's wrong with now? It will take us that long to get dinner ready."

"So now we're having dinner?" Chandler smiled, his blue eyes twinkling.

Sybil pointed to the truck. "I'm going to get back in there and drive away. And then you can eat all by yourself like you do every night."

Chandler took her hand in his. "Please, stay and have dinner. It will be much more pleasurable than what I had planned for this evening."

"And what were your plans?" Sybil pulled her hand away.

"Finish cleaning the stalls since I didn't get to it this morning like I usually do." Chandler wiped at his perspiring forehead once more. "I had some branches come down from that storm the other night. I wanted to get that cleaned up while it was still cool."

"Is there something I can help with so you will be finished more quickly?"

Chandler laughed. "You're going to clean stalls?"

Sybil wrinkled her brow. "How hard can it be? I'm sure Crystal does it."

"Yes, she does. As a matter of fact, she usually takes care of that when she's here so Blu and I can get to more projects." He shook his head. "But she grew up doing that. It's no big deal for her."

Crossing her arms, Sybil blinked rapidly as she stared at the tall cowboy. "Who do you think has been taking care of my father's place while they've been gone?"

Chandler lifted both shoulders. "I assumed they hired someone. I talked to Loren about mowing the grass for him, but he said he had it taken care of."

"That's right, and I'm the one taking care of it." She uncrossed her arms, looking at her fingernails, bare, with dirt along the white crescents. "I've rather enjoyed it actually. It's nice to be outside, and it makes me feel like I've accomplished something at the end of the day."

"Hard work will do that for you."

"Well, anyway, I think Dad and Elvira will be pleased when they return home and find the yard mowed and the garden doing so well." Sybil tapped her fingers on her arm. "So, are you going to teach me how to clean stalls?"

Chandler scratched the back of his head. "Why don't we process one miracle at a time, here."

"Now what does that mean?" Sybil frowned. "You're making some snide comments, and I don't think I like them."

"And you shouldn't. I'll try to be good and keep my sarcastic thoughts to myself." He reached past her and took the basket of tomatoes and started for the house. "Why don't you get these all washed and cut into thick slices while I finish in the barn?" He turned back as she slammed the truck door closed.

"All right, but I'll be back again to have you show me how to clean barns." Sybil jogged up next to him.

"I usually just clean the stalls. I don't do the entire barn every day." Chandler gave her a wink.

Sybil groaned. "I'm thinking I'm going to regret this evening."

THE SUN SLIPPED BEHIND THE cottonwoods lining the river in the distance. The tall trees formed a silhouette against the backdrop of orange, pink, and yellow hues, a touch of violet ribbon intermingled. The humid air hung heavy, but the heat of the day had cooled, offering a warm embrace as the sky darkened.

Sybil leaned her head against the wood slats of the chair and sighed. "It's absolutely beautiful up here on this hill."

Chandler agreed with a nod of his head. "No big city lights down there along the river."

"I know, and I keep thinking I should miss it, but I really don't mind it here too much anymore." She laughed. "I spent my entire childhood growing up and vowing to leave Wheatacre at my earliest opportunity…and I did. Now I'm beginning to wonder what I missed."

"Maybe you didn't miss anything. Maybe God directed you along another path for a while."

"Or maybe it wasn't God at all, but my own will making those choices."

Chandler shrugged. "Could have been. I don't think we know at times."

"You always seem to bring God into the conversation…that is, if we have a long enough one before we annoy one another too much. Why is that? Don't you want to be responsible for yourself, not blame or credit everything with God's guiding hand?"

Chandler shook his head. "Absolutely not. I want everything in my life to be about God and what He has planned for me. I don't want to live any other way."

Sybil looked over to where Chandler sat in the chair next to her. "Maybe you should have been a preacher, instead of a cowboy. You missed your calling."

"I don't think so. I wouldn't mind leading a Bible study, mainly because it would put me in God's Word on a more consistent basis, but Christian cowboys are needed too."

"You can't save the cows." Sybil gave a little laugh.

"No, but I can work among other men and women that have let this lifestyle harden them or make them bitter. It can be a rough crowd. Some of the hands on my father's ranch are pretty rowdy."

"Did your father approve of you trying to liberate his hands from their worldly ways?" Sybil gave another snicker.

"He really didn't mind too much. After all, what I've learned, I've been taught by him. Whenever he could, he hired families. They were just a bit more stable, usually."

Sybil cleared her throat. "I don't get the impression that the Waters family has lived their life in quite the same manner as your family did."

"They didn't. Don't get me wrong, they are still hardworking, upstanding people in the community. But Mr. Waters was always about the money and the prestige, how big he could be. That has worn off on Blu."

"I thought your father's place was rather extensive."

"It is, but that's not what he has strived for. My father has always put God first, then his family, then the ranch." Chandler nodded. "It has worked well for him."

"But you don't want to be part of that."

There was a long pause. "No, I don't. My brothers are well-equipped to take over when my father is ready to retire. I'm more than happy to have it that way. I was very thankful when I heard my uncle had left me this place. So far, it has been all that I hoped it would be, and then some."

Sybil laughed. "And then some. What does that mean?"

Chandler turned to her, her face lit with the golden glow of the dining room lights spreading over the deck. "It means that I've met you. You were not something I anticipated."

Sybil looked away. "It doesn't matter. Crystal made it very clear to me and Blu confirmed it…you are taken. Your families expect it, Crystal's mother has it all planned. You shouldn't say things like that."

"Crystal will not be back in Kansas for a while. She was pretty upset when she left." Chandler leaned forward in his chair, clasping his hands between his legs. "I had a long talk with her and Blu. I made it very clear that I did not love Crystal, that I had not talked about marrying her, and that she needed to get on with her life…without me being a part of it."

Sybil gasped. "She must have been very upset. She told me that her mother had everything planned."

Chandler cleared his throat. "I addressed that as well. I called Mrs. Waters and explained the whole situation to her."

"That must have been fun."

"Not really, but she took it better than I thought she would." Chandler dropped his head. "Basically, I found out that Crystal had been telling people things that were not true about us…leading them to believe the relationship was different than it was."

"Why would she do that? Why would she want someone that didn't want her or reciprocate her feelings?"

Chandler looked back at her. "When people want something badly enough, or they're hurting, they do strange things."

Sybil leaned her elbow on the wide arms of the chair, and propped her chin on the back of her hand. "I don't know what to say."

Chandler stared out into the distance. "You could say that you're interested in getting to know me better."

Sybil closed her eyes, squeezing them tight as she tried to still the erratic beating of her heart. *Did he just say he wanted to get to know me? That he's interested in me?* The beating skipped, followed by a sharp stab. "When did you talk with Blu and Crystal?"

"The Sunday before they left, just after the evening services. Why?"

Sybil's heart sank. *Blu Waters, you knew that Chandler was available. You'd had that confirmed before you rode over.* She opened her eyes, taking a deep breath. *Now, it's not Blu's fault that I gave in. I hadn't expressed any interest in Chandler to anyone. I hadn't even known for sure if I felt anything at all for him… until now.*

"Sybil? Why do you ask?" Chandler turned toward her.

She offered a weak smile. "No reason…I…I was thinking that must have made for a very strained last night together."

"Not really. Crystal went to her room and Blu took Sandy out for a ride. I felt terrible that I had ruined the evening, but it had to be straightened out before they returned to Colorado." He reached out and touched her arm. "Did you hear what I said a moment ago?"

Sybil's eyes found his and she nodded. "I did. How would we go about doing that…getting to know one another better?"

Chandler shrugged. "I haven't really dated, you probably know more about it than I do."

She shook her head. "Not really. I didn't even go to my high school prom. The guys at school were…" She winced. "They were just not my type."

He laughed. "I'm wondering if you have a type. I'm wondering even more if I have any hope of coming close to your criteria." He raised one finger. "But, I did go to my senior prom, with Crystal. I didn't want to ask anyone, and it just seemed like a sisterly thing for her to do at the time. I didn't know it was going to backfire."

Laughing, Sybil leaned forward in her chair. "That was many years ago. I don't think you can be held responsible for that."

"Maybe not." He brushed her arm once more. "So, do you think we could go out for dinner some night, maybe get away from Wheatacre and all the eyes and ears looking for new topics?"

"Good luck with that!" Sybil laughed. "You didn't grow up in a small town if you think driving to another place for a few hours will stop the talk. You're already a hot topic."

"You are too."

Sybil nodded. "I'm afraid so, and most of it is not complimentary. I'm thought of as a shrew, someone that's too good for this place."

Chandler raised a brow. "Isn't that pretty much the case?"

Sybil sighed. "It is, and until now, I haven't really cared too much. It kept people from bothering me. I thought I had more important places to be and people to see, as the saying goes."

"And now you don't?"

Sybil focused on the stars peeking out between the cottonwoods in the distance. "It doesn't seem as important anymore. Tonight has been fun. I learned how to make fried green tomatoes, and I grilled my own hamburger patty."

"Don't forget that you put mayonnaise on that patty, and two slices of cheese." Chandler gave her a wink.

"I'll pay for it later, I'm sure." She leaned her head back and gazed at the dark sky. "It's just nice being here with you, not having to worry about what I look like, or what I'm wearing. Life just seems simpler…and pure, somehow."

Chandler sighed. "And that's just how it should be."

Chapter Twelve

SYBIL SPUN AROUND ONCE MORE, the edges of the cobalt blue dress swirling at her knees. She smiled at Elvira, then laughed. "I'm not doing that again. I'm going to be so dizzy I won't be able to find the front door."

Elvira clasped her hands together and pressed them before her face. "You look so pretty, Sybil. I love seeing that skirt flare out. That blue makes your hair look even more black." Elvira looked away, folding the clothes strewn across Sybil's bed.

"Elvira, what's wrong? You aren't crying, are you?" Sybil sat on the edge of the bed and looked up at the slightly older woman.

Elvira frowned. "Of course not! Why would I be doing such a silly thing?" Her gaze shifted to Sybil. "You're different somehow since your father and I returned from Vermont."

"Different? I'm just the same old Sybil." She fluffed the skirt of the dress, brushing at imaginary lint.

"No, you aren't. You're more relaxed, and content with yourself. It's as if you are at peace with who you are, rather than trying to be an important person." Elvira looked away, biting her lip.

"Well, I *am* a very important person. At least that's what I've always believed."

Elvira turned back, lifting her hand. "See what I mean? If I had said that to you a few months ago…" She shook her head. "Let's just say it wouldn't have happened. None of this would have."

"You mean helping me get ready for my date with Chandler?"

Elvira took a seat next to her stepdaughter. "I knew when I married your father that you didn't like me. You didn't make any secret of your feelings for me. I think referring to me as a *cow* was about as polite as you could get."

Sybil took a deep breath and looked away. "Please don't remind me of that. What a childish thing to say."

"So, my prayer was that we could at some point, many years down the line, have a mutual respect for one another." Elvira sniffed, dabbing at her nose. "But to be a part of this tonight…" She patted the clasped hands in Sybil's lap. "I just want you to know how much it means to me."

Sybil took Elvira's hand. "I know I've been mean and spiteful. I didn't want you to marry my father. I had Tarah slated for that position." Sybil shook her head. "It sounds really crazy now, but I thought I would have control over their relationship. I guess I was too stupid to realize that my father would have never allowed that to happen, even if he and Tarah *had* hooked up."

"Do you think they would have been married if I hadn't shown up?" Elvira pulled her hand away, gripping her knees. "I mean, they would have had so much more in common. Fancy jobs, extravagant vacations—"

"I don't say this very often, but I think God had other plans for my father." Sybil adjusted her position on the bed, looking at Elvira. "I would be blind if I didn't see how much he adores you. You have been so good for him." She shook her head. "I hate to admit it, but he's happier than I ever saw him be with my mother. I think that's another reason I wanted you to just disappear." Sybil sighed. "I also wanted him all to myself, not interested or loving anyone else."

Elvira shook her finger at Sybil as she smiled. "Now *that* is selfish."

Sybil grabbed the finger, shaking it back and forth. "I know, don't remind me."

Elvira cleared her throat. "Why did you say just now that you don't speak of God's plans? Your father said that you've accepted Christ as your Savior. Why wouldn't you believe He is guiding and leading us?"

Sybil raised a brow. "Wow…you're going to tackle it all tonight, aren't you? Why don't you save some for another conversation?"

Elvira pressed her lips together. "I'm really afraid we won't have another opportunity to talk like this."

Sybil stood and walked across the room, wrapping her arms about her waist. The dress sashayed against her calves with each step, the matching high-heeled satin pumps elongating her shapely legs. She stopped in front of the window, staring out at the sun setting in the western sky. "I *have* accepted Christ, and I believe it was a gracious gift. But I get tired of hearing Christians say God's in this and that, almost as if He is responsible for everything, and they have no accountability. When I went to college, I worked hard to become a lawyer. God didn't do that, I did. When I messed up my life with Scott, it was my fault, not God's. If you go to church, all you hear are nice platitudes…simple things that people just repeat because they sound good."

"Is that why you don't attend church?" The question was asked softly, with hesitation.

Sybil nodded. "Partly, but mostly because I just wanted a day to myself with no responsibilities. I worked very hard to get to where I was in that firm. I needed the weekend to prepare for the week ahead."

"I do understand what you're saying, but I look at it from a different perspective. My thoughts come from being saved for only a couple years, not my entire life like you." Elvira cleared her throat once again. "I felt so lost, like I was just wandering through my life.

I had no expectations for a future beyond my physical body dying. I didn't have an important career like you did, but my life just didn't seem worth living most of the time. There was no point to it."

"And I'm sure you'd say that becoming saved solved all those problems for you. Now you have a purpose." Sybil shook her head and drummed her fingers at her elbows. "I've heard it all before, rather like being saved is a magical potion."

Elvira chuckled softly. "No, what being saved, and now learning about God and His provision, has done for me...well, it's given me hope. Hope that I can do all things through Him. Some days are still difficult. I have my less-than-pleasant memories just as everyone else does. But at the end of that day, I know I'm going to Heaven. God has a place waiting for me."

Sybil turned. "I have that too, Elvira. I know that I am going to Heaven when I die. But is God really in control of our lives? Does He *really* care that much about what happens to us? Or is it just some wispy lie a preacher has said over and over?"

Elvira rushed to Sybil's side, taking her by the upper arms. "God *is* with us! He *does* care, and He loves us so much. Neither you or I have had children, but I can imagine the pain of sending your only son to die on a cross. To die for the sins of other people." The tears slipped from Elvira's eyes and trickled down her cheeks. "You know God, Sybil. You know His Son. Now you just have to let that love grow."

Sybil brushed at her own cheeks. "My eyes are going to be a mess."

Elvira smiled. "It's okay, I'm thinking Chandler probably isn't much into makeup."

Laughing, Sybil shook her head. "He's not. He's told me repeatedly he hates the stuff."

Elvira backed away, her eyes examining each aspect of Sybil's appearance. "You are beautiful, Sybil, but it's not the outside that

I'm talking about. You are changing on the inside. That hard shell you've been carrying your entire life is cracking. It's scary, I know, I've been there. But the love I have in my life now, the care and prayers of fellow believers…I don't know how I lived without it before. Your father and I want the same for you."

A knock on the bedroom door caused both of the women to jump, then laugh with relief when Loren stuck his head in the door.

"What are you two doing in here? Chandler's been over at our place for almost half an hour now."

Sybil gasped. "Half an hour? He was supposed to pick me up here at the guest house. What's he doing over there?" She rushed to the opposite side of the bed and retrieved her jewel-encrusted clutch.

Loren rocked back on his heels, crossing his arms. "Well, he said he knocked and knocked over here and no one answered, so he thought he got his instructions mixed up." Loren laughed. "Don't worry about it, we've had a great time talking."

Sybil teetered to the door. "I'm worried because we have dinner reservations and an hour drive to get there! I guess that's what happens when you live in the middle of nowhere."

Elvira raised her brows as Loren took her hand.

Sybil observed the gesture. "Well, you two can stand here all night if you want to, but I'm late. Please shut off the lights and lock the door when you leave." She exited the room, the screen door slamming a few seconds later.

ELVIRA SHOOK HER HEAD. "*WELL*, I thought we had made some progress in our relationship over the past couple of hours, but maybe not."

"You've had enough time to relive the past three years since you met. How much time does it take to get ready for a date?" Loren led Elvira from the bedroom, through the front room and onto the porch. "You slap on some makeup and put on your clothes. Twenty minutes, tops."

Elvira wiggled her hand around the screen door and switched off the front room light. "Sybil asked us to get the lights."

"Well, leave the porch light off for now. I want to watch them leave." Loren pulled Elvira close, patting her shoulder. "But I am happy that you two finally had some time together. I hope it wasn't spent with Sybil snarling and biting at you."

Elvira laughed. "We had a very pleasant conversation. It was a lot of fun helping her choose what to wear and see the process she goes through." She shrugged. "Besides, I think she's beginning to relax and let herself be who she is meant to be."

"Those words would be music to my ears if they were really true." He put his hand over her mouth. "Shh…here they come!"

Elvira laughed, kissing the palm of Loren's hand before taking it in her own. "Isn't she beautiful? I don't think I've ever seen her smile like that before."

Loren nodded. "I did once, when she was a toddler, right before she bit my ankle."

Elvira playfully slapped Loren's shoulder. "Stop that kind of talk. No wonder she feels unloved."

Loren stared down at his wife. "Do you really think that's been the problem all these years?"

Elvira patted her husband's chest. "There, there, I know you love your daughter and I think you've shown her in every way you could. But Sybil is the kind of person that's going to have to learn everything the hard way. Once she has it down, she won't stray. But she'll have to do it on her own."

"I hope you're right. Sybil's mother and I loved her, and gave her everything we thought she needed or wanted. Most of the time it felt as though she was biting the hand that fed her."

"She'll be more appreciative of what she has after she's experienced some obstacles. Life isn't always about what *you've* planned." Elvira crossed her arms as the taillights of the Mercedes faded on the driveway. "Chandler looked pretty handsome in that suit. They make a great-looking couple."

Loren nodded as he reached around the screen door and switched on the front porch light. "They do, but I'm much more concerned about what's in the head under the cowboy hat."

"Are you pleased so far?" Elvira stepped down the stairs leading to the stone-paved walkway.

"I am. I don't think Sybil could go wrong with him. Now, what he's getting in Sybil, that's another matter." Loren joined Elvira on the walkway.

Elvira pointed back at the little house. "You didn't turn off the kitchen light, and you didn't lock the door as Sybil requested."

Loren took Elvira's hand. "I'm the one paying the light bill around here. Besides, I'm going to sit on our terrace until they return home. I'll be watching that door."

Elvira stopped, staring up at her husband. "Are you serious? Sybil is a grown woman. She doesn't need you waiting up for her."

Loren continued their progress to the terrace. "I know she is. But she never dated a soul when she lived at home. I wanted the experience of waiting up at least once in my lifetime."

Laughing, Elvira pulled away from his grip. "Well, if you're going to be out here, I am too. But I get the lounge chair. I'm going to need a nap."

"Hey now, that was supposed to be mine. Do we only have one?" Loren scratched his head, his eyes traveling over the terrace.

"Just one. I think that was poor planning if you ask me." Elvira giggled as she laid back.

"Then move on over, my dear. We're going to have to share. I need a nap as well. They won't be back for hours." Loren sprawled out, pulling her against his long length.

"This is not big enough for the both of us. We're going to end up on the ground." Elvira wiggled against him, snuggling his arm beside her cheek. "It's a good thing it's cooled off a bit. It would have been too hot to do this a couple weeks ago."

"Labor Day is just around the corner." The words were muffled against Elvira's neck. He lifted his head. "You didn't volunteer to make enough food to feed the town that day, did you?"

Elvira giggled. "No, I'm just planning a quiet little get-together right here in our own backyard. Maybe invite your father and Chandler, and Sybil, of course. How does that sound?"

The soft snore answered her question.

"I guess I'll be waiting up for Sybil."

CHANDLER LEANED HIS ARMS ON the linen tablecloth, lowering his voice. "I know I've said this a couple of times already, but you look amazing. I love that color of blue on you."

"Thank you…again. I don't think most women mind being complimented." She leaned back in the upholstered dining chair. "I didn't think I would ever see you in a suit and no cowboy hat. You look pretty amazing as well."

Chandler gave her a wide smile, his teeth gleaming in the low light. "Every now and then I have to drag out my marrying-and-burying suit, make sure it still fits."

Sybil tilted her head. "It does, very well."

"Your hair is real pretty like that, kind of swept up and tousled at the top. That curl hanging beside your cheek is in a very happy place right now." Chandler eyes twinkled as he gazed at her.

Leaning forward, Sybil whispered, "You're making me very self-conscious. Maybe we should finish our meal before the red on my face is clashing with my dress."

Chandler cleared his throat and sat back. "Would you like dessert? When I was reading up on this place, the dessert was a real crowd-pleaser."

"Only if they have something very decadent with lots of chocolate in it. I'm feeling adventurous tonight." Sybil pursed her lips, her eyes flirting with his.

"Now who's making someone self-conscious?" He took a sip of his water, setting the glass back down. "I just wanted you to know that I've really enjoyed getting to know you better over the past few weeks. It's been great having your help with the stall cleaning—"

"The fence-building, deck varnishing, painting…what else have you kept me busy with?" Sybil smiled.

"I must admit, I never thought to see the great Sybil Grafton swinging a paint brush."

Sybil held her hands in front of her face, and then turned them toward him. "My nails are absolutely ruined. They'll never be the same, but there's something very free about not having to worry about them breaking or the polish getting chipped. They are already too short to break, and I haven't had time to paint them. Forget going into town for a manicure."

Chandler shook his head. "I'm sorry, I've probably destroyed your life."

Sybil's face softened, her eyes growing darker. "You've made it better. I didn't know I could enjoy working so hard. It's given me purpose, a reason for being here, rather than just existing." She looked down at her lap. "I've enjoyed getting to know you as well. You've pretty much debunked my thoughts about cowboys…well, some of them."

Chandler smiled, giving her a wink. "Have you had a run-in with a bad cowboy?"

Sybil heaved a sigh, fussing with her napkin. "There's our waiter. Are we ready for dessert?"

Chapter Thirteen

SYBIL WATCHED THE PETITE BLONDE recline in the lounge chair beside hers. The slim body glowed with oil in the late-morning sun as she flirted with the much younger man seated next to her. His muscled arms linked behind his brown head of hair as he stretched, then leaned forward to whisper in her ear, the six-pack crunching nicely.

Tarah giggled, swatting at his shoulder. "You are so bad. I shouldn't even listen to your stories."

The man gave her a wink and a pretend kiss as he stood and sauntered over to the long pool. He dove into the sparkling depths, surfacing several yards away. A bikini-clad redhead tapped him on the shoulder, and he grabbed her hips, pulling her underwater.

Tarah scowled as shook her head. "I never seem to be enough for anyone. Just look at him, flirting with that child." She pushed her black sunglasses up on her nose and stretched against the black towel she laid on.

Sybil raised her sunglasses with two fingers, staring at her friend. "Seriously, Tarah? That guy is *way* too young for you. He deserves that *child* you just observed. And don't look now, but they're leaving the pool hand-in-hand."

Tarah raised her head, then let it drop back down. "I give up! I'm going to be alone the rest of my life. I thought if he was willing to talk with me, maybe it was over between that Barbie and him."

"You mean they're a couple?" Sybil's eyes followed the duo

until they disappeared behind the shrubbery offering privacy around the pool area. "I thought you knew better than to get involved with something like that. At your age, you should have learned some lessons by now."

Tarah's head rolled back and forth on the towel. "Not if I can help it. That would make life much too boring. Besides, I work hard to keep looking young…I need to have some fun." Tarah reached her arm across the space between their lounge chairs, tapping Sybil's arm. "I'm so happy you agreed to spend the weekend with me. I've really missed you. I was hoping when you called the other day that you were going to tell me that you'd had enough of Wheatacre life and you were returning to civilization."

Sybil laughed. "Actually, I'm rather enjoying Wheatacre at the moment. It's much more interesting than I ever knew."

Tarah took Sybil's hand in hers. "What's with the Bohemian look you've got going on here? Your nails are positively ragged."

Sybil jerked her hand away. "I've been learning a lot this summer."

Tarah raised her sunglasses, staring at her friend. "Would these lessons be from a certain cowboy you've mentioned a few times?" She smiled. "Please, tell me more. You can see what my life consists of."

Sybil raised her face to the sun. "Yes, your life is absolutely terrible. You live in one of the most exclusive neighborhoods available." She gestured at the pool. "With beautiful people all around you. What are you complaining about? You have a great job—"

"Yes, I do, at the place you once thought was the cat's meow."

Sybil nodded. "Yes, I did. But that somehow doesn't seem as important anymore."

"So, now you're ready to settle down and live on the farm?" Tarah snorted. "I think that country sun has fried your brain. You would never be happy or content to live in someplace like

Wheatacre the rest of your life. Remember, you left there because you couldn't stand it."

"I know, Tarah…I know that better than anyone. I keep trying to figure out what is happening to me, but I don't understand it. The things I once thought were important don't seem to be so grand any longer."

Tarah shook her finger at her friend. "*I* know what's wrong with you. You've let that cowboy get under your skin. I agree, there's something very romantic about that way of life. Riding off into the sunset with a gorgeous cowboy would be just about any woman's dream."

"I haven't been enjoying a romantic summer. Unless you call cleaning stalls, gardening, painting, and mowing lawn romantic."

Tarah harrumphed. "No wonder your nails look the way they do! I didn't know you'd been working like a common laborer. I'm happy it didn't work out between your father and me. I wouldn't have let him work me that way."

Sybil bent her knees, setting the bottoms of her feet on the lounge chair. "My father didn't make me work." She shrugged. "Well, maybe a little. He asked if I would help with the garden and the mowing, and I was surprised that I rather enjoy it. I also felt a little better about staying there at the guest house. About all I've paid for is my food—"

Tarah sat up, gaping at her friend. "Don't tell me you're all out of money! Why, you had more than enough to live on for a while. You worked a long time to save that little nest egg. Did that cowboy talk you out of your savings?" She pointed to Sybil's hand. "No wonder you stopped getting manicures."

Sybil laced her hands across her middle. "Slow down! I was just trying to say that I haven't been paying any rent or utilities, so I wanted to help in some way. I still have my savings."

Tarah laid back down. "Whew! You know what kind of things happen to us single women. We always have to be cautious and watch out for one another. There's some nefarious character around every corner. Just look at what took place with you and Scott."

"I'd rather not, really. I felt like an idiot when that all happened."

"Well, it's all water under the bridge now." Tarah chortled.

"What are you laughing at?"

"I was thinking that you should just spend a night with that cowboy of yours, you know, get him out of your system. Then you can get back to being the Sybil Grafton I know and love."

"Maybe *this* is the real me. What would be so wrong with that?" Sybil plucked at the black and gold maillot stretched across her middle.

Tarah stood, positioning her sunglasses on top her head. She held a hand out to Sybil. "Come on. We have work to do. Those nails need a belt sander taken to them… fingers *and* toes. I have one day left to get you back in shape. I'm going to hydrate you with lemon and Perrier, and maybe a nice kale salad. You're probably so depressed that you didn't realize you had two bagels this morning, slathered with butter."

Sybil laughed as she stood, arching her back. She took her towel off the lounge chair, draping it across her arm. "You are the only person that I would allow to treat me this way."

"I know! You have to promise me you'll return once a month for refurbishing. It's going to take the rest of the day to get you back in shape." Tarah took her phone off the little table between the lounge chairs and shook it at Sybil. "That's another thing. You never have your phone with you. You wouldn't have walked across the room without it before."

Sybil sighed. "I know…and it's very liberating to not be at someone's beck and call twenty-four hours a day."

Tarah yanked her towel from the chair. "I bet if that Camden—"

"His name is Chandler."

Tarah shook the glittery encased phone in front of Sybil's nose. "Whatever his name is…I bet if *he* was calling, you'd keep it with you."

Sybil shrugged, giving her friend a wide smile before she turned. "Maybe!"

Tarah swatted Sybil's backside with her towel. "You're really obnoxious!"

THE EVENING BREEZE WHISPERED OVER the pasture, the wild sunflowers swaying with the movement. Sandy pranced through the golden field, shaking her head and picking up her feet.

Chandler smiled. *She's loving this cooler weather, just as I am. Before long, it will be downright cold in the morning.* He leaned back in his chair, propping his booted feet on the deck railing, ready to watch the nightly show of the setting sun. He took a deep breath, a wide grin on his face. *This is the life!*

"Knock, knock."

Chandler turned with a start, dropping his feet to the boards. "Sybil! When did you get back?" He stood, long strides taking him to the steps leading to the yard where Sybil waited.

She smiled up at him. "I just arrived. I left Kansas City a little later than I had hoped. Tarah always has so many things planned for us while I'm there. I'm ready to go to bed and get some sleep after my weekend away."

Chandler's eyes swept over her, from head to toe and back again. "You look really citified. Just like the old Sybil."

Sybil pressed her lips together. "It's that bad?"

Shrugging, he extended his hand to her. "Come up here so I can get a closer look."

Sybil navigated the deck stairs with her heeled sandals, her white pants seeming to glow in the setting sun. Her black and white striped top hugged her narrow hips. "Tarah insisted that we eat before I left, and of course every place she goes has a dress code." Sybil gave a shaky laugh as she dropped his hand and supplied a slow twirl.

The whistle drifted away on the breeze. "You're beautiful, as always. I'm happy that your hair didn't fall under the chopping block."

Sybil fluffed the long waves that curled against her shoulders. "I had to fight Tarah on that one. She insisted that I go back to my old haircut, but I won that battle. I did have it trimmed, though. It has always grown like crazy, and bless her heart, Thelma never has been able to cut it the way I instruct her to."

Chuckling, Chandler took her hand and pulled her over to the chair he had vacated. He motioned for her to sit down as he retrieved another, pulling it close. "I've always wondered at that phrase, *bless her heart*. Does that mean you think her simple-minded and incapable of understanding your lofty ways, or do you really wish God's blessing on her?"

Sybil rolled her eyes. "It's just something people say. Not that big of a deal. I just meant that my salon in Kansas City is better acquainted with the styles and new procedures. I don't think Thelma really has the need to stay on top of things here in Wheatacre. Face it, most people just want a cheap haircut and the town's gossip when they go in."

Chandler scratched his head. "That suits me. Especially since I don't see any signs of another barber moving in." He gave her a wink. "I've learned a lot about Wheatacre and its inhabitants over the summer."

"I'm sure." Sybil settled into the chair, tilting her head back against the slats.

"I did miss you, you know." The words came softly, a little hoarse in their hesitation.

The black head turned, the green eyes sparkling as she gave him a smile. "Really?"

Chandler looked away, clearing his throat, his eyes traveling over the distant fields. "Of course. I've become used to your help with the stall cleaning and painting around here."

"So you didn't miss *me*, just the work I contribute to this place." Sybil nodded. "I knew that was probably the case. If I'd stayed away longer, you wouldn't have even known I was gone. Especially if Blu and Crystal return for a visit. Your meals will be taken care of too."

"Mrs. Flores brought me dinner last night, and it was delicious, but it just wasn't the same as the times we've shared a meal." Chandler reached out, brushing her wrist. "I've really enjoyed having you here, preparing a salad for the two of us while I grilled the steaks." His fingers encircled the narrow expanse, his thumb moving over the delicate skin at the base of her palm. He watched as a shiver traveled through her and he smiled. *I don't think you are as immune to me as you try to imply.*

Sybil pulled her hand away, clasping it in her lap. "I can't figure out what is going on between us, Chandler. I think you're being serious, and then you say something that makes it seem unimportant. I don't know whether you care, or you're tolerating me being around because you feel sorry for me."

"Why did you come by here? I'm assuming you haven't been home yet. Why would you stop here before seeing your family?"

"Because it was on the way. You know your place is before ours on the road."

He gave a low laugh. "See, you do it too. Make excuses and try to cover up your feelings. I'm confused as well. I think that's why I make jokes…to try to not be so vulnerable to you, in case you're only feeling sorry for *me*."

She sighed. "Aren't we the pair? Thirty-something years old and we're still playing high school games. No wonder neither of us are married."

"We could remedy that, you know."

Sybil snorted. "Are you suggesting that you follow through with the plan to marry Crystal, and maybe Blu and I can get *hitched*, as you cowboys say? Then all will be well in our worlds?"

Chandler clenched his fists in his lap, taking a deep breath. "I've told you that Crystal and I are not marrying. Do you have an interest in Blu?" He turned to her, his eyes searching her face.

"Really?" Sybil met Chandler's gaze. "I saw him a couple of times. He's a great-looking guy, but not my type. I couldn't spend the rest of my life with someone like him."

"So that rules me out as well?" Chandler rested his head against the chair. *This is crazy talk. You know she doesn't like you or your way of living. These past couple of months have just been a little diversion from her life, not something she would be willing to endure on a daily basis. Run now, before you get in any deeper.*

Sybil pushed from her chair and walked to the railing. She gripped it with both hands. "I don't know what I feel. I'm drawn to this place. I seem to breathe more easily, and feel a sense of protection and trust. As I've said before, life just seems more simple and pure when I'm with you. I didn't come over here practically every day for the past two months because I needed something to do. I *wanted* to be here. I loved being here…with you."

He closed his eyes, his heart beating roughly against his chest. *Those are the words I've waited to hear…and now I don't know what to say!*

Sybil turned, crossing her arms. She stared at the deck floor, moving one sandaled foot over the varnished boards. "See, I've tried to put into words what I'm feeling, and you just sit there." She cleared her throat. "I think I've taken everything you've said in the wrong way, thinking that you might care just a little for me." She nodded. "I understand…really, I do. I'm not a nice person most of the time. I can be pretty vicious. I've watched myself do certain things or say nasty comments, and I just keep right on…nothing stopping me. I'm trying to—"

Chandler stood, cupping her angled jaw as he pulled her into his gaze. "You are talking way too much, *Ms.* Grafton." His lips covered hers, moving slowly as his hands slid over her shoulders and down to her elbows, gripping them firmly. *So sweet! I want to pull her into me.*

She gasped as he broke the kiss, his lips trailing over her cheekbone and to her temple. "I've never felt anything like that before."

He murmured against her hair. "I find it hard to believe that you've never been kissed."

Sybil pushed away, pressing one hand to her chest as she walked further down the length of the deck, the other hand gripping the railing. "There are so many things that I've done that I'm not proud of, Chandler."

"We all have skeletons in our closet." Chandler narrowed his eyes, trying to focus on her retreating form in the gathering dusk. "Please don't walk away."

Sybil stopped at his words, but kept her back to him. "I had never dated anyone, never kissed anyone until last year. Then Scott, a man that I worked with at the firm…" Her voice broke. "My father asked me to wait until I was married to have a physical relationship. I didn't listen. I really regret the things I did with Scott. I didn't love him, barely even cared about him. It just seemed to work for both of us, something to do to keep from being lonely."

"That's the man that took his own life?"

"Yes. He obviously had other problems. What he did to the firm was wrong, and for a time, he was telling our coworkers that I was part of it. I wasn't, but because of our *association*, I was questioned. I was so angry about it at the time, playing the victim, but in reality, I was stupid. I felt sorry for myself, and searched for companionship in the wrong way, and for all the wrong reasons."

Chandler leaned his elbows on the railing, staring out at the darkening pasture. "So, you didn't love this man that you had the relationship with?"

"No."

"I'm not going to say that it's okay with me. It's not, and it hurts to know that you've been with someone else. I know that today's world doesn't hold purity in high esteem, but I think it's important. I was hoping and praying that the woman I married someday would have taken that seriously as well."

Sybil snorted, turning back to Chandler. "So, aren't you the best little Christian! Just as pure as the driven snow. I'm sure your Crystal is as well. You both deserve one another." She stumbled from the deck, her sandals loud in the enveloping darkness.

"Sybil, that's not what I meant. Please don't leave like this." Chandler followed her to the steps, and watched as she got into her car and spun away, gravel scattering. He shook his head. *You never seem to say what you mean, you idiot!*

Chapter Fourteen

THE GUESTHOUSE WAS ABOUT AS welcoming as a swamp as Sybil pushed open the door, and let the stagnant air drift out to the porch. She switched on the light as she tossed her leather overnight bag onto the chair and kicked off her sandals. Taking a box of tissues from the kitchen counter, she went out to the porch, letting the screen door slam behind her. She dropped to the porch swing, pulling her bare feet beneath her. *I guess I deserve a good cry after that one.*

She lowered her head to her hands, and sobbed.

"I thought I heard you drive in. Your father was worried about you…as always." Elvira climbed the steps to the porch.

"Then why didn't he come and welcome me home?" Sybil sniffed and took a tissue from the box, blowing her nose.

"He's taking his shower, so I thought I'd come and check on you and see if you had a nice time in Kansas City." Elvira pointed to the box of tissues. "Those don't make it look so good."

"This isn't from being in Kansas City." She shuddered, another wave of sobs starting. "*This* is from that oaf of a cowboy, Chandler."

Elvira lowered herself to the swing. "So, you must have stopped by there on the way home."

"Yes, and it was about the most stupid thing I've ever done. All it did was give him the chance to kiss me, and then ruin my life all over again. Men are not worth the waste of time." Sniffing and blowing filled the night air.

"So, Chandler kissed you for the first time tonight?" Elvira spoke softly. "This is how it made you feel?"

Sybil shook her head. "No, the kiss was wonderful, unlike anything I've ever felt. It was if he was wrapping me in a warm blanket. I felt so protected and cozy...and then he just ripped that all away."

"Something must have happened after the kiss. I can't imagine Chandler just turning on you for no reason. He's not that kind of person."

"Sure, just take his side of things. It figures you would do that. You've never liked me." The tears flowed freely, dropping to the white pants and making gray splotches. Sybil brushed at them. "My mascara is running down my face, and I don't even care. It'll probably ruin these one hundred-dollar pants Tarah insisted that I buy."

Elvira gasped. "You paid one hundred dollars for a pair of pants?" She rubbed her forehead. "I'm not taking Chandler's side in anything. I'm just trying to listen to what's happened to make you so upset. And for the record, I haven't approved of some of the things you've said or done, but that doesn't mean I don't like *you*."

"You can't separate the person from what their actions are."

"Come on, Sybil, you're a lawyer. You must know that's not true. You can probably think of cases where the person was very nice, had integrity and just got involved in something they shouldn't have."

"Well, I've been tried and sentenced to hang. But I haven't been very nice most of the time, so I probably deserve every bit of what I'm getting now." Sybil gripped the chain of the swing and laid her head on her arm. "My life is a mess, and it's all my fault."

Elvira turned to Sybil. "Well, let's get off the pity party theme and discuss this like two adults. Chandler kissed you tonight?"

Sybil nodded, sniffing.

"You enjoyed it, and then something happened to make you upset."

Sybil sighed. "I told Chandler about Scott and me...the relationship we had."

"I take it that he didn't respond well to that?"

"He wasn't even really upset, just more of disappointed with me. For some reason, that seemed even worse. He told me he had saved himself and wanted to marry someone that had done the same."

"Oh...." Elvira nodded her head. "Has your relationship progressed enough with Chandler to be discussing marriage?"

Sybil lowered her head. "I hadn't really thought of it too much. I just enjoyed being with him. But when he said that about waiting, I knew I could never be in the running, and...and..." She brushed the tears away. "I really care about him, and I don't want to lose what we have. But I don't think I'm good enough for him. He wants a woman that's naïve and innocent." She snorted. "Like he's going to find *that* in this day and age!"

Elvira reached out, rubbing Sybil's shoulder. "I know exactly how you feel, Sybil. But as I had to learn as well, you can't go back and change past mistakes. You have to go on. God is the only thing that can change you, heal the past hurts, and make you the person He has designed you to be."

Sybil brushed Elvira's hand away. "This isn't about God! It's about me. *I* made the decision to have that relationship with Scott. *I* decided to have sex with Blu—"

Elvira's gasp hung in the air.

Sybil stared at her stepmother. "Yes, I did that too. So, if Chandler is upset about Scott, how do you think he's going to feel about his best friend?"

"Why did you do that with Blu? You barely knew the man." Elvira's eyes darkened, tears forming. "You only hurt yourself in those situations, not to mention the risk you take with pregnancy and disease."

Sybil rolled her eyes. "I'm a grown woman. I've had sex education in school." She shook her head. "I don't know why I'm even having this conversation with you. People live together all the time and they aren't scarred for life."

Elvira pressed her lips together. "Not that they will admit, anyway. You can't share the most intimate part of yourself and not have repercussions from it. You become one person. That is something very special, and not to be taken lightly."

Sybil stared at Elvira. "You're not making me feel any better."

Elvira laid her hand over her chest. "*I* can't make you feel better about the decisions you've made. No one can. God's Word is the only thing that's going to change the direction of your life, Sybil. *You* have to submit to what He has for you."

Sybil sneered. "So, if I attend church on a regular basis, wearing a nice dress and smile at everyone, my life will be perfect?"

"You can go to church stark naked every day of the week. But if you keep the same, rebellious attitude you've always had, you'll still be the same old Sybil Grafton you've always disliked and others haven't been too fond of, either." Elvira stood. "I'll be praying for you, and I would advise you telling Chandler about Blu if you have any desire to try to have a relationship with him."

Sybil looked away. "You can pray all day and all night if you wish. It won't help me change. *I* have to do that. And if people like Chandler still think I'm not good enough…what's the point?"

"The *point* is your relationship with God and for all eternity. If you don't have that in your life, you're only existing. I know, I spent my entire life that way, and it was hopeless. People do have the ability to forgive and forget, Sybil. Your father is one of them, and I believe Chandler is too. Don't throw him away so quickly." Elvira turned and left the porch.

THE OCTOBER LEAVES SKIDDED DOWN the sidewalk, brown and crispy in the cool air. Chandler shoved his hands into the pockets of his jean jacket, and strode toward the hardware store. He opened the door to the merry jingle overhead and nodded to the white-haired man behind the long counter. "Good morning, Harold."

Harold placed the pencil he was using behind his ear. "Good morning, Chandler. I haven't seen you in a coon's age."

Chandler chuckled as he walked over to the counter. "Just busy getting the place ready for winter."

"How's the life of a big rancher?" Harold opened a box, peering inside.

"Big rancher I'm not, and I like it that way. My few head of cows and Sandy pretty much keep me on my toes."

"Any plans to expand?" Harold unloaded the box onto the counter, checking the items against a list.

Chandler shook his head. "My friend Blu keeps offering to come and help me with that, but I just want to take my time. Right now, I can pretty much manage on my own. I'm getting by. I have the house the way I want it. I'm looking forward to a relaxing winter watching the snow fall."

Harold nodded. "I hear you, but it's going to be another mighty lonely few months out there. Thinking of anyone special to spend it with?"

Chandler laughed. "Just me and myself. I managed the last two winters. I think I'll be all right."

The bell jingled again, pulling the attention of the two men.

Harold leaned closer to Chandler. "Now there's an option for you. Single, and she breathes enough fire to keep you warm. You should think about it. She'll keep things pretty exciting."

Sybil walked to the counter, eyeing the two men. "Harold, why do I get the impression you're saying bad things about me again?"

Harold laughed. "I've known you since you were waddling around in diapers. I only speak the truth."

Sybil raised her brows.

"Good morning, Sybil." Chandler offered a smile, his eyes sweeping over her.

"Good morning." She turned, focusing on the store owner. "Dad sent me in with this list. Since I don't have a clue what any of it is, would you mind getting it all together for me? No hurry. I have some other errands to run and I'll be back later. Dad asked you to put it on his tab."

Harold took the list Sybil slid across the counter, his eyes scanning it. "No problem. It shouldn't take me too long. It's been kind of slow today. Must be that cold front coming in. Everyone's afraid of the rain."

Sybil smoothed the scarred counter with her hand. "Okay. I'll be back in a couple of hours." She turned, walking toward the door.

Chandler followed, reaching out to open the door. The cool air swept in and swirled around the couple.

Sybil looked up, her eyes meeting Chandler's then darting away. "Thank you."

Harold chuckled. "Hey, you two, go in or out. I'm not turning the heat on yet, and you're letting the cold air in."

Sybil shook her head as she walked through. "That man gets more and more cranky with each passing year. I don't know why my father calls him a friend."

Chandler laughed. "I think he was just giving us a hard time. I like him. He's straightforward and easy to talk to."

"Well, you may go back and talk to him. You must have been

there for some reason when I came in." Sybil walked quickly down the sidewalk, her hair bouncing against the back of her shoulders.

"After seeing you, I don't recall why I was in the store." Chandler's long strides slowed to hers. "I've missed you, Sybil. I haven't seen you for almost a month."

Sybil stopped, shielding her eyes from the sun as she looked up at him. "After what you said to me the last time we talked, I would have thought that would have been just what you wanted."

Chandler shoved his hands into his pockets. "I admit I was upset, but more surprised than anything. I thought it best to be truthful with you. I thought that was what a conversation between two people was all about."

"Maybe it is, or should be. But…" Sybil's eyes traveled over the street. "I don't want to have this conversation in the middle of town where everyone can see us and come up with their own dialogue."

Chandler smiled down at her. "I agree." He tilted his head. "My truck is right over there. We can get a couple sandwiches and have a picnic lunch."

Sybil shivered. "You remember it *is* October? We can have some warm days, but this isn't one of them."

He shrugged. "So we eat in the truck. The important thing is that we talk about the conversation we had a few weeks ago, and make sure there are no misunderstandings."

"Why is that so important to you, Chandler? You pretty much said that because of my past, we have no chance of a future. We need to just get on with our lives." Sybil turned.

Chandler took her arm. "I don't know if we have a future, but I don't want *today* to pass without spending some time with you and talking." He narrowed his eyes, searching her face. "I care about you, Sybil…a lot."

Sybil took a deep breath, looking away. "Okay, I'll go with you."

He grinned. "Well, you can sound a bit more excited about it. I don't bite."

Sybil smiled as she turned back. "I know, but *I* do."

Chandler laughed as he led the way to his truck and opened the passenger door. *Yes, you do! But I don't mind a little nibble every now and then.*

SYBIL POPPED THE LAST BITE of the sandwich into her mouth and chewed slowly, savoring it. "I don't know why I forget that the café will make items to go. I should do that more often, rather than incurring the stares of Wheatacre's finest."

Chandler took a long drink of his Coke, his large hands dwarfing the bottle. "You have to admit that it's fun to go in and interact with people once in a while. It gives some sparkle to the day."

Sybil laughed. "Is that what it does? Why did I just picture you leaping through a field, flinging gold dust?" She shook her head. "Sparkle, a very strange word for a cowboy to use."

He smiled. "I try to broaden my vocabulary every now and then. The cows don't really care, but you never know when you'll be talking with a pretty lady."

Sybil lowered her eyes, rolling up the paper her sandwich had been wrapped in. "That was really delicious. I loved the avocado on it. Just the right amount."

Chandler took the tight ball from her and tossed it into the paper bag. "I'm so happy you enjoyed it. Now, can we discuss what we came here for?"

Sybil turned on the bench seat of the truck, one leg curled

under the other. "I suppose. I'll give you a quick synopsis, you can get upset again, and then we can head back to town and go our separate ways."

Chandler shook his head. "You are so cynical."

"And if you start insulting me, we can just leave now."

Chandler held up both hands. "This isn't going anywhere." He gripped the steering wheel. "I told you during our last conversation that I had been hoping and praying for a woman that had made the same decision to stay pure before marriage that I had."

"And I told *you* that I am not that person. I can't change what has already happened."

"I understand that. I am not expecting you to. The fact that you have regrets about it, or wish that you had made a different decision speaks to me about the kind of person you are. Not the damage that has been done." He faced her. "I would be pretty naïve if I thought that just because I wanted something, or prayed about it, that it would be granted to me. God is working in my life, and He has a path for me to take. It may not be the same one I want."

Sybil frowned. "But wanting a woman that has lived her life in the same way as you in that area is an honorable thing. Not something to be ashamed of, or taken lightly."

He nodded. "I appreciate you saying that." He rubbed his temple. "I'm so afraid of this coming out wrong and making a mess of this like I did the last time." Turning to her, he took her hand in his. "I care about you a lot, Sybil. I don't even understand all the reasons why, because we are so very different. We've led different lives. All I know is that I enjoy being with you, and I can't think of not seeing you. If God's plan is for us to be together, He will work out all the details and confusing aspects. We just need to honor Him."

"But this should be *our* decision, not God's decision. This is *our* life."

Chandler gripped her hand, his eyes darkening as he spoke. "We have this life *because* of Him. We have the ability to fall in love, be happy, succeed in whatever we decide to do because He loved us enough to send His Son. Jesus Christ paid for our sins on that cross, Sybil. *All* of them. So we can live another day to walk with Him, and do what's honoring to Him. Each day that we apply that in our lives, we grow stronger and more mature. I want that in my life. That's even more important to me than whatever past indiscretions you've had."

Sybil looked away, chewing on her bottom lip.

Chandler took her chin and turned her gaze back to him. "I'm falling in love with you, Sybil."

Chapter Fifteen

*T*HE WIND OUTSIDE THE TRUCK whistled through the metal doors, falling leaves hitting the windshield. Rearing back, Sybil brushed his hand away. "Don't say that. You've already told me that I'm not what you want in a woman. What's there to love? It has to be based on something."

Chandler slid his arm along the back of the bench seat and shrugged. "I can't even answer that. You do something to me." He let go of her hand and thumped his chest. "Something in here. I've never felt that way before."

Staring out the window, Sybil shook her head. "It must be heartburn, or acid reflux. That's what you get when you have a chicken sandwich with buffalo sauce on it."

Chandler bent his arm, propping his chin in the palm of his hand. "You make sarcastic comments when you're nervous, or feel threatened. Why do you feel the need to protect yourself like that?"

"I don't know, I'm a lawyer, not a psychiatrist."

Chandler smiled. "See, there you go again. You would think that you were neglected or unloved as a child. But I know your father, and that's not the case."

"If you're looking for any more skeletons in my closet, you have them all." Sybil crossed her arms. "My parents loved me, even if they were busy with their careers. If I wanted something, I had it. My biggest faux pas to date is having a sexual relationship with a man that I wasn't married to." She raised one hand and shook a finger at him. "And that's a problem for you, not me. Everyone is doing it. It's just not that big of a deal."

"You keep saying that, but I think you protest too much. You said you didn't love Scott, and I'm thinking the relationship wasn't much. Just more of a convenience for the two of you."

"I already said that the other night." Sybil shook her head. "Why do we need to keep discussing this? I told you I had my regrets, but I'm not going to let you make me feel any worse than I already do."

"Aha! You do feel badly." Chandler eyes swept over her. "Why do you think that is?"

Sybil gaped. "Oh good grief! Probably because I had dreams like every other girl of meeting my Mr. Right and falling in love. He would ask me to marry him, and I would wear a gorgeous white dress to proclaim my purity before all. Then he would sweep me away, and we would have a blissful night of getting to know one another for the first time. We could explore and learn about one another without the memories and comparisons of past lovers." Tears filled the green eyes and spilled over. "Are you happy now? You've got me crying and feeling like an idiot." She uncrossed her arms, smoothing her fingers over her damp cheeks.

Chandler took her hand in his once more. "You are not an idiot, and the dreams you had are normal and right. It's the way God meant love and marriage to be."

"Well, I've messed that up, haven't I?" Sybil dabbed at her eyes. "Now I have to find someone just as used as I am."

Chandler smoothed his thumb over the back of her hand. "No, you need someone that loves you for all the characteristics that make you Sybil."

She sighed. "I don't think I've ever met a person that enjoys a waspish tongue."

Chandler chuckled. "Probably not." His hand slid up her arm and cupped her cheek. "I think you have a lot of love to give, Sybil. You're a strong woman, sure of yourself, and you know what you want out of life. You've worked hard for the achievements you have." He caressed her chin before dropping his hand back to his lap.

She nodded, brushing at her nose. "I really have."

Chandler smiled. "Instead of thinking that everyone is out to get you, and becoming bitter and lonelier, you need to have confidence in the strengths you have. You need to let that love within you grow."

"And here's where you tell me that God can make that happen." She stared out the window. "Are you going to sign me up for the thirty-day plan? Maybe the ninety-day course would be better." Sybil cleared her throat and lowered her voice mimicking an announcer. "Welcome God into your life and walk the straight and narrow for just ninety days, and you too can love and be loved. All will be right in your world." She turned back and focused her eyes on Chandler. "Is that what you're going to sell me?"

Chandler raised a brow. "Who-ee…there's that waspish tongue and sarcastic attitude in full force."

Sybil shrugged. "You asked, and I delivered."

"No one ever asks to be disrespected. The person dishing it up is the one in the wrong." The words were spoken soft and low.

Sybil groaned. "I'm sorry…but I keep hearing the same things from all of you."

Chandler wrinkled his brow. "All of us?"

She pointed at Chandler. "You, my father, Elvira…" she lifted her shoulders. "Probably my grandfather, if I gave him the opportunity." She waved her hand at the window. "Everyone I encounter in Wheatacre that attends the church I grew up in. You all keep saying that I need to give my life over to God and let Him have control. I accepted Christ as my Savior. I didn't know it was a package deal."

Chandler took a deep breath. "Did you accept Him, or did you just plug in a plan for your life? As if to say, I'm saved, so I'm good, no worries on that score?" Chandler swallowed, running his tongue over his lips. "The Christian walk *is* a package deal. It would be like buying a new car without an engine in it. You're not going to get out of the dealership lot. And if you just accept the gift of salvation, without bringing God into your life, without submitting to Him and learning His Word..." He shook his head. "You'll get just as far. When you accept Christ as your Savior, the Holy Spirit resides within you. That is your direction, your conviction, and your emotions for your Christian walk. Just like you need gas in your car to drive it, you need God's Word. That's the fuel that keeps you going. If you water down your gas, your car doesn't run well. If you water down your Christian life with worldly *stuff*, your life will be a mess."

Sybil blinked, staring back at him. "Leave it to you to compare the Christian life to driving a car. At least you used a car as an analogy. If you had used a horse, I would have really been lost." She narrowed her eyes. "This is very important to you, isn't it?"

Chandler swallowed deeply, his Adam's apple bobbing with the effort. "It is...I have no life without God in it. All that I have, all that I am, is because of Him." He shook his head, rubbing the back of his neck. "There is no thirty- or ninety-day plan. It is a lifelong commitment. It's a daily, hourly giving over of our own will and submitting to God's will. It's difficult at times, we mess up..." he gave her a smile. "Here's where the horse comes in. If you fall off a horse, you get back on. You do the same in the Christian life."

Sybil turned away. "I can't imagine not being in control of my destiny. I always make the plans and see them through."

Chandler raised a brow. "Have you? What happened to your plans when Scott killed himself? When you were accused of things you didn't do?"

Sybil wrapped her arms around her middle, lowering her head.

Chandler gripped the back of the seat, leaning toward Sybil. "I think you planned to marry Scott, even though you didn't love him, and that's why you had a physical relationship with him...to secure that. He would have been a great catch. When he messed that all up, you left your career and Kansas City. You didn't have the resources to patch up your reputation. You ran back to Wheatacre, because even though you say you dislike the town and the people in it...you *have* felt loved and secure here. Which is also the reason behind you treating them so badly. You think they have to tolerate you, mainly because of your father's reputation in this town."

Sybil raised her head, breathing quickly as her eyes met his. "Those are nasty things to say about my motives."

Chandler sat back, taking a deep breath. "The Bible says in Jeremiah 17:9 that 'the heart is more deceitful than all else and is desperately sick; who can understand it?'...that wasn't written only for you, Sybil. It was written for the human race."

Sybil rubbed one hand across her forehead and over her cheek. "Okay, we've established that I'm wicked and evil. You'd be hard put to get anyone in Wheatacre to disagree with that one." Her eyes traveled over the scudding clouds, the fluffy white turning to gray. She gave a shiver. "That storm is coming in. I really need to finish up my errands. Dad and Elvira will be wondering where I disappeared to for so long."

Chandler placed his hand on her shoulder, his thumb caressing along the collarbone. "You are a sinner, saved by grace, just as I am. God hasn't given up on you, and I'm certainly not going to." He smoothed his fingers along a black curl lying on her shoulder. "I think you've sailed along through life, and haven't met much adversity yet. It changes you when you run into it."

Sybil's eyes swept up. "You sound as though you *have* met it."

He nodded. "A time or two. You either become bitter, or you let God direct you through it. I would advise the latter." He shifted over to sit behind the steering wheel. "Well, I'll get you back to town." He brushed her hand, clenched in her lap. "Thank you for having lunch with me. I've enjoyed our talk."

Sybil shook her head, narrowing her eyes at him. "You have a strange way of showing it."

THE TRUCK MEANDERED INTO WHEATACRE. The approaching storm rumbled in the gray skies, causing Chandler to duck his head to look out the front windshield as he steered down the empty street. "It looks like everyone is tucked in at home. Best place to be, in my opinion."

Pointing to a black pickup, Sybil stared out Chandler's window. "Isn't that Blu's truck? It looks just like the one he had here last July."

Chandler made a U-turn, parallel parking behind the truck. "It's his. It has Colorado plates." He shifted the truck into park, shutting off the engine. "But I'd know it anywhere. It matches mine."

Sybil wrinkled her brow. "You drive this old thing. Everyone in town knows it as your uncle's pickup."

Chandler reached out and patted the dusty dashboard. "Now, now, don't be saying mean things about this here truck. She's served me well. My uncle took great care of her."

Sybil snorted. "If you say so. I'd keep the tow truck's number in your wallet." Sybil turned her eyes on Chandler. "So, since this truck is blue and white and in terrible condition—"

"Just the outside is a little rough."

Shifting her position on the seat, Sybil glanced out the back window. "If I jumped hard enough in that truck bed, I'd go right through all that rust. What difference does it make if the engine is in great shape and you have no body?"

Chandler raised an eyebrow. "Do you really want to go back to the vehicle analogies? I thought we already had that discussion today."

"Never mind." Sybil reached for the door handle. "I'm just going to walk around the corner to the hardware store. I'm sure Harold is wondering what in the world happened to me."

Chandler placed his hand on her arm, stopping her. "It's starting to rain, and I have a feeling it will be by the bucketful shortly by the way those clouds look. I can drive you over in a minute." He nodded toward the café. "I'm sure Blu is in getting a bite to eat. Let me see what his plans are."

"There he is. I'll see you later." Sybil reached for the door once again, opening it and hopping out. "Thanks for the sandwich." She slammed the door, rushing down the sidewalk and around the corner.

Blu sauntered over to Chandler's truck, his eyes following Sybil. He opened the passenger door and climbed in. "Wasn't that Sybil Grafton?" He shut the door just as the skies opened, rain hitting hard against the metal.

Chandler nodded. "It was. We had lunch out by the river east of town."

Blu nodded, displaying a huge grin. "I know the place well. Sybil directed me there the Fourth of July. It must be where she takes all her men."

Chandler's hand gripped the steering wheel, the knuckles showing white. "It wasn't like that. Just a pleasant lunch and nice conversation. You should try it sometime."

Blu laughed. "Aw, come on now, I've missed you, Buddy. I don't want to argue with you. We never scrapped like this, and now that's about all we do."

"Why are you here, Blu? You usually call if you're going to visit." Chandler stared at his childhood friend.

"Are you saying I'm not welcome? I thought it was *mi casa, su casa*." Blu shrugged. "At least that's the way it used to be."

Chandler braced his elbow at the base of the window as he rubbed his chin. "You know you're always welcome. You *and* Crystal. It just took me by surprise since you always let me know."

Blu grunted. "Crystal won't be visiting any time soon. You can be sure of that. If she and my mother could have salted you down, you'd be out curing with the rest of the bacon."

Chandler shook his head. "I always did like your mother's bacon."

Blu laughed, narrowing his eyes as he stared out the river flowing over the windshield. "It's really coming down."

"I just hope Sybil got to her car before it hit. I asked her to wait until I talked with you, but she scrambled out of here like she was on fire when she saw you."

Blu grinned. "And here I thought she'd be excited to see me." He shrugged. "I'll just have to catch up with her later. See if she's up to a little fun." He turned to his friend. "I just had a few days free, so I thought I'd drive over and see how you were doing…if you needed any help." He shrugged. "You know how much I enjoy the drive over here. Not much traffic, good roads. Gives a guy a chance to think."

"Well, that's fine, and I can always use an extra pair of hands around the place. You know that." Chandler looked at Blu. "If you don't mind, I'll meet you back at my place. I want to see if Sybil made it to her car without drowning. I'll probably get a few things at the store, since you always eat through my supplies."

Blu patted his flat abdomen. "I'm good for a few hours. That café has great food." He eyed the weather. "But you're really going to kick me out into that?"

Chandler started the truck. "I sure am. Just be glad you have four wheels, and not a horse, beneath you. You've been in worse."

"That's true." Blu opened the door and jogged over to his truck, stooping as the rain pelted him.

Chandler pulled onto the vacant road and rounded the block, looking for Sybil's Mercedes. The hardware store was dark, with no vehicles to be seen. *I sure hope she got her things and headed home before Harold closed. These small towns keep their own hours. I'm going to feel really bad if she or Loren have to make another trip into town because I kept her at the river too long.*

Chandler rubbed his forehead, feeling anger simmer to the top. Blu's words ran through his mind. "It must be where she takes all her men." *I hope for your sake, Blu, that pleasant conversation is all that took place at that river. I also have a terrible feeling that I'm not the only reason you're back in Wheatacre for a visit this time.* He stomped on the gas pedal and raced down the street, skidding on the greasy, wet road.

SYBIL PUSHED THE SOAKED STRANDS of hair away from her face as she leaned over the steering wheel, trying to see the road ahead. *My car is going to be destroyed.* She grimaced at the sound of the mud and rocks against the bottom of the car, the tires seeming to glue themselves to the slippery mess and then slide out of control. *I need to just get a truck like everyone else around here and give up any semblance of having manners or being a lady. I'll probably be chewing tobacco in no time.*

She shook her head, gripping the steering wheel. *Of course, you knew Blu would be back to visit Chandler. You were a simpleton if you thought once with him would be enough and then he'd just go away. He'll just want more and more now. That's how it works. You've heard the talk around the water cooler on more than one occasion. You were always so thankful that you didn't have to deal with that, and then you jumped in with both feet when Scott asked you to dinner. So grateful to have some man pay you the tiniest bit of attention.*

She groaned. *You've made a horrendous mess of everything! Chandler told you this afternoon that he was falling in love with you. Instead of being able to be thrilled by those words, you have Blu lurking at the edges, just waiting to fill Chandler in on everything. And you know he will, just as soon as you tell him you won't see him again. You can't be with him again. Allowing it to happen the one time was bad enough. Blu is Chandler's best friend! What were you thinking? Your lack of self-control is going to be the ruination of your life!* She hit the leather steering wheel with her hand. *Stupid, stupid!*

The front wheels slipped as she inadvertently gave the car too much gas. Overcorrecting, she sent the vehicle into the deep ditch beside the road, where water a couple feet deep was rushing through.

She groaned, shaking her head. *At least I wasn't going too fast. It's about the only thing I've done right lately.* She stared out the front window, wipers swiping quickly, her headlights pointing into the muddy embankment. One look at her door let her know it was going to be a real struggle to open it due to the angle of the car. Glancing at the passenger door, she groaned again. *Well, I can't open that one. It's buried in the ditch. I guess I'll just sit here alone until the storm passes. And hope I don't drown. Although that could make things better.*

The tears began, and she didn't even bother to wipe them away. They fell to the still-soaked sweatshirt that clung to her body. Her eyes wandered to the bag on the passenger seat. *That makes two things I did correctly today. At least Dad will have the items he wanted from the hardware store. I wonder if that will make a difference when he lets me know what an idiot I am?*

Chapter Sixteen

THE WIPERS SQUEAKED ACROSS THE windshield, barely keeping the view clear enough to see the road ahead. Chandler wrinkled his brow as Blu's black truck emerged from the mottled scenery, the taillights glowing in the blurry gray. *What is going on?*

Chandler stopped behind Blu's truck at the edge of the road. Opening his door, he jumped out, slamming the door shut as he made his way through the slippery muck that was now the road.

He pounded on Blu's window as he shouted over the storm, "What's wrong?"

Blu rolled the window down a few inches, pointing along the road to where taillights glowed at an awkward angle above the ditch. "Sybil's car went off the road."

Chandler's head jerked to the scene, his eyes squinting through the rain and wind. "Have you checked on her? Is she hurt? Why are you just sitting in there and not helping her?" He glared back at Blu.

Blu held up his phone and pointed at it. "I'm calling the tow truck now. Of course I checked on her. She's fine…just a little shook up, and worried about her car."

"Why didn't you try to get her out of there?" Chandler's eyes flashed just as gray and stormy as the skies. "She must be scared to death in there, all alone."

Blu rolled his eyes. "She hasn't been there that long. We can't get the car out of the ditch without a tow truck, and with the wind and rain, I couldn't open her door *and* pull her out. Too much resistance.

Now that you're here, we can get her out of the car. I thought it was better that she stayed in there, warm and dry, for as long as possible."

Chandler reached up, settling his cowboy hat lower. "Well, I'm going to see what I can do. Hurry and make that call." He jogged down the road, slipping and sliding.

Gripping the edge of the Mercedes, he guided himself to the driver's door and knocked on the window. "Sybil? Sybil, it's me, Chandler."

The window inched down, Sybil's teary eyes blinking in the small expanse. "Chandler, I'm so glad to see you! Blu wasn't able to hold the door open and pull me out."

"I know. He explained that already." Chandler wrinkled his brow, his eyes darting over her face as water dripped from his chin. "Are you okay? You aren't hurt?"

"No, I'm fine. Just feeling really stupid right now." Green eyes blinked up at him, black hair plastered against her pale cheeks.

Chandler cleared his throat. "Well, let's get you out of there so you can get home where you can change into some dry clothes. Go ahead and shut your window, and then open the door. I'm going to put my back against it to keep it open and try not to slide under the car." He gave her a lopsided grin.

Sybil nodded, pushing the window closed. She opened the door, struggling against the weight of it bearing down at the awkward angle, the wind pounding.

Chandler pulled it open just as Blu slid onto the scene.

Blu shouted over the pelting rain and wind, "It'll be about half an hour before the tow truck arrives!" He turned toward Sybil, taking her hand and pulling her up and out of the car. He knelt down, sweeping her off her feet.

Chandler gripped the car door and shouted, "You're going to

drop her trying to be heroic! Set her down so she can walk!"

Sybil squirmed, burying her face against Blu's chest as the rain hit her. "I can walk, Blu!"

Blu struggled up the steep embankment with his load. "Hold still! I'll have you out of here in just a minute." He turned to Chandler. "You don't mind waiting for the tow truck, right? I told him one of us would be here to give him a hand." He gained the road and strode toward his truck, Sybil's hands gripping his neck as he tried to keep his footing in the mud.

Chandler dropped his hands to his side, the door slamming shut. A loud crack of thunder accompanied a white flash, causing him to duck and scowl up at the skies. *I don't mind. Not at all, Blu…buddy…old pal. You can walk off with the girl I'm falling in love with. You can be the rescuer of damsels in distress. I'll take care of all the minor details. Just as I always have.*

Blu honked as his truck sped away, spraying mud over Chandler's backside.

Wringing your neck is looking better by the minute, Blu. He opened the door, reaching into Sybil's car to shut off the engine. *No sense in running all the gas out.*

SYBIL'S EYES FOLLOWED CHANDLER'S DRENCHED form as they drove away. She turned back to Blu. "I should have waited with him until the tow truck arrived. It is *my* car, after all."

Blu brushed her comment away. "He'll be fine. He enjoys doing things like that." He gave her a wink. "Really…he does. Makes him feel as though he is helping mankind." He grinned. "Or womankind, in this case."

Sybil crossed her arms and looked away. "He's going to catch pneumonia standing out there like that."

"I would hope he'd get back in his truck to wait. He *is* blond, but he has a pretty good head on his shoulders most of the time."

Glancing at Blu, she tightened her arms against her chest. "You aren't very nice to him. Why is that?"

Blu shrugged. "It's just our way. He can give as good as he gets, believe me. He's not as innocent as you're making him out to be." He gave her another wink. "I don't want to talk about Chandler. I'd rather talk about us. My place or yours?"

Gasping, Sybil stared at Blu. "For one thing, you don't have a *place* to go to. Secondly, that one time is the *only* time for us…and that was a mistake."

Blu made a fist and hit his chest, thumb first. "That was like a knife through my heart. You can't be serious." He took his eyes off the road, the truck swerving.

Sybil grabbed the steering wheel, giving a screech. "What are you doing? I don't plan on ending up in the ditch again…even if I do have company this time."

Blu brushed her hand away. "Don't grab the wheel when I'm driving. Understood?" He raised a brow at her. "That's a very dangerous thing to do."

"Well, you're driving like a crazy person, and talking even worse."

Blu shook his head. "That one time was very special for me. I've never felt that way before." He rubbed his forehead, tilting his cowboy hat back and then adjusting it. "This is coming out all wrong." He put on his blinker, turning down her driveway and then stopping. He took her hand in his. "I came back to talk to you about us getting married."

"Married!" The word overpowered the raging storm. She

threw his hand back to his lap. "You *have* lost your mind, Blu Waters. I don't even know you."

He grinned. "I thought you knew all of me pretty well."

Sybil turned red, her eyes flashing. "You're pushing the limits of my sweet personality."

Blu chuckled. "See, that's what I like about you. You're rather like this storm. Full of energy and loud. I think you'd keep life pretty interesting for me. I need someone like you to help me run my parents' ranch someday." He nudged her arm. "A lawyer would come in handy for those sticky negotiations."

Sybil nodded. "I've heard that one before. It usually means an innocent party is about to get—" She shook her head. "Never mind. You and me getting married is absolutely insane. I don't love you, and I'm not sure I even like you, after some of the things you've said. You're pretty full of yourself."

"You are too. See? A perfect match." His hand snaked over to her thigh. "We could have a lot of fun getting to know one another better."

Sybil slapped the hand away. "No, Blu! If that's the reason you returned to Wheatacre, I'm sorry you wasted your time. I don't want to be a rancher's wife, I don't want to live in Colorado, and I want to love the person I marry...*before* I marry him."

Blu lowered his voice. "Chandler is a rancher...born and raised. I think if it was him doing the asking right now, you'd have a different answer."

"I would not!" Sybil looked away, chewing on her bottom lip. "Besides, that's two different things. I've known Chandler for a while now. I have a clue about what kind of man he is, and I respect him."

"But you can't say that about me?" The half-whine grated through the truck.

Sybil sighed. "No, I can't. Just the fact that we've already been together physically says that you're not the same kind of person."

Blu snorted. "So now you're going to play the innocent party? You had been down that road before, pretty lady. You knew just where you were going, and how fast you wanted to get there."

Sybil's eyes flashed as they met Blu's. "You're not telling me anything I don't already know. I'm not proud of it, either. I think waiting until you're married is pretty special, but I've ruined it."

Blu reached over, his hand cupping the back of her neck as he took her right shoulder, pulling her against him. His lips covered hers, moving slowly.

Sybil pushed at his chest. "What are you doing?" She covered her mouth, wiping the kiss away.

Blu chuckled as he continued down the driveway. "Just taking one last taste. Showing you what you're going to be missing. There's plenty of pretty little fish in the pond for me. But not for you, Sybil. People don't wait until they're married anymore. That's as old-fashioned as singing hymns in church on a Sunday morning. You're going to be waiting a long time for another offer of marriage." He turned the truck into the parking area beside the guest house. "Chandler's about the only guy I know that fidelity means everything to." He gave her a wink and a twist of his lips. "When he finds out what you and I did together, he's going to throw you right back into the pond."

"Is that a threat?"

Blu shrugged. "I'll be around for a few days if you change your mind about the marriage proposal, or even a few hours of fun." He grabbed her knee and squeezed. "You *do* make my blood heat up, Sybil Grafton. I know we could be great together."

Sybil snorted, jerking her knee away. "Yep, until the next one came along. That's the way a guy like you thinks." She opened her door and jumped out, slamming it behind her. She ran to the porch, ignoring the good-bye honk of the truck.

Her chest heaved, tears mingling with the rain dripping down her face. *Chandler's not going to find out what we did, Blu Waters. You wouldn't tell your best friend what a jerk you were, and I'm going to change the person that I am. Even if I have to attend church three times a week and bake cookies for the elderly, I'm going to change and be the kind of woman Chandler would want to share his life with. The old way of doing things sure hasn't worked for me.*

She pushed the door open and walked into the little house, pressing the door closed and leaning against it. *You are one of a kind, Chandler. Crystal saw it, and so do I. But I'm not going to let you slip through my fingers.*

CHANDLER ROLLED DOWN HIS WINDOW as Blu's truck approached. He leaned his elbow on the wet surface, squinting up at the clearing skies.

"She's at her place." Blu spoke over the roar of his engine. "Safe and sound and as prickly as ever."

Chandler smiled. "Yeah, she can throw a few spines every now and then. They're taking Sybil's car into town. The axle's bent from landing on a large rock in the ditch. I'll have to give her a call to let her know what's going on."

"Well, you have fun with that. I'll see you back at your place. I'm going to assume I can bunk down where I always do."

Chandler nodded. "Make yourself at home. Since the storm has passed, we can grill steaks outside."

"Sounds good to me. See you in a few." Blu roared off, mud churning behind his tires.

Chandler watched the black truck disappear down the road, the taillights tiny in the rearview mirror. *If it weren't for you being here, I'd go and check on Sybil. Hope that she would invite me in for a cup of coffee. Now I'll have to settle for a phone call. She's probably had enough of cowboys for one day.*

He started his truck and shifted into gear, spinning a modified K-turn. He roared down the road. *I've had enough of cowboys, especially ones with a smart mouth and arrogance so thick you can slice it with a steak knife. Our friendship is wearing thin, old Blu. Or maybe it's just me, getting older and lonely for some female companionship. The prospect of cows, Sandy, and an occasional visit from The Cowboy of the Year as my only entertainment isn't sounding so good anymore.* He shook his head, turning onto his long driveway.

SYBIL STEPPED THROUGH THE WOODEN doors of the church sanctuary, her eyes darting over the crowd of people visiting in the pews. *And I thought I would be just late enough to avoid all the senseless chatter.*

"Well, good morning, Sybil!" Burgundy-colored hair glowed pink at the ends with the sunlight shining through the tall windows. The older woman gave Sybil a side hug, pressing her cheek against Sybil's shoulder. "It's so good to see you! It's been ages."

Sybil forced a smile. "Good morning, Thelma." She patted the back of her shoulder-length hair. "I'm in need of a trim, but I just haven't had the time, for some reason."

Thelma smiled, fluffing a black curl on Sybil's shoulder. "You look lovely. I prefer you with longer hair. It really softens your whole demeanor."

Cissy teetered over, her skinny heels making dents in the padded carpet. "I thought that was you." She smiled, her eyes traveling over the crowded room. "These women here aren't going to be happy with another contender."

Thelma shook her head. "Don't talk silly. Most of these women should be attending church for the right reasons, not searching for a husband."

Sybil pressed her lips together and tightened her fingers around the strap of her purse. "I never heard of anything so ridiculous. You'd think we were living back forty or more years ago when a woman was only good for marrying and having children. Women have so many options these days, only one of which is getting married." Sybil's eyes scanned the pews once again.

Cissy giggled, pointing to the front of the church. "Chandler's right over there, Sybil. He always sits in that second pew."

Sybil grabbed Cissy finger and pressed it to the blonde's side. "I could care less where Chandler Byron is sitting. I didn't come to church to see *him*, after all." Sybil dropped the offending finger and adjusted the silky material of her blouse at her narrow waist. "Good grief. You act as though you're sixteen years old."

Thelma sighed, shaking her head. "You two! Are you ever going to act your ages?" She gave Sybil another smile. "It *is* good to see you here. We've missed you. I'm going to take my seat before Pastor taps the microphone to get our attention. It makes my insides shiver when he does that." She grabbed Cissy's hand. "I think there's an empty spot right beside me."

Sybil covered her smile as she watched the older woman pulling the tall blonde down the aisle. People scrambled to their seats as the music ended, the low rumble of chatter disappearing into quiet. Sybil took a few steps down the aisle, her eyes searching for a vacant pew to hide in. *When did this place become such a popular spot on a Sunday morning? There was always a vacant pew or two.*

Her eyes met Elvira's as her stepmother shrugged and worded "sorry", their pew packed with several small children.

That's just fine with me, Elvira! I don't want to spend the entire service with sticky fingers on my silk blouse and shoes running up and down my pantyhose until they're shredded. There has to be a place to sit well away from children and mumbling elderly.

The pastor tapped the microphone, silencing the last talkers. Sybil winced at the shrill shriek from the feedback.

"Sybil, there is a place right over here." The pastor gave her a wide smile, pointing to the second pew on his right side.

Sybil's eyes followed the gesture, meeting Chandler's warm grin. He patted the spot next to him.

Sybil ducked her head, walking quickly down the aisle and over to the narrow space. *At least it's at the end of the pew. I won't have to crawl over several people to get there.* Sybil sat down, noting the young woman smashed against Chandler's right side. *Well, isn't that cozy!*

Chandler's aftershave drifted over as he whispered, "Good morning."

Sybil took a deep breath, her heart racing with his nearness. "Good morning. But you really didn't need to make room for me here. I'm sure I would have found a place eventually."

Chandler took a quick look around. "It's standing room only, I believe."

"I've never seen so many people here. You'd think it was Christmas or Easter." Sybil leaned forward, glancing at the row of college-aged girls crowded into the pew. "I thought it was in style to sit at the back of the church. Not up front where everyone can see you."

Chandler smiled down at her. "The times are changing."

The pastor cleared his throat, raising one eyebrow as he watched the exchange. He addressed the large congregation. "Let's bow our heads in prayer as we begin this morning's service."

Sybil sat back, pressing herself into the corner of the hard pew. She ducked her head, arranging her purse and Bible upon her lap. *Remember…you're here to change, to be the kind of woman Chandler would be proud to call his wife.* She rolled her eyes. *Now you're sounding just as ridiculous as Cissy or most of these other women. You have an education, you've been a successful lawyer…you don't need to be married to show you're worth something.* Her eyes traveled to Chandler's bowed head, the eyelashes lying against his lean, tanned cheeks. She took in his strong jaw and the crisp line of his sideburns. *But it would be wonderful to wake up next to him every morning!*

As the pastor said, "Amen", Sybil closed her eyes, saying a quick prayer that her plan for attending church would work. After all, whenever she made plans, they usually went just as she wished.

Chapter Seventeen

SYBIL DEPOSITED A TONG-FULL OF salad onto her plate and then passed the large bowl of brightly colored greens and tomatoes to her father. "I don't understand why none of you ever told me that Chandler is the youth leader at church."

Elvira cleared her throat as she passed a platter of baked chicken to Sybil. "It's more of a college-age group. Those that are single—"

Sybil glared and interrupted. "By the way they were crowding the pew, I don't think any of them want to remain single for long. I think every one of those girls has a crush on Chandler. Aren't there any other eligible men in Wheatacre? Did they all move away?"

William Grafton chuckled as he plunked a heaping scoop of mashed potatoes on his plate. "Either they moved away, married, or have had too many visits to my court room. Wheatacre is a little short in the marriageable men area." The white-haired man gave Elvira a wink. "Have I told you how much I appreciate Sunday dinners here?"

Elvira laughed. "Only every Sunday."

William nodded. "Well, it's true. And I'm going to say it every time I'm invited." He jabbed his fork in Loren's direction. "I asked that son of mine over and over to fix me dinner, or even meet me at the café after church. He just left this poor old man to starve each and every Sunday before you two were married."

Loren shook his head, raising his brow at the older man's midsection. "From the way your middle is expanding, I don't think you've done too much starving, Dad."

William patted the slightly rounded area. "This? I'm storing up for winter." He returned his gaze to Elvira. "Tell me you baked a pie for dessert…or two."

Elvira smiled. "I did. One apple pie and one mincemeat."

Loren grinned, exhaling a dramatic sigh. "And it's not even Thanksgiving yet." Loren reached across the corner of the table and nudged Sybil's arm. "I bet it's the real deal, too. None of that meatless mincemeat you tried to pass off on me that year."

"Yes, Dad, you're just the luckiest man on earth. A good woman to feed your ego *and* your stomach. A match made in heaven." Sybil stabbed her chicken breast with her fork, tearing the meat from the bones.

William eyed his granddaughter. "I'm afraid that poor bird is already dead. Maybe you should tell us what's eating on you and give the chicken a bit of dignity." He tore a small piece of meat from the bone and dropped it to the floor.

Loren raised an eyebrow. "Are you feeding Grayson?"

William chuckled. "Just a bite or two every now and then. He's a part of this family too, and I have to stay in his good graces. When he stays with me in July, he won't let me sit on the furniture if I don't include him at meal times."

Elvira smiled, giving William a wink. "That's perfectly all right. He *is* part of this family. I would give him a small place at the table if I had my way."

Sybil rolled her eyes. "You wouldn't have to worry about me coming for dinner anymore. He's a cat, and a very stuck-up one at that."

Loren mumbled and then popped a big bite of food into his mouth.

"I heard that, Dad. I'm not stuck-up, and I don't appreciate being compared to a cat." Sybil laid her fork on the edge of her plate. "I was *trying* to talk to all of you. I don't know why I'm the last to find out anything that goes on in this family. I've been here since April, and now it's October. That's seven months, and no one has said a thing about Chandler being the mascot for the college group, or that he sings, as well." She took a deep breath, laying her hands in her lap. "It seems like he's not even a real person. He's much too perfect."

Elvira dabbed the napkin across her lips. "Chandler shared with the church that he played guitar and sang, only a couple of months ago. He doesn't talk too much about himself."

William took the platter of chicken from the middle of the table. "I thought it was pretty brave of him to stand up with that gaggle of girls and sing. They did a beautiful job."

Sybil glanced at her grandfather. "Yes, it was very nice. But that's not the point. Why is everything such a secret around here?" She pointed to Elvira and then Loren. "You two didn't even let me know Chandler was going to our church all those months ago."

William shrugged, passing the chicken to Loren. "They probably thought you'd check it out if you were really interested. If I remember correctly, you haven't shown much desire for church in a few years. You only went when you were in town to appease your father."

Sybil gasped. "That's not true!"

William raised his white, bushy brows. "Really? What church were you attending in Kansas City?"

Sybil spewed and sputtered. "You know I was very busy when I was living in Kansas City. Sundays were my day to relax and have some time for *me*."

William shrugged. "My Bible doesn't say a thing about

spending time for ourselves. It does say a lot about giving our time and attention to His Word, and to Him."

Elvira slid her chair away from the table. "I think I'll get those pies. Would you give me a hand in the kitchen, Sybil?"

Sybil shoved away from the table. "Of course! Anything to get away from being interrogated."

William chuckled. "I thought you were supposed to get *out* of the kitchen when you couldn't stand the fire."

Loren smiled, looking up at his daughter. "Simmer down, Sybil. You know he likes to poke at you."

Sybil tossed her napkin on the table, as she took short breaths. "Yes, I know. He likes to intimidate, as well." She met her grandfather's eyes. "I've faced a few cranky judges in my time. You don't scare me. I did what I thought was best. Now I think it's best for me to attend church. I don't have the work load that I had in Kansas City. I can handle being at church on a Sunday."

William laughed. "Just making sure you're going for the right reasons. Chandler is a smart fellow. He will see right through any manipulations you have up your sleeve. You'd better be concentrating on the teaching of God's Word, and what He has in mind for you. He'll work it all out…whether it involves Chandler Byron or not."

Sybil groaned. "You've always been insufferable, and you're only getting worse as you get older."

William scooped up a bite of mashed potatoes. "Just preparing for my nursing-home years. I want to keep those pretty little nurses on their toes." He popped it into his mouth and gave Sybil a wink.

Sybil stomped from the table on her high heels, rounding the island separating the dining area from the kitchen. She braced her hands against the counter as she watched Elvira slice the pies. "I can't believe this town still allows him to be the judge. That man is half-crazy!"

William's voice carried into the two women. "I'm full-crazy, my girl. Have been for years."

Sybil rolled her eyes as Elvira giggled. "Whoever thought of the open concept for living spaces must have lived alone. It's nice to have somewhere to go and have privacy once in a while."

Elvira nudged Sybil's arm with her elbow. "It sure is!"

Sybil smiled. "Not you too. I have to have someone to talk to every now and then."

Elvira grinned. "I'm here whenever you need to talk, Sybil. I might not always have the answers, but I'm a great listener."

Sybil placed her hand on her hip. "Is it unreasonable of me to be hurt that no one thought to tell me about Chandler? I mean, the guy is practically an icon at the church, and now I find out he can really sing. Is there anything he can't do?"

Elvira met Sybil's gaze. "He's pretty special. But it all shines through because of Chandler's love for the Lord." Elvira took the apple pie from the counter. "You're special in your own way, Sybil. I think Chandler sees that. Chandler isn't too good for you, or a better person than you are. He's just letting God direct his path, while you're still stumbling a bit."

Sybil dropped the hand from her hip. "You make it sound so simple."

Elvira headed for the dining area, looking over her shoulder. "It's not. You just have to humble yourself and submit to what God has for you. Please bring in the dessert forks and plates."

Sybil stared after Elvira. *Submit? What a demeaning word. It makes it sound as though you have no input to give in the situation.* She snatched the plates and forks from the counter.

CHANDLER KNOCKED ON THE DOOR of the log home, rubbing his hands together. The chill in the air spoke of the coming winter, as did the trees losing their leaves in the late-October wind. He smiled. *The color here is nothing like the aspens in the mountains of Colorado, but at least there is a hint of autumn, my favorite time of year.*

The heavy door whooshed open, Loren smiling and extending his hand. "Chandler, this is a surprise. I didn't think we'd see you until church tonight. Come on in." Loren stepped aside, gesturing the younger man into the living room.

Chandler swept the hat from his head and entered the house, a fire snapping merrily in the huge stone fireplace. He nodded to Elvira, sitting on the leather sofa. "Good afternoon. I hope I'm not barging in."

Elvira smiled. "Of course not. You know you're always welcome. As a matter of fact, I was just telling Loren that we should include you in our Sunday meals after church. It's always nice to have one more person to cook for."

Chandler grinned. "That's a different take on meals, but one I like to hear. My mother wasn't always so happy about cooking on a Sunday after she'd done it all week. Our family usually ate out on a Sunday to give her a break."

"Not me!" Elvira shook her head. "I was an only child, and church was an occasional activity for my mother and me. I dreamed of huge Sunday dinners with lots of family around." She pointed a finger at Chandler. "So, remember, next Sunday after morning services, our place. Loren's father usually joins us, and Sybil was here today as well. It was nice to have everyone together."

Loren crossed his arms, rocking back on his heels. "Well...it was nice most of the time. My father and Sybil tend to peck at one another."

Chandler ducked his head, giving a slow smile. "I could see that being a problem. Judge Grafton has a way of stirring the pot."

Loren nodded. "Yes, he does, and Sybil wants to be the only one stirring her pot."

Elvira frowned. "Loren!"

Chandler chuckled, moving the brim of his hat through his hands. "Actually, I was hoping Sybil was here. I didn't know if she would be returning to church tonight since she was there this morning, but I wanted to offer her a ride."

Loren raised his left wrist, looking at his watch. "It's three-thirty. Church doesn't start until seven." He met Chandler's eyes, his own twinkling with merriment.

Chandler's face blushed. "I…I know. I thought she might like to go for a drive, or sit and talk for a while. But…but if you think she's busy, I'll just see her tonight…or next Sunday morning."

Loren tilted his head back, laughing.

Elvira wrinkled her brow once again. "Loren!" She turned to Chandler. "Sybil is over at her place. She didn't mention whether she would be at church tonight or not. I'm sure she would enjoy the company."

Loren raised a brow, staring at his wife. "Didn't she say she was going to take a nap? Getting up so early for church apparently exhausted her."

Elvira uncurled her leg from beneath her and stood. "Yes, she did mention a nap. I'm going to give her a quick call and let her know you're on your way over. I'm sure she'd be delighted to see you, Chandler." She patted the pocket of her jeans. "If I can just find my phone."

Loren gestured down the hall. "It's on the nightstand in our bedroom."

Elvira smoothed her hand down Loren's arm as she passed

him. "Thank you. I'll be right back."

The two men exchanged shrugs and raised brows.

Chandler winced. "Do *you* think it's all right for me to go over? I mean, I don't want to get her at a bad time."

Loren snorted. "Me neither. But your guess is as good as mine. I'm trying to wrap my mind around it, but Elvira seems to understand Sybil better than I ever could. Maybe it's because they're both women." He reached out and gripped Chandler's shoulder. "You know the way to her place. If you really want to see her that badly, armor up and head over. We're here if you need anything."

Chandler gave a lopsided grin. "You really make it sound bad. Do you think I'm crazy to be interested in Sybil? I mean, she's *your* daughter."

Loren walked over to the door and opened it, the cool air drifting into the cozy room. "Yes, she *is* my daughter, and I would be delighted to call you more than a friend. But I also know Sybil and her little quirks. It's going to take a brave and courageous man to live with her." He smiled. "But you just may be the fellow to tackle that."

Chandler stepped onto the wide porch, setting the hat upon his head. "So, I have your permission to get to know Sybil…to maybe pursue a relationship if she's willing?"

Loren smiled. "You have my permission, my blessing, my prayers, and whatever else you need to help you along your way. You're going to need all of them."

Chandler nodded. "Thank you…I think."

ELVIRA ENTERED THE ROOM AS Loren closed the door. He laughed as he walked to the sofa and sat down.

"What did you say or do now?" Elvira crossed her arms and tapped her foot. "It can't be good. I shouldn't leave you alone…ever."

He shook his head as he positioned his elbows on his knees, clasping his hands in the empty space. He grinned up at his wife. "No, you shouldn't." He sat back, patting his knee. "Come and sit with me."

Elvira laughed. "Sit *with* you or *on* you?" She walked over, sliding down next to Loren.

He shrugged. "I was hoping for the latter," he maneuvered his arm around her shoulder, pulling her close, "but this is nice too."

She leaned back, meeting his eyes. "What was so funny when I walked in?"

"That young man is falling in love with Sybil. Sybil…my cantankerous, bossy daughter." Loren's eyes widened as he shook his head. "God really does answer prayer."

Elvira smacked Loren's knee. "Don't be blasphemous. God may be working this all out, and we need to be praying that He works in Sybil. Changes her heart."

"Well, if that happens, I'll believe in miracles, as well."

Elvira gasped. "You really need to watch your tongue, Loren Grafton. You know that God works in mysterious ways, even better than I do. I'm only beginning to understand the power of life with Him."

Loren kissed Elvira's forehead. "I'll be good, I promise. But I pray Sybil doesn't mess this up. Chandler is a bright young man, hardworking, and strong in his faith. I think he would take care of Sybil, and that she'd be happy with him."

"But?" Elvira stroked the fingers that lay against her collarbone.

"She's just so stubborn, and set in her ways. I sometimes wonder if she has the ability to love anyone other than herself."

"Only time will tell. But I know God can change a person's way of thinking. He changed mine. I know He uses circumstances and people to bring that about." She pressed Loren's fingers to her lips. "I firmly believe that God allowed me to find those letters that Libby wrote. Even though she was gone, her words spoke to me, and turned my eyes and heart to God. She wasn't physically here, but she helped lead me to Christ." Elvira looked up. "He brought you into my life. If you remember, I was a bit stubborn and cranky, as well."

Loren nodded. "Yes, you were. There were times I thought I had better just go my own way."

Elvira snuggled against her husband. "I'm so happy that you didn't."

Loren pulled her closer, laying his cheek against the top of her head. "Me too."

Chapter Eighteen

*S*YBIL PULLED THE BRUSH THROUGH her hair, fluffing it about her head. Leaning forward, she widened her eyes dabbing at the smudged eye shadow at the corners. *Of course Chandler decides to visit on the one day I take a nap. At least Elvira had the good sense to give me a call and let me know. Even so, I look like I just crawled out from under a rock! Oh well, no time for a complete redo. At least he saw me this morning when I was actually put together.*

She sighed with the knock on the front door. "Coming!" *Just be happy he decided to visit. You didn't have to go over there, looking desperate for companionship.* She switched off the bathroom light, smoothing her hands down over her hips and the long, shirt-style dress she wore. *It doesn't do much for the figure, but it's certainly comfortable.*

Opening the front door, she gave a smile. "What a surprise!"

Chandler raised a brow. "I thought Elvira called you, letting you know I was coming."

Sybil waved her hand. "Yes, she did. I guess it just seemed like the thing to say. Won't you come in?"

Chandler's eyes slid around her thin form to the room beyond. "Actually, I would rather sit outside. It's a beautiful afternoon. Maybe you'd like to go for a drive?"

Sybil shook her head. "I don't think I want to be cooped up in an old truck right now." Her eyes traveled up and down the length of the driveway. "Where *is* your truck?"

Chandler pointed to the front of the large log home across the driveway. The bed of a bright red truck extended beyond the edge of the porch. "Right there. I stopped at your father's place first…as you know. So I just walked over."

Sybil frowned. "But that's not the blue and white one you usually drive. The one that was your uncle's."

He shook his head. "No, it's *my* truck, the one that matches Blu's. I only take it out for special occasions, like church and visiting." He rubbed the back of his neck. "We were having this conversation the day we had the picnic at the river. We got back into town—"

"And I saw Blu's truck parked in front of the café. You said you knew it was his because it was just like your truck." Sybil nodded. "I remember now, just not understanding very well." She gave a shiver, pointing to the porch swing. "I'm going to grab a sweater and I'll be right back. Can I get you anything to drink?"

"No, I'm fine." Chandler smiled down at her. "Maybe after some time out here I'll feel like a cup of hot coffee, but right now, the cool air is really nice."

She smiled. "I'll put a pot on while I'm in there so it'll be ready, just in case."

"Sounds good!"

Sybil went into the house, measured coffee into the basket and poured water into the reservoir. Grabbing her red cardigan off the back of a chair, she slid her arms into it. *It's the bag-lady-look for today, I guess.* She glanced down at her fleece-lined moccasins and sighed. *It's Wheatacre, Kansas. Who do you have to impress? Just one great-looking cowboy!*

Shutting the door behind her, she approached the porch swing, Chandler's long length dwarfing it considerably. "Coffee's on. It'll be ready whenever you want it." She sat down, pressing into the corner. "So, tell me why you and Blu have the exact same truck…other than a different color."

"When we were in high school, we took an auto body class. We each purchased an old truck, finding the same model and year. Blu's didn't need as much work as mine did, so he helped me out a lot." Chandler smiled. "We worked on those beat up piles of rust a lot of years. Now, they're practically brand new, inside and out."

"Which explains why you don't just drive it all over the place and haul furniture in it."

He nodded. "Exactly. Big Red has spent much of the past couple of years in the barn with a tarp over her. I get her out on nice days and air her out. She enjoys it, and so do I."

Sybil tilted her head, raising one black eyebrow. "It sounds as though you two have the perfect relationship."

He chuckled. "We do. She's just not much for cuddling…" he looked at her, "or making coffee."

Sybil cleared her throat, looking away. *Those blue eyes drill a hole right through me! I can't hardly take a breath when he looks at me like that.* "I enjoyed the special music at church today. I didn't know you could play the guitar or sing. It seems as though you have all sorts of surprises hidden away."

"Not something I advertise. My guitar playing is usually just for Sandy and the cows. They aren't too critical if I mess up." He shrugged. "But the girls wanted to work on a song together, so I obliged. They did a really nice job. They worked hard to get the harmony down."

Sybil's eyes met his. "You do know that those *girls,* as you call them, have a crush on you. They probably draw straws every Sunday to see who gets to sit next to you."

Chandler laughed. "They were only in that pew today because of the special."

Sybil scoffed.

"Really! They usually *do* sit at the back of the church, and many of them have boyfriends that attend the college-age classes that I teach on Wednesday nights." He leaned back, stretching his arm along the back of the swing. "They are a bit young for me anyway. Believe me, I would much rather have a wife help me with the class. I think a woman would give a different, much-needed perspective on some of the questions they ask."

"So how did you end up teaching the class if you weren't comfortable with it? Couldn't you have just said *no?*"

He nodded, chewing on the edge of his lip. "I could have. The couple that led the class for several years moved out of the area. The board was going to discontinue it because the numbers were down. But I just didn't feel right about that. I prayed about it for several weeks, and then I knew God was asking me to take it over."

Sybil pulled the sweater together at the front. "Did God whisper to you one night, 'Chandler, you're the next college-age class teacher'?"

Chandler rocked the swing with his booted foot. "Still a bit cynical when it comes to God, I see." He nodded. "I understand. I once was too. But until you have experienced what it's like to trust and follow, it's very hard to explain. It's just one of those things you have to live through personally."

Sybil clasped her hands in her lap. "Well, you're about the same age as I am, so I don't know how you could have racked up all these learning experiences to make you so trusting of something you can't see. I believe that Christ died on the cross, but I can't say as I've ever heard Him *speak* to me in any way. As I've said before, I've pretty much run my life, making my own decisions. God hasn't whispered to me, or shone a flashlight on the path I need to take. I just don't understand what you're saying."

Chandler adjusted his body to face her, his left arm extending to her back. "When you practiced law, did you research what your client told you?"

"Of course. I got as many facts as I could."

"When that client told you his or her side of their story, did you observe them carrying out what they told you?"

Sybil laughed. "Well, of course not. The actions had already taken place. I had to trust—"

Chandler raised a brow.

"I understand what you're trying to say. I had to believe…trust…have faith in what my client was telling me in order to represent them."

"What if they were lying?"

"I still had to base my case on the facts given and researched." She rubbed her forehead. "I wasn't that kind of lawyer. I wanted truth to be upheld. But I'm sure there were times that I was wrong. It goes along with the territory."

"So," Chandler rubbed the faint blond stubble on his chin. "You're telling me that you would have faith, trust, and believe a client…a mere person, but you can't do that with God? You aren't able to hear or feel the Holy Spirit within you, directing you?"

She shook her head. "Not that I'm aware of."

"Can I ask you another personal question?"

Sybil shrugged her thin shoulders. "You can ask, but I don't know if I'll answer."

"How much time have you spent learning God's Word?"

She frowned at him. "I haven't attended church services very much over the years, if that's what you're asking. I've told you that before."

He shook his head. "That's not what I asked. You don't learn God's Word by going to church. You can meet some lovely people, and you can encounter some real rascals. Christians own a corner of stupidity, too. You can sing beautiful songs, fellowship with your friends, and generally feel pretty good if you want to. But unless there is some good teaching going on, you're not learning any more than what you could get at a fun party."

"I think you have a messed-up view of what church is all about."

"No, I pray I have the view that God wants every Christian to have. The one that Paul taught so much about. Think of it this way." Chandler leaned toward her, his eyes darkening. "When you took a class in school, any class, you had to be taught what the class was about. You had a book or two to study. Right?"

Sybil nodded.

"If you were in algebra, the teacher taught about that. You had homework, and you used a textbook."

Sybil wrapped her arms about her waist. "I really despised math while I was in school. So that analogy isn't really working for me, wherever you're going with it."

Chandler closed his eyes and took a deep breath as he opened them. "I enjoyed history when I was in school. I had a terrific teacher that made history fun. She had us act out scenes so they became a reality to us. We drew and colored maps, learned about the people during those times. Whenever we were in her class, all that we did was based around history. It became a part of me after a while. I can still remember certain things from all those years ago."

"So you had a great history teacher. I had a couple teachers I liked as well. I don't know how that relates to church."

"My question to you was *how much time have you spent learning God's Word*. How many hours of homework have you spent, what kind of grades have you received on your tests? When you *are* at church, *if* you go, are you being taught God's Word, and how to apply it in your life?" Chandler sat back. "If you aren't reading God's Word, if you aren't being taught His Word, how can you expect to know about Him? How can you hear Him?"

Sybil slumped against the boards of the swing, clasping her hands in her lap. "Wow! Maybe you should have considered being a lawyer."

Chandler rubbed his forehead. "I'm sorry. I get a little intense. It's just so important to me. I think people have gone far away from what church is supposed to be about. You can't learn to drive a car by sitting in the sandbox building castles. You have to get in and drive, and you have to *study* the book about driving in order to pass the written test."

Sybil smiled. "I get what you're saying. Believe me, I've spent years studying. I know a lot about the law." She grimaced. "But not so much about the Bible."

Chandler reached out, laying his hand over hers. "All of us are at different places in our Christian walk. There are times when we fall and have to pick ourselves up, but we continue. You've already accepted Christ as your Savior, now you need to study." His eyes searched her face.

Sybil looked away, staring down at their hands. "How did you get to be so smart? Were you just born this way…ready to take on the world, able to handle anything that came along?"

Sitting back, Chandler took the hat from his head and set it on the porch railing. He ran his fingers through the short, blond waves. "Not by a long shot. I had to learn everything the hard way. But I'm thankful for the route I had to take to get to where I am. It's made me appreciate it more."

Sybil ran her tongue over her lips. "I think that's true with anything in life that's worthwhile. It wasn't easy to become a lawyer. As a woman, I had to work just that little bit harder to be taken seriously." Her eyes drifted over Chandler's profile. He stared out over the stone terrace behind the large log house, the wrought iron furniture tarped for the winter. The brown fields beyond undulated in the wind, the tips of the tall grass glowing in the late afternoon sun. "What are you thinking?"

"Just about this afternoon, the things we've been talking about. When I look back over my own life so far, there are times that I wish I could change. Decisions that I had made differently. But I suppose we all want that."

Nodding, Sybil leaned forward, crossing her arms over her knees. She bent her right arm, and braced her chin with the palm of her hand. "That's for sure."

"When I think of having children of my own one day, I want to be able to save them from the stupidity that ran my life when I was a teenager. There must be a way to instill a respectful, more mature attitude into a young adult."

Sybil laughed. "If you figure that one out, you should write a book. I think being a teenager and doing stupid things is just part of the growing up process." She swayed toward him, bumping her shoulder against his arm. "Come on, it's not like you killed someone, or were in jail. I think Blu would have shared such information. Your teenage years couldn't have been that bad."

Chandler's voice softened. "No, I didn't kill someone, but I lost something very dear to me because of my selfish, arrogant behavior. I can't take that time back and redo it. It's gone forever, but the pain and scars still remain."

Sybil straightened, laying her hand on his arm. "If you'd like to talk about it, I'm here. When my mother died of cancer, I walled myself away, not wanting anyone around. If I had shared my grief and anger with someone, it would have made it easier to bear. It was a very difficult time for my father and me."

Chandler looked back at her. "I'm sorry. I didn't realize your mother had died of cancer. That's hard when you're a child."

Sybil shrugged. "I wasn't a child. I was just beginning my life as a lawyer, a profession I had chosen because it was what my mother had done with her life. It was very important to my mother to see women succeed at such things. I was at school, and then living in Kansas City. My father had the complete burden of caring for her." She wrinkled her brow. "You know…one of those times you would like to go back and change. Each time I talked with my mother, she assured me she was getting better, and that she wanted me to keep fighting for my dreams." Sybil sniffed. "More her dreams than mine, truth be told. Then…she was gone. I regretted that I hadn't gone home to be with her, to care for her. By the time Elvira moved here and entered my father's life, I was pretty bitter that he would just take up with someone else. It was like my mother had meant nothing to him all those years."

"Unless we have lost a spouse, I don't think any of us would understand what the other person goes through. To spend years with someone, sharing your life with them…and then they're gone." He gave a half-smile. "I guess I hope that my wife outlives me. Isn't that selfish?"

"Understandable."

Chandler cleared his throat. "I'm smelling that coffee."

"Me too. It has to be one of the best aromas in the world."

Chandler raised a brow. "*If* you like coffee."

Sybil laughed, pushing up from the swing. "I wish I had some of the pie Elvira served at dinner today. About the best I can do is some packaged cookies."

"I know you're going to find this hard to believe, but packaged cookies are usually my go-to with coffee. I don't spend a lot of time baking."

Sybil set her hands on her hips, tilting her head. "You don't? Crystal went on and on about what a great cook you were and how your mother had taught you how to bake. You would have thought that Julia Child had been your mentor."

Chandler laughed. "I admired the woman and her culinary abilities, but that's about as far as it goes. I do manage a nice pound cake every now and then. My mother's recipe is very easy, and it takes a while to bake. Not so time-consuming as babysitting cookies."

Sybil patted her tummy. "All this talk is making me hungry."

Chandler stood, stretching his back. "So, let's go get something to eat before church tonight. I'm sure we still have an hour or so before it starts."

Sybil looked away, wrapping her arms about her waist.

Chandler put one hand up. "I'm sorry, I didn't even ask if you were going to church. I just assumed..." He sighed. "I'm going to be quiet now and look forward to a nice cup of hot coffee with some cookies." He winced. "Unless that's not an option any longer."

Sybil met his gaze. "You know, I wasn't going to go to church tonight, thinking that Sunday morning was more than enough church in one week. But you describing it as studying kind of has me intrigued. I've always been up for a challenge. I also love research, and finding the correct answers."

Chandler grinned. "Happy to have been of service. I enjoy Sunday nights especially because the congregation chooses the songs. We sing for a half hour or so after the message."

Sybil frowned. "*After* the message? I don't remember it that way. Songs always came first, rather like the warm-up band getting you ready for the message."

He nodded. "That's the usual way of it. But we have teaching *first*...getting our minds prepared to worship. But that's only on Sunday nights."

Sybil looked down at her slippers, wiggling her toes. "I had better put on some shoes, and turn off the coffee maker." She smiled up at him. "I'll only be a minute...if the invitation is still open for something to eat before church."

Chandler nodded, his grin showing a line of perfect, white teeth. His blue eyes sparkled in the dimming light of the day. "It's open and waiting."

"Great! I'll be right back." Sybil went into the house, her heart beating triple time. *It's only a quick bite to eat before church. Not dinner at the Waldorf. Calm down!*

Chapter Nineteen

SANDY PAWED THE DIRT AISLE of the old barn. Chandler continued brushing her butterscotch sides, smoothing his hand along her back. "I know you're ready to go into your stall, but you don't want to go to bed dirty. We had some fun this afternoon, but now it's time to do the boring stuff." Chandler smiled, running his hand over her velvet nose. "You know you love the attention."

Sandy whickered, shaking her head and pawing the ground once more.

"May I come in?"

Chandler jumped, turning to the large sliding doors at the end of the barn. Sybil stood framed between, her jean-clad legs ending in brown leather boots. Her leather jacket hugged her waist, and black tendrils of hair draped over her shoulder. Rosy cheeks glowed, and her eyes sparked at his smile. *She just gets prettier and prettier! You're falling hard, and other than Sybil being really friendly and stopping by every now and then, she's said nothing about her feelings for you. She could be interested, or just really lonely.*

"Of course! You know you're always welcome. Sandy and I always like a good visit." Chandler continued grooming Sandy. "I didn't think I'd see you until Sunday morning."

Sybil stepped into the barn and pulled the door closed. "Surprise! I think you'll be even more happy to see me when you hear that I brought supper for you." Sybil stopped beside

Chandler, reaching out to pat Sandy's rump. "Nothing for you though, Sandy. I was fresh out of hay and grain at my place."

Chandler smiled. "You know she enjoys a carrot or apple." He gave her a wink. "Didn't you learn anything about horses while you were cleaning all those stalls last summer?"

Sybil wrinkled her nose. "Yes, I learned a lot, and some of it not so pleasant. But I'll remember the carrot or apple for next time. I didn't think you'd be in the barn this time of day."

Chandler unhooked the cross tie from Sandy's halter and led her into her stall. "Normally I wouldn't be. But Sandy and I had a nice long ride, and I wanted her groomed and settled in for the evening. It's supposed to go below freezing tonight."

"What about all those poor cows out there? Do they just have to stand and shiver all winter? Don't they have someplace to go to get in out of the cold?" Sybil gripped one of the metal bars framing the upper half of Sandy's stall as she watched him fill Sandy's water pail.

Chandler shook his head. "I'm afraid not." He gave her a smile as he put the grain scoop away. "I'm sure you've noticed cows out in all sorts of weather. Most of the time horses, too. Sandy's pretty lucky to have her own little space. And my cows have lots of places to go for shelter in the heat and the cold, so don't be worrying about them."

Sybil shook her head. "It just doesn't seem right. I've seen mothers give birth in freezing weather and calves barely old enough to walk try to navigate frozen mud."

"That's how it goes. It can be a rough life."

"Spoken like a true cowboy." Sybil muttered the words as she followed Chandler from the barn.

He turned, slowing his gait. "Just how many cowboys have you've known over the years?"

"You and Blu are the only two I've personally known. But I've done a lot of observing. It just seems like a hard existence and a lot of work. Not something I would ever want to do."

Chandler stopped, his eyes traveling over her face. "It *is* a lot of work, but it's honest work. I'm proud of the way I make my living. It's just a way of life that gets into your bones, and I don't want to live any other way. I wouldn't know how to, for that matter."

Sybil looked away, clearing her throat. "How about some supper? That's something I know a little about."

"That sounds good to me. I'm hungry, and I wasn't looking forward to trying to scrounge something up in my kitchen." Chandler continued toward the house. "If you don't mind, I'd like to take a quick shower so you don't have to smell Sandy while we eat."

Sybil paused beside her car. "If *you* don't mind, I can run into town while you do that. I just thought of something I forgot. You could take the crockpot in and set it on low. I'll be right back." She opened the door and took a large crockpot from the floor.

Chandler sniffed, closing his eyes as she passed the appliance to him. "That smells just like my mother's kitchen. What did you make?"

Sybil laughed as she slid into her car. "No peeking! Just plug it in and turn it on low."

Chandler gave her a puppy-dog look. "You are coming back, right? I mean, I won't be eating this alone or waiting for hours?" He shrugged. "You kind of got my hopes up about eating a home-cooked meal and spending the evening with you."

Sybil smiled. "I'll be back." She gave him a flirty grin. "I was looking forward to the evening with you, as well. I'll hurry." She closed her door and turned down the driveway, her taillights disappearing in the gathering darkness.

You just about blew that one! Telling Sybil that you wouldn't do anything else for a living, and how much this life meant to you…and after she told you she wouldn't do it! Idiotic stuff just flows out of your mouth. You should give yourself a good slap, Chandler! That's no way to win her over.

He climbed the steps to the deck, his boots thumping in the stillness. Opening the door, he backed his way into the dining room and set the crockpot on the kitchen island before closing the door. *But what else could you have said. You aren't going to live any other way. This place is your life. This house is where you want to raise your family. You know it will be miserable if you marry someone that doesn't appreciate what you've accomplished here.*

His mind raced back to the conversation he had had with Crystal all those months ago.

Chandler shook his head. *You're right, Crystal. Sybil doesn't have a clue about this life. All those points you brought up make perfect, logical sense. I can't disagree with them.* His eyes tracked to the crockpot and he sniffed. *Except Sybil's a pretty good cook.* He groaned, tossing his hat onto the dining room table and ruffling his hair into spiky points. *But I never felt about Crystal the way I do about Sybil. I was never physically attracted her, and Sybil makes my heart race just by hearing her voice, or catching her looking at me. Falling in love with Crystal and marrying her would have been the best, most simple solution for me and for the Waters family. Everyone would have been happy. Yes, even me! I hadn't known anything else, until…*

Sybil's snapping green eyes came into focus, and he smiled at remembered, sarcastic quips. Her red lips curved into a smile, and he wanted to feel their softness with his own. He wanted her near him…always.

God, none of this makes logical sense. I know You're a God of order, but I also understand that You work in ways not known to us. Marrying Crystal and living my life with her would have made sense. Loving Sybil makes no sense to me. But I do love her! You're going to have to show me how this is all going to work out. Sybil just told me she doesn't want to spend her life doing what I do. She's a lawyer! She doesn't have to clean stalls, make endless meals for grumpy men, and sit up all night with sick children and animals. She has made more money in the past few years than I'll ever see. But it's in Your hands. I'm following You!

PARKING HER CAR OUTSIDE THE café, Sybil rushed in and stopped Genie by placing a hand on her shoulder.

Genie looked down at the four plates of steaming food she had staggered on her arms. "If you'd like to find a seat, I'll be right with you, Sybil."

Sybil backed away, taking a deep breath. "I'm sorry, Genie. I'm in a bit of a hurry. I forgot all about dessert, and I know he really likes dessert. I should have thought about it. I mean, I had all day to prepare the chicken—" Sybil winced. "I'll let you finish what you were doing." She pointed to the dessert display case. "I'll be right over there."

Genie raised a brow. "Thank you, Sybil, that's right nice of you, considering I have third-degree burns on my arms from standing here passing the day with you." She hissed as she continued to the table. "You're not the only one in the world, you know!"

Sybil rolled her eyes, and greeted the customers that had overheard the conversation. "I heard it's supposed to be getting cold tonight."

They nodded, then shook their heads as they went back to their food.

Genie came up behind the counter and set her hands on her hips.

"What do you need, Sybil? Are you all out of lettuce at your place?"

Sybil grimaced as she gestured at Genie's forearms. "You *are* red. Maybe you should put some cold water on them."

Genie crossed her arms. "Yes, I could do that, and put my feet to soaking at the same time. They're killing me. But unlike you, I have to work. You must remember how busy we are on a Friday night. You worked here once upon a time."

Sybil glanced at the ceiling. "Don't remind me. It was the most miserable summer of my life."

"I really need to get back to work. We had a waitress call in tonight, so along with being busy, we're shorthanded."

The cook poked his head through the space separating the dining room and kitchen. "Genie, you have plates backing up over here. These people don't want cold food."

"I'm coming!" Genie turned back to Sybil. "See? I don't have all night. What do you need?"

"Well, it's kind of a strange request—"

"Genie!" The cook's voice traveled through the dining room.

Sybil took off her leather jacket and draped it over the high stool at the counter. "Please, let me help you get those plates out, then I'll tell you what I need. This rush can't last forever, right?"

"Seriously?" Genie's eyes looked Sybil up and down. "You're not afraid of getting your pretty shirt all dirty?"

Sybil glanced down at the chocolate brown silk. "I didn't volunteer to do the dishes…just carry out a few plates."

"Genie!"

The older woman turned and took two plates from the stainless steel shelf. "These go to that table right over there. Be sure to ask if they need anything else. I'll be around with more coffee after I get these plates out."

Sybil tilted her head and stared at Genie. "I can handle coffee refills."

Genie gave a lopsided grin. "Yes, you can. You keep acting like this, and I'll have to be nice to you…and not just on Sundays at church."

Sybil laughed as she walked to the table.

TURNING THE CAR OFF, SYBIL grabbed the large bag from the seat and slid from the warm leather. The light coming from the back deck of Chandler's house beckoned her. Rushing up the steps, she stopped when she saw him hunched over in a chair, his fleece-lined denim jacket collar pulled up to his ears. "Why are you sitting out here? You're going to freeze. The temperature has dropped a lot since—"

Chandler stood, his height even more intimidating with the bulky jacket and cowboy hat. He shoved his hands into his jean pockets. "I didn't think you were coming back. I took my shower, and I waited inside the house for a while. Then I came out here. I just kept thinking that I had misheard you, and maybe you left the food for me to eat…alone." The corners of his mouth drooped down. "That made me really sad."

Sybil pressed her lips together, tears forming as she walked to him. "You look so pitiful. Please don't be sad." She set the large plastic bag on the chair next to the one Chandler had vacated. "You didn't peek in the crockpot, did you?"

Chandler shook his head. "Not even once." He took her by the elbows and pulled her toward him. "Where have you been? You left here almost two hours ago! Do you know how worried I've been?"

Sybil moved her head back and forth, looking up at him through her lashes. "I'm really sorry. I didn't even think to call. I was in such a hurry, rushing to get back here as quickly as possible so we could spend the evening together."

"I thought something had happened to you. Maybe a car accident…" Chandler gripped her elbows tighter, staring down at her.

Sybil met his gaze, her eyes sliding down to the lips so very close to her own.

Chandler groaned, pulling her close as he kissed her, his lips moving over hers and then to her cheek, then her temple. He pulled back, taking her face in his hands, his eyes inches from hers. "I can't lose you, Sybil. I don't want to live without you. Even if you hate this place, I want you to be here, with me."

Tears spilled over, sliding down Sybil's cheeks. "I don't hate this place. I love it here. Would there be another reason I come over so often? I feel at home here. Why do you think I learned to clean stalls and paint and do all sorts of stuff I've never done before? I wanted to be here…with you!"

He kissed her again, his lips drinking her in, pulling her into his soul. "I love you, Sybil!" The words were whispered soft and low against the corner of her mouth.

Rearing back, Sybil looked up at him, her eyes wide and shimmering. "Really?"

Chandler grinned, his hands sliding up her arms to grip her shoulders. "Yes…really! Is that so difficult for you to grasp?"

"No man has ever said that to me before." Sybil glanced away. "I realize I can be rather unlovable sometimes."

Chandler cleared his throat, brushing her chin with his thumb. "Sometimes?"

She nodded. "Okay, maybe more than sometimes. But…" she

held up one finger, "I am working on that. I think I may have made some progress tonight."

Chandler scratched his forehead. "Tonight?"

Sybil sighed, gesturing at the large bag on the chair. "I realized after I got here that I didn't plan anything for dessert. I worked all day on the chicken and dumplings—"

"*You* made chicken and dumplings?" Chandler raised a brow.

"Well, don't sound so shocked! I can cook. I usually keep it more on the simple side, and I try not to eat flour, sugar, and dairy—"

"That about rules out anything that tastes good." Chandler grinned. "No wonder you're the size of a stick."

"If I ate all that *stuff* on a regular basis, I'd be the size of a house." She shrugged. "I understand that not everyone eats the same way. I know there is a balance, and I'm really trying. That's why I made you chicken and dumplings. It seemed like a dish you would enjoy."

"It's only my favorite. I requested it every year for my birthday. That and—"

"Chocolate cake?" Sybil tilted her head. "How does that sound for dessert?"

Chandler laughed. "Yes, chocolate was always my birthday cake choice. But how'd you know that?"

Sybil crossed her arms, shivering with the cold. "I went in—"

Chandler grabbed the bag from the chair and took her arm, leading her to the bright lights illuminating the French doors. "You can tell me inside. It's crazy to stand out here when there's a perfectly warm house within a couple steps."

"Thank you! I was wondering how long it took to get frostbite." Sybil laughed as she walked through the door and into the cozy dining room. Her eyes swept over the table. "You even set the table." She put one hand on her hip. "How did you know to put soup bowls on? You really did peek."

Chandler set the bag at the end of the table and raised his hands. "I didn't. I figured if something was in a crockpot, it had to be soup-like. That's as far as it went." He walked up behind her. "Let me take your coat, and then you can finish telling me how you knew I liked chocolate cake."

Sybil shrugged out of her coat. "Genie said you *loved* their chocolate cake."

Chandler groaned. "I must admit, I think it's even better than my mother's. But don't ever tell her I said that."

Sybil went to the crockpot and lifted the lid, checking the contents. "So, I went into Wheatacre to check the grocery store for something dessert-like. Then I remembered that the café sold cakes, cookies and pies. I thought they had to be better than what I could find at the store. When I arrived at the café, Genie was swamped. Friday night is one of their busiest nights, and a waitress had called in." She motioned for Chandler to bring the bowls. "I thought I could hand out some of the orders backing up, and then I'd ask Genie what you liked for dessert. It ended up taking a lot longer than I expected."

Chandler braced one hand on the counter and watched as she ladled the stew into the bowls. "I wouldn't mind a couple more of those dumplings. Since you don't care for flour and milk, I'm more than happy to eat your share."

Sybil laughed. "You can have seconds, you know. I made plenty." She winced as she scooped a dumpling into his bowl. "Although these may be a little on the rubbery side after cooking for so long. I should have thought about that when I was playing waitress."

"They look delicious to me." Chandler walked the bowls to

the table. "I still can't believe you stayed and helped through the dinner rush. Have you ever waitressed?"

Sybil filled the water glasses. "Of course! I worked at the café the summer before I left for college. I wouldn't have offered to help otherwise. Genie was a real grouch some days, but she knew her job and she trained me well."

Chandler pulled out her chair and gestured for her to sit down. "So, the café has a new waitress. I'll have to go in there more often."

Sybil scowled at him. "Are you kidding? It has to be one of the worst jobs a person could have. The tips are terrible, and people can be just rude at times."

"I would think a good waitress could turn that all around." He gave her a wink. "I would tip you *very* well."

Sybil took a deep breath. *If you had stared at me like that, I would have probably dropped your plate! No tip for me! Those blue eyes make me so flustered that I can't even think straight.* She laid her napkin in her lap. "Well, my pay for tonight was a chocolate cake. Genie made sure the frosting was nice and thick and she sent a container of whipped cream along. She said you really liked it that way."

Chandler smiled. "I sure do!" He rubbed his hands together. "Let's pray so I can get started on this first bowl. I'm hungry!" He held his hand out to her. "Would you hold my hand while I pray?"

Sybil obliged, sliding her slim fingers into his.

Chapter Twenty

CHANDLER LEANED BACK AND PATTED his lean abdomen. "That was really good. You make great coffee." His eyes swept over her face. "If you remember, I never had a chance to try your coffee that Sunday I stopped by. We were in a rush to eat and get to church."

"I remember. I used it for iced coffee the next day. Coffee with a splash of almond milk, and a tiny dash of caramel syrup all poured over ice is wonderful."

"I'll take your word for it. Coffee should stand well on its own, nice and dark, and very strong."

Scooping the last bite of cake from her plate, Sybil smiled. "You sound like my father. He doesn't see the point of drinking it any other way."

"I think your father and I have a lot in common. I really like it the way my father makes it over a campfire. Just dump the coffee in after you bring the water to a boil and let it sit for a few minutes. The grounds will sink to the bottom."

Sybil winced. "Doesn't sound too difficult, but you probably need to know what you're doing. I just picture a mouthful of nasty coffee grounds. I know I don't like to chew my coffee."

Chandler laughed. "You get one every now and then, but nothing serious. I knew one fellow that put hot water in a thermos and added coffee. By the time he was ready for a break after riding for a couple hours, the coffee was ready."

Sybil slid her chair back. "That sounds relatively disgusting."

"Where are you going?" Chandler's eyes followed her slim figure as she stood, laying her napkin on the table.

"I'm going to clear the table and do the dishes." Sybil gathered the cake plates and forks.

Chandler leaned forward, placing his hand over her arm. "I don't want you to do that…really. You made the meal, and I'll clean up…later." His hand slid down her arm, taking her wrist as he stood. "We have some things we need to discuss."

Sybil's eyes widened. "I don't know what you mean."

Chandler led her into the front room and motioned for her to take a seat on the sofa. He braced his legs, shoving his hands into the pockets of his jeans as he stared down at her. "You can't dance around the subject all evening, Sybil."

She clasped her hands in her lap and repeated her last sentence. "I don't know what you mean."

Chandler knelt down, meeting her eye-to-eye. He covered her hands with his. "I told you that I loved you."

She nodded, looking away from him. "I heard you."

He reached out, turning her face back to him with a gentle nudge on the chin. "I kissed you twice, and I told you I loved you."

Sybil pressed her lips together. "Those kisses were very…nice."

Chandler raised a brow. "They were *nice*?" He stood, running his fingers over the back of his neck. He sat down in the chair across from the sofa.

She raised her shoulders. "I don't know what else to say. I told you earlier that no man had ever said those words to me."

Rubbing his forehead, Chandler closed his eyes for a moment. *Maybe I've read this all wrong. After all, she didn't say she loved me, but I thought she seemed excited after I said the words to her. Maybe she really* is *just lonely, and I'm the guy to fill in her time until the right one comes along. Meaning the guy who has a six-figure income and a huge house...and drives a really nice sports car.* The sound of crying jerked his eyes open.

"Sybil, what is it? What have I done wrong?" Chandler stood, rushing to her side. "I can't take the words back, but I won't say them again if they make you unhappy. I...I thought maybe you cared a little for me. I didn't mean to offend you." He sat down and slumped back against the sofa, rubbing his hands up and down his face. "I don't know what I'm doing here. I have no experience with all of this dating stuff. I haven't been given a list of the proper things to say to a woman that you care about. All I know is how I feel inside when I'm with you."

Sybil swiped at her cheeks. "And you think I'm any better? I never dated. I had a relationship with one other man, and it was for all the wrong reasons. We didn't love one another, we were just there and convenient."

"That's more than I've had."

Sybil turned to face him. "Exactly! How can I be happy that you love me, or say you love me? You told me I wasn't good enough for you."

"I never said those words!" Chandler gaped at her.

"You told me you had saved yourself for your wife. I'm already damaged goods. I can't undo that part of my life. I'm not what you've waited for."

Chandler shook his head. "We talked about this that day in the truck. I love you, and I want to marry you, Sybil. Your past doesn't matter to me."

Sybil gasped, staring at him. "You would be letting yourself down to love me, to marry me. You deserve better than what I can give you."

"Why do you keep saying that?"

Tears trickled down her cheeks. "Because it's true. You and Crystal should be together. She understands you, knows about being a rancher's wife, and she loves you so much."

Chandler swallowed deeply, clearing his throat. "So you don't care about me at all? I know you said that you would never live this way, but you could still practice law. I can run this place by myself. I have for a couple years now. You don't have to be a part of it."

Sybil offered a weak smile. "But isn't that what marriage is all about? Wanting to share the other person's life?"

Chandler looked away. "I'm just trying to find workable solutions. But if you have no interest, if you don't care about me, then we have nothing to discuss."

Sybil took his hand in hers. "I do care, Chandler. I have for several months now."

He returned his gaze to her. "Then what's the problem?"

Taking a deep breath, Sybil bit her lip. "Blu and I were together."

Chandler laughed. "Is that what this is all about? I know, he told me you went to the river that night. He also informed me that you wouldn't have anything to do with him." He smiled. "I think his words were, *when I tried to get friendly, the claws came out.*"

Sybil gulped. "Chandler, Blu and I were *together* another time. That Sunday before they left, back around Independence Day."

Chandler wrinkled his brow. "That evening that Blu took Sandy for a ride, and didn't return until almost midnight?"

Sybil nodded, the tears flowing freely. "I don't know why I did it." She shook her head. "No, that's not true. I was upset about the conversation I'd had with Crystal at the café, and I was lonely. I wanted to feel close to someone again...in that way. Because I'd already had that kind of relationship with Scott, it felt like it didn't matter." She covered her face. "See, that's what I've been trying to tell you. I'm not good enough for you. I can't change the things I've done."

She dropped her hands, her eyes flashing as she stared at him. "And I can't stand that you make me feel that way! Not all of us are perfect like you, Chandler Byron! Some of us have done stupid things…maybe more than one time." She struggled to her feet. "Where's my coat?"

Chandler's eyes were dark pools, reflecting the hurt and pain as he looked up at her. "Blu never said anything to me. He always bragged about his conquests."

"Well, maybe I'm just bad at that too. There was no reason for him to crow." Her eyes traveled the room. "Where's my coat? I need to leave before I make a complete idiot out of myself. I don't cry in front of people, and I've already done way too much of that tonight."

Chandler stood, taking her arm. "Your coat's on the back of the chair, but you can't leave, Sybil. We need to talk about this. Running away won't solve anything."

Sybil's lips became a red line on her pale face. "Really? Do you still love me after knowing what Blu and I did together? Do you want to marry me now?"

Chandler blinked, and then looked away as he let her arm go.

Sneering, Sybil turned, throwing over her shoulder, "That's what I thought." She rushed to grab her jacket.

Chandler followed her to the French doors leading to the deck. "Please, Sybil, give me a chance."

His answer was the sound of her boots on the deck as she disappeared into the dark.

SYBIL RAN TO HER CAR, slipping on the grass gleaming with tiny crystals. Her back met the hard ground and she gasped. Pushing to her feet, she groped for her leather jacket, finding it a few feet from where she had landed. She shoved her arms into the sleeves, continuing to the car. In seconds she had left the glow from the windows of Chandler's house and headed into the inky night, her headlights bouncing off the tall grass beside the driveway.

At the road, she stopped, gripping the steering wheel as she laid her head against it. Sobs shook her thin frame. *You've done it. You have destroyed any chance with Chandler. Always worrying about yourself and what makes you feel good. Well, you did what felt good with Blu, and now you're going to pay the price. The only man you've ever loved just turned away from you in disgust. Can you blame him? Blu is his best friend. You've never sunk so low.*

She leaned back against the leather, letting her head roll back and forth. *Happiness was so close…within my reach. I've let it all sift right through my hands.* She sneered. *No, I threw it right in Chandler's face. All that he offered.* Tears streamed down her face as she sat up, staring into the dark night. *You asked me to give you a chance. I am. For the first time in my life, I'm going to walk away and do what's best for the other person. I'm giving you the chance to have a life with someone else. A woman that has lived her life for God, a woman that can understand your life and your ways.*

Sybil buried her face in her hands. *I love you, Chandler, but Crystal is waiting. I will give you the chance to be happy with her, build a life together, and do all those things you're so good at.*

CHANDLER RUBBED HIS EYE AND blinked, the rising sun pinkening the sky in his rearview mirror. His eyes traveled over the eastern Colorado landscape, so similar to what he'd been driving through in Kansas. *Just a couple more hours, Blu. I'll get to the bottom of this.*

He narrowed his eyes as he concentrated on the view out his windshield and then smiled. *There they are.* The mountains rose out of the awakening land, their white peaks tinged a cantaloupe hue. *How I have missed this glorious view!* He rolled down his window, thrusting his left hand out as he took a deep breath. *Colorado air, chilly and no humidity. How I wish you could be here with me, Sybil, to see this beautiful morning painting the skies.*

He rubbed his forehead. *That's crazy thinking! You're tired from driving all night. Sybil wants nothing to do with you. She wouldn't even give you a chance.*

Almost two hours later, he turned south off of Highway 24, his tires crunching on the gravel road. Several miles passed, and he stopped the red truck just before the stone arch welcoming visitors to the Rocky Waters Ranch. Chandler gritted his teeth and took a deep, cleansing breath. *Remember, Blu's your best friend, and has been all of your life. Don't do anything stupid.*

He closed his eyes and bowed his head. *Father, help me to stay calm. Give me patience and understanding of what has taken place with Blu and the woman I love. Help me to have faith in You, and know that You are in control. I don't understand how this is going to all work out. All I know is that I love Sybil, and I want her to be my wife. That seems crazy to me given the circumstances, but I have peace that is what is supposed to take place.* He squeezed his eyes together. *And Father, keep a restraining hand on me concerning Blu. Because right now I want to strangle him! In Your Son's name, amen.*

Chandler opened his eyes, his gaze drifting over the landscape. The Waters and Byron ranches were separated by the graveled road he sat on. The long road beginning at the stone arch wound its way into the dark pine trees. He smiled with the memory of long walks up the drive leading to the Waters' impressive log home. But more often than not, he and Blu had been on horseback, racing to see who arrived first, amidst the dust they stirred up.

At the sound of a vehicle approaching, Chandler watched out his side mirror as the truck roared down the road and skidded to a stop just behind Chandler's. *Of course, it would have to be you, Blu. I don't even have the privilege of a few more minutes to compose my thoughts and actions. Might as well get this over with.* Chandler grabbed his hat from the bench seat and set it on his head as he climbed from the truck. He slammed his door shut, setting his hands on his hips as he turned to face Blu.

"I thought that looked like Big Red! How's it going? You haven't been in these parts for a long time, friend." Blu grinned as he strode up, swiping at Chandler's arm. "You should have let me know you were coming. We could have had breakfast in town."

Chandler fisted the hands on his hips. "My trip wasn't exactly planned. Sybil told me all about you and her getting together that night you took Sandy for a ride. That takes some nerve to borrow my horse and then…" Chandler swallowed, looking away. His gaze returned to Blu as he cleared his throat. "You had sex with the woman you knew I cared about."

Blu swept the cowboy hat from his head, and smoothed his hand through his hair before replacing it. "Don't tell me you drove all the way over here…" he gestured to Chandler's stubbled cheeks, "and in the middle of the night, by the looks of it, to talk about something that happened last summer."

Chandler's eyes darkened as he leveled his gaze at Blu. "That's exactly what I'm telling you."

Blu shook his head. "Well, if you don't mind me saying, that was real stupid. You could have called me on the phone if you wanted to know what that little tease was up to."

Chandler's fist swung, catching the side of Blu's chin. "I couldn't have done that over the phone…friend."

Blu reeled back, his hat knocked to the road. He put his hand to his jaw. "You shouldn't have done that, Chandler. Not after the way you led my sister on for years and then dumped her in the dust for that little hussy."

Chandler thumped his finger against Blu's chest. "Don't call her that! It's not true."

Blu snorted, scooping his hat from the road. He brushed it off. "It wasn't the first time Sybil had ridden that particular horse. She knew what she was doing."

"And you took complete advantage of that, just like you always have." Chandler rubbed his knuckles. "I always knew you were hard-headed."

"Yes, I am. And you'd better be thankful that I didn't punch you back. I don't take kindly to being hit. You're the only person that would get away with it."

Chandler ground his finger against Blu's chest once more. "And *you'd* better be thankful that I didn't strangle you with my bare hands like I thought of doing all night. Good thing it was a long drive over here."

"Not long enough, in my opinion." Blu pushed his hat back down on his head. "Now, are you going to talk about this like a man, or are we going to just punch it out right here in the middle of the road?"

Chandler thumbed his own chest. "You're asking *me* that? I'm the one with my head glued on straight. You're the one going around having relationships with women that you shouldn't be doing anything with. You knew how vulnerable Sybil was after everything that happened last winter in Kansas City. You should have stayed away. Not gone in for the kill."

Blu shrugged. "She wanted it just as much as I did. I'm not going to feel sorry about anything, Chandler. Sybil's a grown woman, and she can make up her mind for herself. If you wanted someone as pure as the driven snow, you could have had Crystal, but you didn't want her."

"I told you last summer that I never said anything to Crystal implying that I loved her or that we were going to get married. It's what she made up in her mind." Chandler sighed. "Like I said, I never wanted to hurt Crystal, but I can't feel something that's not there."

"But you can get all high and mighty about Sybil...the kind of woman you said you would never have a thing to do with." Blu shook his head. "You're messed up."

"Not as messed up as someone that goes around having sex with women for fun. No commitment, no love, no sacrifice on your part." Chandler looked away, rolling his eyes.

Blu laughed. "You just don't get it, do you? I told you back in high school that I didn't think about sex the same way you did. I'm fine with having some fun with someone that wants to do the same." He shrugged. "It might last a night like it did with Sybil, or maybe a few weeks. If you're real lucky you find someone that makes it good for longer. I don't think that something that feels so *good* should be for the happily wedded only."

Chandler nodded. "I recall you saying that back when we were teenagers. I thought you'd grown up by now. But I guess not."

Blu pointed a finger at Chandler. "For your information, I asked Sybil to marry me—"

"What?" Chandler gaped at Blu. "Based on one night together? Did you even talk to her?"

Blu lifted his shoulders as he shoved his hands into his jean pockets. "Sure, we talked that night down by the river. Enough to know that I liked her…a lot. I thought we had some things in common. She was the first woman that I thought I could get used to seeing every morning when I woke up."

"You went after her because you knew I was interested. Plain and simple. You like a challenge, which is why you pursued Sybil."

Blu nodded. "Probably."

Chandler scoffed. "What was her answer? Or were the two of you keeping that a secret as well? Do I need to wait for my wedding invitation in the mail?"

Blu walked over to his truck and braced his elbows on the hood. "She told me I was insane. That we didn't love one another."

Chandler nodded, crossing his arms. "Well, at least one of you has some sense."

Chapter Twenty-One

SYBIL TOSSED THE GARLAND ONTO the leather sofa and crossed her arms. "I'm sorry, Elvira, but I can't just pretend that nothing is wrong. I'm not in the mood to decorate for Christmas."

Elvira twisted her hair and anchored it with a clip. "I know it's difficult, but keeping your mind off of Chandler will help. If you stay busy, you won't have so much time to think about what he's doing." She motioned to the large window. "The flurries outside make it seem just like winter. Never mind that's about as far as it will go. It still makes it seem festive." She retrieved the garland that Sybil had tossed. "I can make us some hot chocolate."

Sybil offered a smile. "I know you're really trying to make me feel better." Her eyes scanned the room. "And normally I would be thrilled to help you decorate and make something beautiful out of my father's fifty-year-old collection of plastic greenery—"

Elvira gasped, fingering the dark green holly leaf. "There's a lot of life left in these. You can't buy quality garlands and wreaths like this anymore."

Sybil rolled her eyes. "Thank goodness!"

Elvira dropped the garland back to the sofa and sat down next to it. "Sybil, if you're really wanting to see Chandler that badly, just go over there and talk to him. Sitting here and moping around doesn't solve anything."

Sybil plopped into the leather chair. "I shouldn't have to go over there. He should have come here, or even called by now. He's the one that said he loved me and wanted to marry me." She scoffed. "What a joke that was! They were just empty words."

Grayson entered the room, strolling over to Sybil as he flicked his gray tail. He sat at her feet and looked up at her. "Meow."

"Oh, no you don't. I don't want to be covered with cat hair." Sybil crossed her legs.

Grayson stood, his tail standing straight as he turned with a look back at Sybil. He put his nose in the air.

Elvira called him over. "I'm sorry she's so rude. But you know she's not much of a cat person—"

"Or dog, rabbit, gerbil..." Sybil shook her head. "That doesn't make me rude or mean. Just not an animal lover."

Elvira smiled, green eyes twinkling. "How about horses and cows?"

Sybil looked away, staring out the window. "That's different. They stay outside." She propped one elbow on the wide arm of the chair and rested her chin in the palm of her hand. "I wonder if Chandler's cows are able to get out of the storm?"

Elvira bent down, lifting Grayson to her lap. "What storm? We're having a few snow flurries. It's about time, too. It's December, after all." She patted Grayson's head. "You are welcome to sit here as long as you like. It's nice to snuggle on a cold winter's day."

Sybil stood, smoothing her sweater down over her hips. "You know what? I'm going to drive over there and talk to that man. He can't just say he loves me and tell me he wants to get married and then ignore me for a month. I'm not going to stand for that."

Elvira wrinkled her brow, her eyes still twinkling. "I wouldn't either. He needs to make good on those words."

Sybil scowled. "Now you're making fun of me."

Elvira shook her head. "Really, I'm not. It's just rather nice to see you vulnerable, and in love."

Sybil dropped her shoulders. "Does it really show that much? I don't want to seem too eager...like I've been waiting here for him."

"But you have been, Sybil." Elvira smoothed her hand over Grayson's plump tummy. "Don't play games. It almost always backfires, and then you get burned."

"So I'm just supposed to go over there and spill all my feelings out for him to sort through and pick which ones are good enough for him to accept?"

"Chandler is not like that, and you know it. I'm sure he's just giving you some time and space to sort out what you feel for him. He's probably spending a bit of time wrapping his mind around what you told him about you and Blu." Elvira's eyes met Sybil's. "If he really does care for you like I think he does, that had to have been very hurtful to him."

Sybil rubbed her forehead. "I know, and I wish I could go back and make different choices." She crossed her arms and walked over to the window. The flurries drifted lazily to the ground, melting as they touched. The afternoon was dreary and cold, causing her to shiver and turn away from the window. "I *am* going over. Life is too short for me to let my pride get in the way. Chandler wanted to talk that night, and I should have stayed. But I let all my emotions get in the way again."

"I think that sounds like a great idea." Elvira scratched Grayson under the chin. The cat purred, closing his eyes.

Sybil paused by the sofa. "Thanks for the offer of hot chocolate. Do you have any of those cookies you made the other day? Maybe if I bring a peace offering it will ease the way."

Elvira laughed. "You can look in that ice cream bucket on the counter. But your father may have eaten them all. I keep telling him I want to do some Christmas baking, but I'm afraid it won't even make it until then."

Sybil smiled. "That sounds like Dad. All sweets are his friends."

SYBIL MANEUVERED THE MERCEDES OVER the graveled driveway, topping the hill in front of Chandler's house. She frowned at the unfamiliar truck in front of the barn. She stopped beside it and got out, pulling the fur-lined hood of her coat over her head. The wind whistled around the big building, snatching brown leaves from against it and tossing them into the air. They danced with random snowflakes before continuing their journey down the hill.

An older man slid the barn door open and exited the dark interior. He glanced over at Sybil as he pulled the door closed. "Can I help you?"

Sybil's eyes traveled around the yard between the barn and house. "Um… I was looking for Chandler Byron. This is *his* place, after all." Her green eyes scanned the figure from his grizzled beard to his worn-out cowboy boots.

He opened the truck door and threw his work gloves onto the seat. "Who's looking for him?" He added another wrinkle to the lined forehead with a lift of a salt-and-pepper-colored brow.

Sybil straightened on her heeled boots, looking down on the bow-legged man. "I'm Sybil Grafton. I'm a friend of Chandler's."

He slammed the door shut, putting one gnarled hand on the rim of the truck bed. "I thought I recognized you." He pointed to her hood. "Not many people dress like that around here." He spit a stream of tobacco juice toward the barn doors. Wiping his hand across his chin, he narrowed his eyes at her. "You say you're a friend of Chandler's, but I would think that a *friend* would know that he's in Colorado. Has been for about a month now."

She gasped. "No, he didn't say anything about going to Colorado." Her eyes looked toward the pasture. "What about Sandy?"

"She's over at my place. Whenever Chandler visits family he brings her over. Likes it, too, she does. There's other horses for her to talk to."

Sybil cleared her throat. "Does he visit family often?"

Another stream of tobacco interrupted the conversation. "No. When he first moved here he went home two, three times a year. But it's been a long time now. I take care of Sandy and the cows, just like I did for Black Byron when this was his place."

Sybil pressed her lips together, flicking a strand of hair out of her lipstick. "Um…do you know when he's returning?"

The man chuckled, shaking his head. "All I know is he came by my place with Sandy kind of late on a Friday night. He bedded her down and took off. Said something about a pretty lady and a wedding." He motioned toward her. "But I guess if you're standing here, you're not the pretty lady." He thumped his hand on the truck. "I have to get going. Tell your grandpa I said hello. He'll know who Spry is."

Sybil gaped as she watched the old cowboy get into his truck and rumble away.

You did it. You went home and married Crystal…and all because I let my pride get in the way of staying to talk that night. I should have told you how much I love you, how much I want to be a part of your life. She turned tear-swollen eyes to take in the little house on the hill, and the view of the silver river weaving among the bare cottonwoods. *We could have shared this together, Chandler. I would have grown to love it here.*

She put her back against the aged, rough walls of the barn. *I've lost it all. I was hateful, only thinking of myself, just as I've always done. I used Blu.* She closed her eyes. *I even used Scott. I've taken advantage of my father and Elvira. Where does the list end of all that I've done wrong, the people that I've harmed with my waspish tongue and selfish ways?*

Swallowing, Sybil squeezed her eyes tight, tears seeping through. *I need You, God. I really do. I can't fix my life on my own. I've tried for years to run from You. Again, my pride and arrogance getting in the way. I have nothing more to lose. I have no job, no place of my own, and I've done all that I can to chase away family and friends. I don't have the answers to fix my life…but I know You do. Please show me how. I've lost Chandler, and I don't want to live with the person that I am. I really don't like…me.*

The snowflakes became bigger, drifting softly to the ground. Sybil stood against the barn, crying gently in the cold air as the sun lowered over the cottonwoods.

CHANDLER TOSSED THE DUFFEL BAG into the truck and slammed the door, turning to Blu. "I've forgiven you, but you understand if I don't ask you to be my best man or invite you to the wedding, right?"

Blu rubbed the back of his neck as he nodded. "Yeah, I can see how that may be a problem for Sybil."

Chandler scoffed, squinting in the predawn light. "Not just Sybil. I'm still just a second away from giving you a good thrashing." One corner of his mouth lifted up.

Blu pursed his lips. "I guess I can understand that. If I was in love with a woman, and you'd done what I did, I'd be kind of sore for a while." Blu kicked at the blanket of snow covering the ground. "I do appreciate you coming back and facing me…even if you were angry. We've been friends for a long time. I'd like to keep it that way." He tilted his head. "You're sure you won't stay for Christmas? It's only a couple more weeks. I know your parents would really like that."

Chandler shook his head. "It's time for me to go. I've been here too long already. I don't want to take advantage of Spry, and I have my class at church." He gave a lopsided grin. "Besides, my parents have enough family at their house Christmas morning. My brothers are trying to populate this end of Colorado all by themselves."

Blu chuckled. "It'll be hard for you to catch up at the rate they're going." Blu cleared his throat. "Seriously, Chandler...I do appreciate you coming. I'm really sorry about what happened with Sybil. But some good may have come out of it. I think it put our friendship on a different level. I kind of enjoyed our time of prayer in the mornings, and I'll be looking into those verses you shared with me."

Chandler nodded. "I'm really happy to hear that."

Lifting his shoulders, Blu took a deep breath. "I guess it's time for me to grow up. Almost losing my best friend because of my selfishness...well, it was an eye-opener." He swallowed, looking away. "You'd better get on the road, and I've got chores to do." He turned back. "I always thought I'd be at your wedding, giving you a hard time..." he grinned, "and just making the day miserable for you."

"Thanks, I appreciate the sentiment." Chandler walked around Big Red and opened the door.

Blu kicked at the snow once again. "It might not mean much coming from me under the circumstances, but I wish you and Sybil all the best. She has attitude, but I can see you two making it work." He shrugged. "Just saying my two-cents' worth."

Chandler glanced up at the pinkening sky. "Don't get ahead of yourself, Blu. She hasn't said she'd marry me yet. And if she does, knowing Sybil, it will be a drawn-out lavish affair." He propped both arms on the top of the door. "I'll be back, and you're always welcome to visit. You may have to bunk down in the barn, though." He pressed his lips together. "You're on the right track, Blu. Just keep it up, and remember that God's always there to direct you." He jumped into the truck and started the engine as he pulled the door shut. He tipped his hat at Blu and began the journey home.

JOGGING UP THE STEPS TO the log house, Chandler took a deep breath as he crossed the porch and knocked on the door.

The door opened, Loren loosening his tie as he gave Chandler a smile. "Well, hello, stranger! Come on in. Elvira was just getting ready to put dinner on the table. You're welcome to eat with us."

Chandler took his hat from his head and crossed the threshold into the warm room. The fire snapped merrily in the stone fireplace. Chandler took a sniff. "It does smell delicious in here, but I'm kind of in a hurry. I do appreciate the invitation to dinner, though. I'll have to take a raincheck on that, if I may."

Elvira walked from the dining room, drying her hands on a towel. "Certainly! You know you're always welcome." She gestured one thumb toward the kitchen. "I have biscuits in the oven, just about ready to come out, so I'll let you two visit while I finish up. It's nice to have you home."

"Thank you, it's great to be back."

Loren stripped the tie from his neck and gave a sigh. "Never have liked those things. When did you get into town?"

"Just now, as a matter of fact. I haven't even checked on Sandy yet. I came straight here." Chandler moved his fingers around the brim of his hat. "Actually, I stopped at Sybil's place first. When she didn't answer, I thought she might be here. Would you happen to know where she is?"

Loren raised a brow. "I guess you didn't get her letter if you haven't been home." Loren cleared his throat. "Chandler, she moved back to Kansas City about two weeks ago. She just started working at a legal clinic there—"

"She's doing pro bono work?" Chandler gaped, dropping his hat to the floor.

Loren chuckled. "It was a bit of a surprise for us as well. She's staying with her friend Tarah until she finds a place of her own. It may take a while to find something she can afford."

Chandler picked up his hat and slumped into the chair. "I don't understand. What would make her just up and move like that? I mean, that's a big decision…and working pro bono? Sybil?" He shook his head.

Loren took a seat on the sofa, leaning forward to perch his elbows on his knees. "Chandler, she was convinced that you went back to Colorado to marry Crystal."

Chandler held up his left hand, pointing to his ring finger. "But I didn't! That's not why I went to Colorado." He leaned his head against the back of the chair, staring up at the loft. *What have I done, Father? I thought for sure You were going to work this all out. I prayed about it the whole way home. I thought she'd be here and I could explain everything.* Chandler straightened, leveling his gaze at Loren. "How did she get the idea that I was going to Colorado to get married? I've told her over and over that I wasn't going to marry Crystal."

Loren nodded. "I know, both Elvira and I tried to talk to her about that. She kept saying that Spry had said something about a pretty lady and a wedding, and that's why you had left."

Chandler slumped further down in the chair. "The night I dropped Sandy off at his place I told him I had some things to work out, but I would be marrying the prettiest lady around if she would have me." He groaned. "Spry was half asleep when I talked to him. You know him, he hears half of what you say and makes up the other half."

"That's Spry. I always figured that was part of the reason he never married. Women don't take kindly to that kind of behavior."

Elvira entered the room. "Are you talking about me again, dear husband of mine?"

Loren looked up at his wife, giving her a wink. "Certainly not. Chandler and I are trying to make sense of why Sybil left."

Elvira took a seat next to Loren. "She left because she was hurt and thought there was no chance with her and Chandler."

Chandler nodded. "I'm getting that part. But I don't understand why she would take another job doing something so out of character."

Elvira smiled. "Sybil and I had some long talks before she moved. She wasn't very happy with herself and the decisions she had made. She wanted to start over, in a sense. Be a better person."

Chandler rubbed his fingers over his forehead. "But she could have done that here."

Elvira raised a brow. "Just like you could have worked out your problems with Blu right here in Wheatacre?"

Chandler gaped.

Nodding, Elvira slid one hand to her husband's knee and gave it a pat. "Sybil told me all about it, and I'll explain everything to you later, Loren."

Loren sighed. "The husband is always the last to know."

Elvira met Chandler's eyes. "Do you love Sybil?"

Chandler's eyes did not waver. "Yes."

"Are you willing to marry her, knowing all that has happened in her life?"

"Yes!" Chandler's eyes darkened. "It is part of who she is. We all have past mistakes, burdens, and hurts that we carry with us. I want us to learn and grow together."

Elvira smiled. "I had a feeling you were going to say something like that." She glanced at Loren. "The love of a good person has a remarkable influence on a damaged soul. I know."

Elvira stood. "Sybil is hardest on herself, just as I was. But her moving back to Kansas City, facing her past there, and taking a job to solely help others, speaks volumes of what's changing in her heart." Elvira pointed at Chandler. "Now, she just needs God's guidance and your love."

Chapter Twenty-Two

*I*T SEEMS AS THOUGH I'M *always standing outside someone's door and knocking. Maybe I was called to be a door-to-door salesman instead of a cowboy.* Chandler smiled at his thoughts and then wrinkled his brow when he heard several bolts being unlocked.

The door opened just as wide as the chain would allow. An older, attractive face peeked around the door frame. "May I help you?" Her eyes slid over him, from the top of his blond head to his ropers and back up. The door shut.

Chandler stepped back with a frown, placing his hat on his head. *I must have read the address wrong.* He turned, fumbling in his shirt pocket for the piece of paper Loren had given him.

The door opened with a click. "Where are you going in such a hurry, cowboy?"

Looking over his shoulder, Chandler swept his hat off and turned, facing the petite woman. She wore a sapphire blue dressing gown, the deep 'v' gaping. He focused his eyes on her pert nose. "I'm sorry to bother you, ma'am. Loren Grafton gave me this address. I'm looking for his daughter, Sybil Grafton. I was told she was staying here."

The woman gave a slow smile, her eyes sweeping over him once more. "My name is Tarah, Tarah Clayton." Her tongue smoothed over her bottom lip. "So *you're* the handsome cowboy. I can see why Sybil has been in such a dither."

Chandler gulped. "This *is* where Sybil is staying?"

Tarah nodded, stepping to the side and gesturing him in. "By the looks of it, she'll be here a while. She's not going to be able to afford peanuts on that job she took. Please, come in."

"Is Sybil here, Miss Clayton? I don't want to bother you, ma'am, if she isn't. I can return another time." Chandler took a deep breath, feeling sweat gathering on his forehead.

"Please, my name's Tarah. I don't answer to ma'am." She crossed her arms, leaning against the door jamb. "No, Sybil isn't here. It's a Sunday night, so she's over helping at a squalid little church. Some program for children where she helps them memorize Bible verses." She shook her head. "I don't know what's gotten into that girl, but I'm beginning to think she's lost her mind."

"Would you happen to know the address of the church? I'd like to meet her there if possible."

Tarah rolled her eyes. "Not you too. Why is it that all the good ones are either married or religious?"

Chandler shrugged. "I think you already answered your own question." He pulled the piece of paper from his pocket. "If you have a pen, I can write down the name of the church, if you don't know the address."

Tarah pushed away from the door. "I have a pen you can use. I'll give you the name and the address. I drive by it every day on my way to work. It's about five miles from here."

"Thank you, ma'am."

Tarah scowled over her shoulder. "You're too polite for your own good."

Chandler smiled. "Thank you, ma'am. I think my mother taught me well."

Tarah walked back across the foyer, her arm extended, a piece of paper dangling from her fingers. "I wrote it down for you."

Chandler took the paper, studying the flowing penmanship. "Thank you—"

"Don't say it…please. I feel as though I've aged ten years just standing here talking to you." She took up her stance beside the door jamb. "I really don't mind you waiting here for Sybil. We can get to know one another better. It's not every day that I have a great-looking cowboy in my apartment."

Chandler's eyes traveled over the contemporary design of the hallway and the rich carpet beneath his feet. "No, I bet you don't. This isn't really a cowboy's style. My horse would hate this décor." He flashed the paper up between two fingers as he set his hat upon his head. "Thank you, ma'am."

THE SEVEN-YEAR-OLD GIRL GAVE SYBIL a huge grin, pink gums showing where two teeth should have been. "I'm just like that song, Miss Sybil. All I want for Christmas is my two front teeth." She bent in half, giggling, her brown ponytail swinging forward and brushing Sybil's cheek.

Sybil reared back. "Be careful, Laura. You're going to hurt someone, and it just might be me." She laughed, laying her Bible on the chair beside her.

Laura jumped at Sybil, burying her face against her side. "I'm so glad you're my helper. I memorize better with you."

Sybil swallowed around the lump in her throat. "I'm happy that you're doing so well." She patted Laura's shoulder. "You know what?"

"What?" Laura popped up, staring up at Sybil, her wide, brown eyes blinking.

"I also memorize those verses when I'm helping you." Sybil gave her a smile.

Laura frowned. "You didn't learn them when you were a little girl like me?"

Sybil shook her head. "I didn't."

"Didn't you go to church?" Laura leaned on Sybil's knee, moving her little body back and forth.

"I went to church sometimes."

Laura formed a wide 'o' with her mouth. "My daddy says we should go to church every time the doors are open." She wrinkled her small brow and shook her head. "But sometimes I don't like to go because it's boring. Pastor just talks and talks."

Sybil laughed. "I understand what you're saying. I felt the same way when I was your age." Sybil smoothed Laura's ponytail. "But you just keep listening and learning all these verses, and when you're old like me, you'll be happy that you did. I wish I had paid better attention when I was younger."

"Laura, it's time to go. Your mother is waiting in the car."

Laura looked up at the tall man standing in the doorway to the Sunday school room. "Okay, Daddy." She hugged Sybil and skipped away.

"Have a Merry Christmas, Laura," Sybil called after the small figure.

"Merry Christmas, Miss Sybil!"

Sybil gathered her Bible and purse and left the classroom, heading for the main entrance.

The pastor's wife greeted her as they passed each other. "Will we see you for our Christmas Eve service?"

Sybil shook her head. "I'm afraid not. I'll be going home for Christmas…just through the New Year, and then I'll return."

"Well, have a blessed Christmas, and I'll look forward to seeing you when you get back. We have appreciated your help on Sunday nights. We have so many children, and the more adults we have, the better."

"I've enjoyed it." Sybil laughed. "I'm learning right along with them."

The pastor's wife laid her hand on Sybil's arm. "That's the truth! We all need a refresher." She gave Sybil a hug. "Merry Christmas!"

"Merry Christmas!" Sybil smiled.

Wow! Even the pastor's wife is learning. Where did I ever get the idea that you either just knew God's Word or you didn't? I've made so many wrong assumptions about the Christian life.

She walked to her car, unlocking it with the remote. As the lights flashed, a tall figure wearing a cowboy hat came into view. Gripping the Bible in her hand, she brought it to her chest.

"Chandler?"

"Yes, ma'am, it's me."

The words were spoken soft and low, a velvet blanket being wrapped around her soul.

"What…what are you doing here? How did you find me?" Sybil gripped the Bible tighter, praying for strength against the tidal wave of emotions rolling over her.

She closed her eyes. *Please, God, help me to understand what's going on. Give me the strength to congratulate Chandler on his marriage. Help me to do what's best for Chandler and not myself. Please God…help me not to love him! Help me to remember all that I've learned from You these past weeks. I can't do this alone.*

Blinking, she stared up at Chandler, only inches from her, the brim of his hat a covering against the dancing snowflakes. His aftershave was warm and enticing, sending her pulse racing. She swayed toward him, straightening her back against the weakness at having him so near.

His hands reached up and framed her face, calloused and so warm. Sybil's eyes widened as he leaned near and whispered against her lips.

"I've missed you, *Ms.* Grafton." His lips met hers for a second.

"I love you." His lips descended once more.

"And I'm asking again if you would marry me." His lips lingered longer the third time, melting into hers.

Sybil, turned her head, breathing deeply. "You aren't married to Crystal?"

Chandler laughed. "Would I be kissing you, telling you I love you, and that I wanted to marry you if I was already married?"

Sybil sighed. "I hope not, because that last part would be technically illegal." She closed her eyes, meeting his lips, her Bible held tightly against their hearts.

Chapter Twenty-Three

THE LOW RUMBLE OF THUNDER shook the wall sconces, the lights flickering in the foyer of the church.

Sybil raised her black brows, giving Elvira a radiant smile. "It *is* May in Kansas. What could be more exciting than to be under a tornado watch when you're walking down the aisle? I bet not many brides could say that."

Elvira fussed with the white chiffon of Sybil's gown. "It will be a day to remember in many ways, that's for sure." She turned concerned eyes to the long front windows. "You said you've never seen a tornado in Wheatacre…right?"

Sybil brushed Elvira's arm. "No, we haven't. They've been close a few times. Today we'll just have faith that God will take care of us."

Tarah snorted as she walked away from the double doors of the church. "I won't be thinking about God. I'll be running for shelter if those sirens go off." She glanced down at her heeled silver sandals. "Even in these." She fluffed the skirt of her tea-length, taupe-colored dress, the chiffon floating about her legs. "I was going to see what the temperature was like outside. But I guess I'll wait until after the downpour." She shook her perfectly coiffed head. "No sunny, bird-chirping day for your wedding, Sybil. If you'd waited just one more month, maybe the weather would have cooperated better."

Sybil adjusted the jeweled bracelet on her wrist. "Chandler and I have waited long enough. If he'd had his way, we would have been married at Christmastime when he asked me to marry him."

She smiled. "But God's timing is perfect. I was able to help at the church in Kansas City until the end of the school year, plus work for a while. Now I have a little more experience with pro bono work. The hours I put in at the firm were helpful, but nothing like what I did at the legal clinic these past six months."

Tarah crossed her arms, shaking her head. "I still think you're nuts. The firm would have taken you back, and you could have had the lifestyle you enjoyed before you returned to hayseed land last year."

"The name's Wheatacre, Tarah." Elvira flashed a look in Tarah's direction before facing Sybil. "*I* think it all worked out perfectly. Your father is so pleased to have you in the office with him a couple days a week. By the time you return from your honeymoon, he'll have your desk piled high."

Sybil laughed. "I'm afraid of that! But I'm happy to be working with the people here in Wheatacre. Maybe I'll be able to change their impressions of me…over time." She raised a brow, looking into Elvira's eyes. "You know, be a Grafton that can be respected, like my grandfather and father."

Elvira smoothed a stray hair from Sybil's face. "You'll be a Byron now…and that's just as important."

Sybil's eyes glowed. "This is really happening, isn't it?"

Tears welled in Elvira's eyes. "It is!" She stepped back, her eyes sweeping over Sybil's gown and the elaborate chignon at the back of her head.

Sybil brushed at the flowing layers of chiffon. Her fingers moved to the elegant, tiny gemstones imbedded in the soutache adorning the illusion neckline and fluttery cap sleeves. "Do you think it's too much? Maybe too gaudy? I probably should have worn a veil, but then it would have covered this beautiful…" Sybil's hand fluttered up to the matching jeweled hair accessory.

"It's you, Sybil." Elvira took Sybil's hands in hers. "You're a beautiful bride."

Tarah gave her friend a hug. "I know I complain a lot, and I *do* think you're crazy…" she pulled back, dabbing at her eyes. "But I've really loved having you stay with me these past months. Even if we did almost tear each other's hair out a few times. I'm going to miss you." The tears spilled over. She pointed a silver-painted nail at Sybil. "And I don't care what that cowboy of yours says, you'd better come and visit me…a lot."

Sybil nodded, blinking rapidly. "Now you both have to stop. We'll all be blubbering in here. With the sound of the storm outside and our racket, we'll never know when to go in."

Elvira sniffed. "Your father will be here to get you, remember?"

Sybil waved a hand at Tarah. "Go see if Chandler and Blu are at the front of the church. If they are, it's almost time."

Tarah rolled her eyes. "Well, I guess I *am* the maid of honor. I probably should do something."

Elvira's eyes followed the slim figure down the hall. "Yes, she should."

Sybil responded with a lopsided grin. "Now, now, be nice. I appreciate all you've done since Tarah's been here. I know she can get on your nerves."

Elvira scowled. "That's one way to put it." She stepped to the long table, picking up Sybil's bouquet of red roses. She held it to her nose. "Roses don't smell the way they once did. Especially roses from the florist. But they are still gorgeous." She placed it in Sybil's hands.

Tarah rushed back. "Chandler and Blu are standing there just as relaxed as you please. I don't think those two have a nervous bone in their bodies." She pressed her lips together, sighing. "There's just something about a cowboy all dressed up."

Sybil laughed. "*Any* man, dressed in *anything* makes you say that."

Tarah shrugged. "What can I tell you? I like men." She turned as Loren came down the hall. "Here's another one now." Her eyes slid over Loren.

Loren nodded to Tarah and placed a kiss on Elvira's cheek. "You ladies look lovely." Taking Sybil's hand, he smoothed his thumb over the pale skin. "But you steal the show today."

Sybil's eyes darkened. "Aw, Daddy. Thank you!" She flicked at her eyelash with one finger. "You all are determined to ruin my makeup."

Loren cleared his throat. "The music is playing, and I believe we're up next."

Tarah kissed Sybil's cheek. "You're gorgeous! I'll see you up front." She teetered away, her arms swinging as she balanced on the wood floor.

Elvira spun around. "I should be sitting down!" She blew a kiss to Sybil before rushing from the foyer, the long skirt of her champagne-colored gown swirling at her feet.

Sybil laughed as they watched Elvira's retreating figure. "You did the right thing when you married Elvira. She's good for you, and I know she loves you dearly."

Loren nodded, his expression soft and warm. "As I do her." He turned back to Sybil, gripping her hand tightly. "My life is just about perfect. I am married to a wonderful woman. My daughter is growing and changing in ways I never thought possible. In a few minutes, I will have a son that I admire and respect. The very best part of all is that God is the center of all those lives." His voice became rough. "You don't know how many years I've prayed for this day."

Sybil smiled, rolling her lips together. "I might have a clue." She wrapped her father in a hug, the bouquet balanced against his back. "I'm sorry for all those years of making a mess of things. And I know the old Sybil will come out every now and then with claws bared." She stepped back, meeting her father's gaze. "But as my understanding of God and His ways becomes clearer, my love just seems to grow for Him…and all those around me."

Loren nodded. "Yes it does, my girl. Yes it does." He extended his left arm, giving her a wink. "That's your song playing."

Sybil entwined her arm through her father's as the sun's watery rays illuminated the long windows dappled with rain.

THE DOORS AT THE BACK of the sanctuary opened, and Tarah walked in, offering smiles to both sides of the aisle. Chandler looked away, nudging Blu in the side as he whispered, "Watch out for that one. She's like a piranha."

Blu chuckled. "An attractive little piranha, but point taken."

Chandler nudged him again. "By the way, I'm really happy that I changed my mind about you being my best man. I couldn't have done this without you."

Blu smiled. "I know." He tilted his head toward the back of the room filled with guests. "You're one lucky man."

Chandler's gaze swept down the red-rose-bedecked aisle. He grinned when his eyes took in Sybil's flowing dress, the bodice twinkling in the light. *My Sybil, my bride, with your elegance shining through!* Her upswept black hair shimmered, her cheeks pink, and her green eyes sparkled above her glorious smile. Her gaze captured his and didn't let go until they stood side by side.

Loren placed Sybil's hand in Chandler's as he stepped back.

The pastor's voice filled the room. "Who gives this woman to be married to this man?"

"I do," Loren replied loud and clear, but Chandler caught the whispered, "With pleasure."

Chandler grinned, nodding his head at Loren as he turned to be seated. His eyes caressed Sybil's face. "Are we ready to do this?"

Sybil's smile beamed. "More than ready!"

SYBIL TIED THE DELICATE RED bow on the empire waist of the gossamer robe, then leaned over to look at her reflection in the bathroom mirror. She fluffed the long layers of hair framing her face, dark waves flowing over her shoulders. Smiling at her reflection, she went to find her husband, white lace swirling around her bare feet with each step.

Walking through the kitchen, she noted the pot of fresh-brewed coffee and sniffed with appreciation as she crossed into the dining room. She opened the French doors leading to the deck and peeked her head out.

Chandler sat beyond the table and chairs grouped to one side of the doors, his arms draped over the chair, his blond head resting against the slatted back. His bare chest rose and fell with each sleeping breath.

She crept to his side, jumping when his hand reached out and took her by the wrist. "You scared me! I thought you were sleeping."

He smiled up at her. "I was, and then my dreams became reality when I smelled your sweet perfume." He dropped his jean-clad legs from their perch on the deck railing. "I missed you!"

Sybil laughed. "You haven't been gone that long."

Chandler groaned as he pulled her over, positioning her on his lap. "It seemed like ages to me." He took her lips with his, moving softly over them.

Sybil pulled back. "You taste a bit like coffee."

"Since you like coffee, that's a good thing, right?" He smiled, his hand moving in slow circles across her back. "I'm about to have my second cup. How about you?"

"I'll get it in just a minute. Right now, I just want to sit and enjoy this gorgeous view." She raised one brow at him. "I've never seen it before, remember?"

He chuckled. "Believe me, I know. There were plenty of mornings I sat out here wanting you with me." His arm slid around her waist, snuggling her close. "What was it like waking up this morning and knowing you were married? Your first day as Sybil Byron…*Mrs.* Byron."

Sighing, Sybil closed her eyes, laying her head on his shoulder. "It was magnificent!" She sat up, meeting his gaze. "What about you?"

He grinned, his white teeth gleaming against his tanned face. "My name's still the same…but it was pretty marvelous. Even better than I was expecting." He nuzzled her neck. "But not nearly as good as last night."

Sybil blushed red. "You can't say those things right out here in broad daylight."

Chandler wrinkled his brow, scanning the deck and skies. "The sun is barely up. I don't think that qualifies for broad daylight." His finger brushed her cheek. "I've waited a long time for last night…and I'm happy I did. I wouldn't have wanted to experience that with anyone else."

Sybil took a deep breath and looked away, stiffening her body.

"Hey, now." Chandler turned her back to face him. "We've discussed this more than a few times over the past months."

Sybil's eyes dropped to the red bow. "I...I know. Believe me, I didn't think about it last night, but this morning, I couldn't help but compare." She shrugged. "Just the human in me, I guess."

He raised a brow, lifting her chin so her eyes met his. "And?"

Sybil's eyes became dark pools and spilled over. "I love you, Chandler. With you, it was not only an act, something that just felt good. Because of our soul relationship, it was if we really were becoming one person. I melded into you." She shook her head. "I can't even explain it."

He smiled. "I think you're doing a pretty good job." He snuggled her against his chest, his chin resting on the top of her head. "It's a physical relationship that God designed. He wanted it to be enjoyable, something to be shared intimately. I haven't tried it, but I can't help but think that a physical relationship with someone you love and are committed to is very different than a one-night stand."

"Or months of living with someone because everyone else is doing it." She sat up, looking into his eyes. "I know this has to hurt you. How are you dealing with it so well?"

He gave a crooked grin. "Believe me...I haven't at times. Blu can attest to that." He fingered the red bow. "While waiting to be married was difficult, we both needed that time." He dropped his hand to her leg, stroking it back and forth over the silky softness of the peignoir set. His eyes went to the line of cottonwoods beside the distant river, the vibrancy of their green leaves exposed in the rising sun. "Do you remember that Sunday afternoon when I came by your place? You made me coffee, and we never drank it. We went into Wheatacre to eat before church."

She nodded. "Of course I remember. That was when I first started questioning what I believed, and the way I was living my life."

"We had that conversation about raising children—"

"I told you that doing stupid things as a teenager was just part of the growing-up process."

He laughed. "Yeah, something like that. But like most teenagers, I had to go the trial-and-error route. My learning curve was a little steeper. It really changed my attitude and the way I perceived life." He rubbed his forehead. "So, it would be really unfair of me to judge someone else and the way they handled decisions in their lives. We all have to learn."

"Yes, we do, but here's where I remind you of what I said that day. I can't imagine that you did anything too terrible. That's just not *you*."

"No, I didn't do something that was listed among the 'bad' items. I didn't murder, steal, take drugs, smoke, or go to jail—"

"See, what did I say? You were a parent's perfect dream." Sybil laid her hand over his.

"I think the sins of the mind, the thoughts, are almost worse. Not submitting in your head to what you know is right. I had a big problem with that one. Sometimes that becomes outward, but not always. Some people are pretty good at putting up a spiritual front."

Sybil nodded. "I agree. I've seen that a lot. Enough that I knew I didn't want to be that way." She laughed, giving him a nudge. "So, we're married now. I can't run away. What's your deep, dark past?"

"It's not really deep and dark…just what formed the person I am today." Chandler sighed, laying his head against the back of the chair. "I had a horse that I raised from a colt. He was born when I was twelve years old. He was a black Quarter Horse, and I named him Thunder."

"Did he have the attitude to match?"

Chandler nodded, smiling. "Yes, he did. He didn't take kindly to anyone else riding him. Blu tried a few times, and usually met the ground at some point." Chandler cleared his throat. "But with me, he was obedient to a fault, and loyal. I loved him." He straightened in the chair, adjusting her on his lap. "Blu and I were about two weeks from leaving for college. We were full of ourselves back then, nothing standing in our way of having fun. We were invincible."

"Again, rather normal teenage behavior. I can remember feeling that way." Smiling, Sybil laid her head on his shoulder. "You may continue."

"Thank you. Good thing we have all day. It's going to take me that long to get this all out." He kissed her forehead. "Blu and I had finished our chores. It was almost dusk, and we decided to take a ride. My father suggested that we not go since it was almost dark. He warned me to be careful, that it would be hard to see." He shook his head. "I laughed it off, telling him I knew what I was doing, that I'd been riding for years…all stuff my father already knew, of course."

Sybil smiled. "Parents don't know a thing, in a child's mind."

"This is sadly true." Chandler's voice deepened. "Blu and I rarely just *rode* our horses. Which is why my father was concerned. We raced and jumped…anything crazy. I'm amazed one of us wasn't killed." He raised a brow. "That's why my father warned me to be cautious…several times." He cleared his throat. "Racing across the pasture, we came to a small gulley…a place my father had pointed out to me just a few days before. Blu rode on, but Thunder hit it…and…" Chandler took a deep breath. "We both went down."

Sybil gasped, sitting up and cupping his cheek. "That's terrible! Were you hurt?"

Chandler nodded, his eyes welling up. "I ended up with a broken collarbone and wrist, and a kneecap in a couple of pieces. Thunder didn't fare so well. He broke his leg…pretty badly. Blu went for help, and when my father arrived, he had to put Thunder down."

Sybil gaped. "But why? I thought that with today's medical advancements, a broken leg could be fixed. That sounds archaic, like something you would see in an old western."

Chandler shook his head. "A horse's legs are rather fragile, a lot of bones in them. Thunder's leg was…" Chandler looked away, tears trickling down his cheeks. "He was in so much pain. I sat there with him in the dark, hearing him, not able to do anything…knowing it was my fault."

Sybil smoothed her thumb over his cheekbone. "You couldn't have known that was going to happen."

"I *should* have listened to my father. I *should* have been more aware. I shouldn't have been racing in the dark." He wrinkled his brow. "But we can't live by what we *should* have done. We live with what we *have* done." He looked into her eyes. "How could I judge anyone's motives or actions? A friend that I loved dearly died because of mine."

"But you were injured as well. You didn't just escape unscathed."

Chandler nodded. "A very small price to pay for what I did. I had surgery on my knee, and instead of starting college, I was home recovering." He bit his lower lip. "And Blu postponed going to school until we could start together. He came over every day, did my chores, and went to therapy with me. I don't know if I could have survived those months without him." He smiled. "He kicked me in the pants more than a few times when I started feeling sorry for myself."

Sybil stood, walking to the railing. She turned and faced her husband. "Blu would not have spent that night with me if he thought you loved me."

Chandler returned her gaze. "No, he wouldn't have."

Sybil crossed her arms, looking up at the brilliant colors in the sky. "You needed him beside you at the wedding. I'm happy he was there for you."

"I am too." Chandler clasped his hands in front of his lean abdomen. "I haven't always agreed with the way Blu's handled his life...especially the relationships he's had with women over the years. But he's loyal, and there when you need him. He's been as much of a brother to me as my biological brothers." He lifted one tanned shoulder. "Maybe even more so."

"I was wondering about the pattern of scars on your knee."

He smiled up at her, narrowing his eye in the rising sun. "Now you know. When I'm old and gray, the arthritis is going to kill me." He gave a light chuckle.

Sybil's eyes flew to his leg. "Do you still have pain in it? I never would have known. You don't limp."

"Hours and hours of therapy. When I'm really tired, or have a long day on my feet, it bothers me." He stared down at his hands. "But that pain is nothing compared to the loss of Thunder."

Smiling up at her, he reached out. "You're much too far away."

Sybil glided to him, taking his hand. "I thought I should make us some breakfast. You must be hungry."

His eyes slid over her. "Starving, actually."

Sybil blushed, taking a deep breath. "You don't realize what you do to me when you look at me like that."

"I'm learning." He tilted his head. "I didn't really think you were the blushing type."

Sybil laughed. "I'm not! Now back to breakfast. It won't take me very long. I can do something simple like scrambled eggs—"

Chandler pulled her down to his lap, nuzzling her neck. "You look too delicious standing there in that nightgown. I don't want you in the kitchen right now. We have years ahead when you can make me breakfast." He untied the little red bow. "Besides, Mrs. Flores made us some meals to have until we leave for Colorado in the morning."

Sybil struggled to sit up, staring at Chandler. "*Our* Mrs. Flores…Gloria…our maid?"

He raised a brow. "You're sounding a bit like your old self."

"Sorry, I didn't mean it like that." She creased her brow. "I'm just surprised she would be willing to do anything here if I was involved. She didn't say anything about it at the wedding yesterday."

"Mrs. Flores asked me to keep it a surprise…a little wedding gift for us." He skimmed a finger over her collarbone. "She mentioned that you were going to help her son Jorge with some trouble he's gotten himself into."

Sybil brushed his comment away. "That…it's not a big deal. A few letters, a couple phone calls, and it should be taken care of."

"It was a big deal for Mrs. Flores." Chandler's finger slid under the robe, pushing it from her shoulder. "She told me that she never thought she'd see the day when her little Chiquita would become a woman of honor. But you had arrived."

Sybil put her hand to her chest. "She said that about *me?*"

Chandler nodded. "She did." His warm hand cupped her shoulder. "Now, I don't want to talk anymore. We can't solve all of the world's problems today. But we can learn so much more about this." His hand slid to the back of her neck.

She shivered.

"Are you cold?" His lips trailed over her jaw, down her neck to the little hollow at the base of her throat.

Sighing, she tilted her head back, giving him access to the long column. "No, I'm burning up inside."

Chandler groaned, soft and low. "Me too." He struggled to his bare feet, gripping her against his chest. Bouncing her up, he repositioned her in his arms.

Shrieking, Sybil clasped her arms about his neck. "You're going to drop me."

His lips met hers, moving slowly as he braced his feet upon the stained boards. "Never, my dear," he whispered against her rosy lips. He strode to the French doors, the full skirt of her gossamer robe trailing across his legs and onto the deck.

Sybil laid her head upon his shoulder, breathing deeply of his own unique scent. She closed her eyes and sighed. "I love you, Chandler Byron."

He replied with a kiss as they crossed the threshold.

About the Author

Deborah Ann Dykeman has over five published books available through major online retailers. Her Rubyville series has been loved by many readers. Deborah strives to get at the heart of a person's walk with God. Through her stories, characters face many issues that are rarely discussed in Christian circles. Deborah's nonfiction short stories, "Twice in a Lifetime" and "Joshua's Story", have both placed second at the Called to Write Conference. Deborah has been married for thirty-two years, has five children, three sons-in-law, and five grandchildren (and two more on the way). Deborah has homeschooled her children and taught Sunday School, and has been an AWANA director and a pastor's wife. When not writing, marketing or attending events, she is working on home renovation projects. She loves to meet with her readers and hear their stories. She resides in the beautiful Flint Hills region of the state of Kansas.

When Love Grows is the sequel to *When Hope Blooms*.

Also by DEBORAH ANN DYKEMAN

Jason and Kathy Miller are brimming with hope and excitement for their future together as husband and wife on their wedding day in June of 1983.

Twenty years later life isn't so carefree anymore. Three children, several pounds, and graying hair have dampened enthusiasm, and Kathy is feeling it. Caring for a home, husband, and teenagers isn't always as fulfilling as a woman would want it to be . . . and that's where problems begin for the Millers.

Kathy now travels a road she would never have considered walking as a young, exuberant bride. Jason struggles along, clearing a path through the thorns that have become their marriage. Will a new baby repair all the damage done or shred the last ties binding them together?

THE COMPLETE Rubyville SERIES

BY DEBORAH ANN DYKEMAN

Rubyville: A Place to Call Home — Deborah Ann Dykeman

Rubyville: A Place of Refuge — Deborah Ann Dykeman

Rubyville: A Place to Heal — Deborah Ann Dykeman

Rubyville: A Place in my Heart — Deborah Ann Dykeman

Made in the USA
Columbia, SC
12 January 2018